Dedications

For Cassie, for Denis and for my beautiful bump – whoever
you shall be.
ND

For Jase, Mat and Unca Dunca, the fabulous Beaconsfield Boys.
And for Sean O'Meara, for wasting a summer
so many years ago
SC

Relax, the Doctor told himself. Everything's under control. Well, if you could call two people hurtling blindly through space in a tiny metal canister built for one 'under control'.

It was as if something in the life capsule had responded to his panic, to the need to escape. He'd felt a sickening lurch as the vessel launched itself on an apparently preset course, and had panicked even more. But the little ship's systems had sought to understand his thoughts, and in turn had given him impressions of the space they all were travelling through: the harsh radiation of a fat sun. The comfort of a small planet, nearby. A large, dark world, far away, that the stars had shied from.

He realised this was an interface of some kind, that his thoughts could be routed through the capsule's basic flight computer. It was difficult at first: he wasn't thinking clearly enough –

Relax. You could steer something like this in your sleep. You *are* steering it in your sleep. He'd shut down his cardiovascular system; he imagined the thick gel he and Compassion lay in was designed to protect and nourish only a single occupant.

He was able to bypass the imprinted co-ordinates. He didn't want to get to where the capsule was meant to go – he had to bring it back home. Had to find people who could help him get back to Fitz – assuming Fitz hadn't been launched off into space himself – and back to the TARDIS. To ask them some quite unpleasant questions, to which, he suspected, there would be equally nasty answers.

The life capsule sped on, Compassion kept sleeping, and the Doctor wondered if their transport was designed for a soft landing; if the bump might disturb him, or if he would lie here half aware in the dark until something came to wake him up.

Part One
Getting On

Chapter One
On the Edge of a Storm

Karl Dam shifted uncomfortably in the staff car, looking out from a rocky outcrop over the pallid expanse of water. An old army maxim declared that a soldier's arse was for kicking, not sitting on; hence the uncushioned plastic bucket seats of all army transport. Maybe that was fair enough for new recruits like Higs, sitting quietly beside him in the driver's seat, but Dam couldn't see quite why he should be made to suffer in the same way. As Security Chief of Facility One, his backside was already in a more precarious position than most.

It wasn't just the seating that discomfited him as he surveyed the soldiers swarming over the vast, grey shale shores of the Northern Waters.

'Look like ants from here, don't they, sir?' Higs observed.

Dam grunted noncommittally. 'This is all way too obvious,' he said quietly as vehicle followed vehicle heavily on to the beach. 'The spy cams of every Parallel on the globe must be trained on us now.'

The loudspeaker system sounded yet again: '*Will Facility Head please report to Main Control... Will Facility Head please...*'

'All right, I'm coming,' Narkompros muttered irritably as he strode along the corridor. Idiots. The tiniest problem and Terma and his mob were on to him these days, dragging him out of his bed at all hours. It couldn't be good for his health.

Narkompros tapped out his security code on the keypad outside Main Control and composed himself. He'd had thirty years to master the expression of the natural leader, thoroughly aware of his indispensability and ever so slightly bored by it. When the door to Main slid open at last that expression was firmly in place.

Not that anyone noticed today. The forty-strong team of scientists and controllers seemed entirely absorbed by their work, staring at giant monitors, keying in reports, regulating endless flows of data. All incomprehensible to him, of course. They might as well be keying magic spells into the circuitry to make Main light up like this: a thousand LEDs twinkled like the stars they were reaching up to under the drab, flat lighting of the fluorescents.

Was it his imagination or was it stupidly hot in here?

Narkompros remembered back when this place had seemed ludicrously huge, as vast as a launch bay but with only a skeleton staff to operate it. He'd watched operators skitter from terminal to terminal like children racing about in a playground. Developing systems. Making the dream possible.

He located Terma in front of the main strat-screen and marched over. While operators and supervisors alike noticed him at last and saluted respectfully, Terma was still hunched over the controls, sweat beading the back of his neck.

'Singularity and strength in you, Controlling Deputy Terma,' Narkompros said, stiffly.

Terma turned to him. 'And in all 59, Head Narkompros. I'm sorry to disturb you during a rest period. You're well, I trust?'

Narkompros forced a smile. 'Never better.'

'We've got a problem.' Terma handed him a datapad. 'That last glitch in the network gave us more of a problem than we'd thought. A number of life capsules have launched themselves unbidden from one of the Bastions, overriding the control protocols.'

Narkompros regarded the datapad. Its screen was crowded with incomprehensible figures and jargon. He nodded sagely, hoping that was appropriate.

'Flight program of these capsules?'

Terma looked cagey. 'As intended; ahead of schedule, but that can be allowed for and balanced out elsewhere.'

Narkompros shifted uncomfortably, worried he was missing something. 'So the problem is?'

'One of the capsules started manoeuvring in space. It's changed course. Coming back here.'

Narkompros stared at him. 'To Skale?'

'I mean *here* here. On its present course, the capsule will splash down in the Northern Waters.'

'Our side?'

Terma nodded. 'About ten clicks off North Shore. We're computing an exact grid reference now.'

'If one of our capsules were to fall 67's side of the divide…' Narkompros felt his stomach twist. 'Well, we must speak to Government. Get hold of a platoon and dispatch it to intercept –'

Terma held up his hands. 'Head Narkompros, I took the liberty of speaking to Government myself last night.'

Narkompros stared at him. 'Did you, indeed?'

'Deputising in your absence is my duty, is it not?'

'I wasn't absent, I was asleep.'

'I saw no cause to trouble you,' Terma said, handing him a copy of the communiqué. 'Once we had calculated the landing site, arranging for the craft's interception seemed a sensible precaution to take. You'd have done the same, surely?'

Narkompros glowered at him. 'I trust Dam is aware of the situation?'

'Very aware,' Terma said, snatching a report from an operator's hand. 'Dam knows what to do.'

The military presence was still building on the beach.

'We don't even need all these men,' Dam muttered. 'This is a ridiculous display.'

'Show of strength,' Higs said. 'Government will explain it away, sir. No one would dare push it with us.'

Dam glanced at his driver. The lad couldn't be much older than sixteen. Fresh from the military camps, pumped full of propaganda and national pride, Higs doubtless believed that he and his homeland would go on for ever. But Dam saw it himself. The soldiers *did* look a little like ants to anyone watching from up above. And ants could be stepped on.

'Hours left till splashdown…' He looked glumly at the pale sky, a brief and futile search for some sign of the capsule's impending arrival. 'Let's hope the thing just explodes on impact.'

'Sir?'

'Bang. End of story. If your lot have to locate it and tug it in, we'll be stuck here for hours more.' Dam sighed. 'Not at all conspicuous.'

'Let Skale take a good long look. We're too strong to be touched.'

Every Parallel on the globe was too strong to be touched, Dam reflected, but it didn't stop them coming close. And, while the forces gathered on the beach were general army, the Facility was a secret installation, undeclared, contravening the spirit of at least ten treaties. A convoy like that on the beach transporting the capsule back would lead every spy cam straight to the Facility's door – but it was less likely anyone would notice one transport and a staff car leave the trail back to Great City and vanish. It was his own responsibility to ensure that the Facility's security was not compromised. If this little lot started a skirmish, the Project could be set back years. Dam shuddered at the thought of being reposted to this wilderness for another five-stretch when his assignment was coming to an end in six months.

He had a wife in Great City, Ilsa, and had found himself actually looking forward to spending a stretch of time with her again. They'd been paired up and partnered by the State seven years ago, on his twenty-eighth birthday, and had spent two years learning how to get on with each other before he'd been stationed here. As part of the population programme, they'd been targeted to produce two children by the time Ilsa was thirty, and one more every two years after that until she was too old to bear more. Strict penalties affecting both income and social status were incurred if targets weren't met.

But Dam, as ever, hadn't rushed things. He'd always hoped he would fall in love with his partner before having children. Ilsa, eight years his junior, had been relieved. A romantic, she'd called him, and they'd both agreed to wait. To postpone things until the last possible moment.

'Won't be long now,' Higs observed, peering through the windscreen.

Dam shifted in his seat again. Higs, clearly already hardened to army life, sat staring straight ahead. The sky, gunmetal grey, stretched over the sea and the marshlands like a dowdy blanket.

'Wonder where the capsule will burn through,' Dam thought aloud. 'And who'll be watching when it does.'

Narkompros noticed sourly that Terma looked up from his report only at the sound of Chief Supervisor Yve approaching rapidly with another.

She handed the data to Terma. 'Here's the latest from the defence net,' Yve stated, smoothing back loose strands of dark hair from her high forehead. 'Even assuming we could destroy the capsule remotely, an explosion of that magnitude could easily be construed by Parallel 67 as an act of aggression.'

'*Assuming* we could destroy it?' Narkompros questioned.

Terma glared briefly at Yve, who met his stare quite innocently with wide brown eyes. 'The capsule is not responding to our programming signals,' he said. 'Detonation isn't an option.'

Narkompros clenched his fists. 'How long till impact?'

'Not long enough,' Terma replied, handing him Yve's report.

'What caused it to launch?'

'We don't know. Not yet.'

'We're reading some kind of operating error in the Bastion's systems,' Yve said. 'An accidental launch is possible within certain parameters.'

'And its coming back here suggests possibly the psych-drive is damaged,' Terma added.

'As technical hitches go, it's… unfortunate,' said Yve. 'But the shielding should ensure it remains unobserved until splashdown.'

Narkompros was finding it hard to keep his composure in this heat. 'And then?'

'If it doesn't go off, we bring it back here and try to work out what's gone wrong. If it does, well… put it down to controlled waste disposal at sea,' Terma suggested. 'A bigger bang than normal, but no one in that backward Parallel would suspect the truth.'

Narkompros watched as Yve fiddled with the collar of her green supervisor's tunic, holding it open to let out some heat from her willowy body. 'Why *is* it so hot in here, anyway?' he demanded.

Terma clearly felt such a question beneath him. 'Makkersvil, any news on air con?' he asked of an operator.

'Still down, Deputy Terma,' Makkersvil replied, ruefully. 'It's the same over half the Facility. Engineering's got its hands full with the sanitation systems down. The strat-screen's on the flicker, too.'

'Engineering assures us a fix by this afternoon,' said Yve quietly.

Turning to view the screen himself, Narkompros kept his features carefully impassive. He was well aware he'd personally agreed to a trimming down of the engineering section to channel more funds into Systems.

Operators moved aside deferentially as he approached the strat-screen to inspect it himself. He could see blank strips in the resolution, but could see too the tiny yellow point that had detached itself from the bright mass of the Bastions and which was floating slowly down to Skale.

'We'll all have our hands full when that thing hits,' he muttered. Operating errors… Glitches… Incompetent engineers and a faulty heating system. They were reaching for the stars, but it was a child's reach, barely able to grab empty space.

After so many years of effort, they should be stronger. *He* should be stronger. He'd spent his life seeing the Project through to glorious completion, while the Project had seen him grow old in secret shelters and military establishments, years at a time spent away from the sun.

He supposed there was always a price for fulfilling your aims.

'Full briefing in Strategy One, thirty minutes from now,' Narkompros announced. 'I want to know everything that is, could be or should be affecting that capsule. Have the Bastions scanned for any sign of further glitches; if there are any I want layman's data on any further projected problems.' He strode from the room, self-assured. In control. Keeping the front well up. 'And get air con fixed in here before I have someone shot.'

Yve watched Narkompros leave Main, then turned back to Terma.

9

'You really believe the launch was accidental?'

Terma snorted in irritation. 'What else should I believe? Sabotage and subterfuge? That little grey men from Haltiel have come to invade us?' He looked down at her sardonically. The dedicated scientist who kept Narkompros off their backs had given way to the more familiar bully who mopped the floor with anyone foolish enough to irritate him.

Except her.

'Alien invasion could be our best bet,' Yve persisted, lightly. 'Get *us* in the clear, anyway. Narkompros won't be satisfied till we prove this was a one-off.'

'He just doesn't want us to realise our iron leader is actually made of straw,' Terma said, snatching some printouts from an operator and scrutinising them. 'All that bluster, that tough man façade. Can barely make it through a work-stretch without having a lie down.'

Yve looked away. Terma was back on his favourite subject. Years of being trapped in the role of deputy when he felt he was doing the real work, that *he* was the one who kept the Facility functional despite Narkompros's best efforts to bring it to a grinding halt. She watched him wander off to upset some operators on Second Level.

The two old men were close enough in their own way, she was sure of it – Narkompros, the ruthlessly efficient visionary, and Terma the hands-on scientific genius. The theory and the practice. Perhaps Terma just didn't want to admit how similar he and Narkompros were. Both had to be in their early sixties, and had devoted their lives to the furthering of the aims and agendas of Parallel 59 – in return for the furthering of their own prestige and power, naturally.

It was a good game to play, Yve thought. With this pair around she'd learned the rules quickly. And now, with the end finally in sight and more and more corners being cut, mistakes were becoming more and more commonplace. Perhaps the old men had assumed after all this time that they were above reproach, that the errors would be eclipsed by the glory of success.

Yve was confident she'd be able to make someone in Government realise just how much she'd had to carry the pair of them these last years.

She moved closer to the strat-screen. 'Makkersvil, I want this fault fixed within the hour,' she called as the operator hurried past to attend to a cluster of red-faced supervisors.

'No sweat,' Makkersvil called. Then he wiped his brow. 'Well…'

She turned away, primly shaking her head. She'd fix the flicker herself, but then Narkompros would only claim he could lay off more engineers. Then she'd end up repairing the air con and the sanitation systems on top of everything else.

On the screen, the tiny yellow bullet continued its inexorable fall.

Chapter Two
Landing

It happened just as dusk was falling. The capsule described a vivid arc, as if a knife was scraping the flint sky, sparking crazily all the way down to the sea. The waters surged and foamed over the tiny vessel, and the rent air boomed like thunder.

The noise was incredible, as if the heavens had stolen the explosion from the fallen craft. Higs turned to Dam in alarm. Dam just sighed heavily, imagining all Skale woken up by the din, that the whole planet was now watching the Northern Waters, fingers twitching over firing buttons. He slid open his communicator and set it to scrambler.

'Commander Havdar, what have you got ?'

Havdar's voice came through so clearly he might've been standing outside the car. 'Clear fix, Security. Object came down whole.'

Dam cursed silently. 'Can you get some illumination out there?'

Even as he spoke, the phosphor arcs snapped on, and a sickly light spread over the sea. Looking through binoculars Dam could make out the cause of all this: a giant scorched bullet bobbing on the waves.

Havdar's voice sounded again, making Higs jump. 'Reclamation team going in.'

Acknowledging, then breaking contact, Dam peered through the binoculars again. He wasn't a superstitious man, but he couldn't help but think of that coffin in the sea as symbolic of 59's great dream of space travel falling from the sky. He didn't want to take it back to the Facility. Why couldn't they just leave it to slip under the waves, pretend none of it had ever happened?

He realised how adept he'd become these last few years at pretending that way; then he caught a strange movement. The capsule seemed suddenly darker, somehow.

Dam quickly passed the binoculars to Higs. 'What do you make of that?'

The boy's hands were shaking so much Dam was surprised he could see anything. 'I... I think the lid's open, sir.'

Dam grabbed back the binoculars in time to see what looked like an arm emerge from the capsule, groping in the yellow night that had fallen over the churning water.

Dam swore. Another complication he didn't need. He spoke hoarsely into the communicator. 'Havdar, alert your men. Capsule occupant has survived re-entry.'

As it became clear there had been no explosion following the capsule's splashdown, a ragged cheer went up round Main with a muted round of applause.

'All right,' Yve called out to her staff. 'We can all turn our attention back to the skies now. We need answers, and quickly.'

She began her patrol of Main's lower level, and noticed Operator Makkersvil trying to catch her attention, all furtive looks and twitches. She walked past him and back to the strat-screen. Now the capsule had been tracked successfully, they could disconnect the monitor to perform a more decisive overhaul of the imaging systems.

Makkersvil appeared at her side. 'Ignoring me, Chief Supervisor Yve?'

Yve glanced at him briefly. 'What?'

'I knew it,' he said, his voice the driest thing in this wretched heat. 'Terma's endless moaning's finally made you deaf.'

Yve didn't spare him a second glance. She concentrated on exploring image-resolution options on the strat-screen remote pad.

Makkersvil gently took her wrist and pulled her hand away from the controls. 'Shouldn't you be letting an operator do that for you, Chief Supervisor Yve? I've already patched it up best I could without disconnecting.'

She turned to face him now. He was staring at her, green eyes almost luminous with the reflected light of the screen. The snub nose, the blond hair, that little gap in his front teeth… She'd found him quite attractive, once. Relationships between staff in the Facility were strictly forbidden, and the danger of discovery had made the drudgery of operator stretches a lot more bearable for a time. She recalled how bitter he'd been when it ended; not because she'd made supervisor, but because she could just leave him behind without another word, moving on to seize the better life the higher rank allowed her.

What else had he expected her to do?

'You're right, of course,'Yve said, coolly. 'It wouldn't be right not to use my operators.' Her voice hardened. 'Power down the strat-screen. Get the imaging system fixed up and an engineer on to that flicker, now.'

There was the faintest of smiles on Makkersvil's face as he keyed in the shutdown procedure. 'So easy to switch off, isn't it?' he said. 'Do you recall?'

'I think we each remember things somewhat differently,' she said. He really hadn't changed. He probably didn't want to. He'd keep his precious integrity, and stay down here with the operators until doomsday. 'But I trust you won't forget yourself this way again, Operator Makkersvil.'

Makkersvil smiled. 'My apologies, Chief Supervisor. Must be the heat.'

'Capsule's down,' said Terma. 'Retrieval has begun.'

Narkompros gave a heavy sigh of relief, but Terma was still looking at him expectantly over the polished marble of the conference table. He realised he had no idea how to react to this situation. Terma's briefing had only depressed him with how little they understood what was happening, so he'd occupied himself working on a Government cover story for the enormous military presence they'd sent out to the Waters. Deserters, he'd decided. Dangerous men, clearly. Couldn't risk their reaching 67. Now the matter would soon be wrapped up, with not a shot fired. The army forces would be dispersed before warning voices could be raised from any other Parallel.

He was quite pleased with the deception. They'd get away with it. Soon, a solitary car and a guard transport would be carrying their secret here.

'That's excellent news, Terma,' Narkompros finally managed, rubbing his eyes. He felt dreadful this evening, not that anyone would care. 'Isn't it?'

'I suppose so,' said Terma, nodding stiffly. 'Still better news is that the bloody air conditioning's up and running in Main again. Might help us keep a cool head while we try to decipher what the hell's going on with that Bastion.'

'You're still reading…' Narkompros groped for the precise words. 'Operating errors?'

Terma's thin lips twitched. 'It's nothing we can't handle.'

The Doctor felt water splash his face, caught a crazy jigsaw piece of bright sky through half-closed eyes. He grinned automatically, just to welcome sensation again.

The capsule was letting them out, which meant the air had to be breathable. He took a snatch of it into his lungs to be sure as he felt Compassion's neck for a pulse. The capsule lurched and spun sickeningly, and more water slopped over him, getting in his mouth. It had an acrid, chemical taste and he spat it back out. They were at sea. All at sea.

He found the beat in Compassion's throat – faint, but that was probably down to the foul-smelling goo they were coated in, some kind of preserving fluid no doubt. She'd be just fine, as usual.

He reached an arm up into the light. The yellow haze didn't seem natural. There was a bit of a breeze, the sound of waves lapping at the capsule's hull… and machinery, too. Something moving at a regular speed through the water, he could detect the vibrations.

Trying not to squash Compassion still further, the Doctor sat up, wincing as the lights – which were coming from the shore, a mile or so away – dazzled him completely. He put up a dripping wet arm to shield his eyes, just as a dark shape burst up from the water in front of him.

The Doctor squinted against the glare. It was a man, probably, done up in a protective suit, perched doggedly on some kind of submersible. He heard others emerge from the foaming water, surrounding the capsule.

'Hello,' the Doctor said, his voice a little croaky. 'I don't suppose you'd mind turning off that light, would you?' The man was staring at him. 'Only my friend here's not awake yet, and I don't think she should be disturbed unless you know what you're doing. Do you know what you're doing?' He turned to address those behind him. 'Do *you*? You see, there's no time to lose, there's a friend of ours who...'

He tailed off. The glare was a little less intense this side of the capsule. He could see the men in the water were all carrying guns.

This visual clue, and the whistle of air released under pressure, made it easier for the Doctor to guess what had just embedded itself in the back of his neck. He tutted, as the lurid haze about him faded again into blackness.

Chapter Three
The Earthling Patient

Fitz woke up in a hospital bed.

The whitewashed ward was empty, and a faint smell of disinfectant and soap suds lingered in the air. The smell was familiar from endless visits to his mum. Fitz wondered if hospitals smelt the same everywhere.

He was alone. The Doctor and Compassion were nowhere to be seen, and he remembered in bleary flashes what had happened. Landing on the space station. The white capsules lining the room like coffins, sticking out sideways like man-sized nails waiting to be hammered into the walls. The alarm blaring and the lights changing, ultraviolet with a dash of blue. Compassion's freckles burning grey on her chubby face. A shout as the wall slid down and the TARDIS was lost to them, then his tongue going dry and everything darkening. Being hefted into what felt like a vat of cold custard, and the Doctor saying something about lifeboats...

That had to be what had happened. He'd been bundled into a lifeboat and set adrift through space. And this was where he'd wound up.

He was naked under the covers, and checked for any signs of injury. None that he could see. In fact, he felt pretty good. The ghost of the tan he'd picked up on Drebnar was still vaguely in evidence, so he couldn't have been here too long.

When the nurses came in he was relieved: they were human-looking, and attractive with it. He'd been imagining hideous big green things giving him a bed bath, and getting more and more rattled just lying there with no way of knowing how much time was passing.

Then the nurses came and sat on his bed, and told him everything he wanted to know. They were very helpful.

Fitz knew that the Doctor would rescue him in the end; it was inevitable, on past form. But there was no guarantee how long that would take. If Fitz was stuck here, well then, just as on Drebnar, he would have to make a life for himself somehow until it was time to move on. So he lay and listened, and let his situation sink in.

This was Mechta, a utopia that was state-owned; not in an aggressive, limiting way, as when he'd stayed in China, but as part of a grandiose health service. There was no need to worry about social status – all jobs paid the same, all housing was identical. There was no need to worry about possessions and keeping up with the Joneses – everything you had was state-supplied. The biggest choice you had was what to eat and drink and from where – but even that was only decided upon geographically, as all menus were the same. Basically, choice was humanely removed from your life – you just concentrated on getting to know yourself and on getting to know the others around you. Community. Fellowship. Until the doctors said you could go back home.

Fitz had been here a few days, quite unconscious. The life capsule that brought him here had crash-landed, but his injuries were only superficial and had soon healed. To his surprise, the nurses didn't seem to care who he was; there were no forms to fill in, no questions asked.

'You're here now, and you're who you are *now*,' one said. 'Forget the rest. It's all part of the treatment.'

'No one here has ID?' Fitz said, unable to believe his luck.

'You wouldn't be here if you didn't need the treatment,' the other nurse said. 'No one else can reach us here.'

'Are you sure?' Fitz said, a little nervously.

'You're from the Bastion, aren't you?' the nurse enquired, smiling.

'Of course I am,' Fitz said, grateful for the hint.

That seemed to settle it.

A few hours later, all tests on Fitz checking out A-OK, he was decked out in a jazzy space-age whistle off the peg and walking outside into a city of white concrete pyramids and sunshine. The air was fresh, and the pavements were busy with people. He shook his head, smiling broadly. The nurses had told him he'd been assigned housing and a job, as simple as that, and could pick up the details from Central, the Mechtan equivalent of City Hall.

There was a small vehicle parked by the road, about the size of a motorbike side-car, open topped and with three wheels. There were no keys for the ignition, only a large red power button. Fitz looked about him shiftily. He'd been told the cars belonged to everyone. You just parked them by the side of the road when you were finished with them. It felt totally alien to him to be freely encouraged to nick a car, but after he'd sat inside and still no one came to arrest him, he decided the hell with it. As an electric whine started building up - a car that ran on batteries, weird, maybe that helped explain why the air smelt so fresh here - he pressed one of the two pedals experimentally, and lurched off down the street, pulling into the traffic. The cars moved a little faster than a milk float, but at least they were convertibles. All part of the therapy, Fitz supposed. Take life slowly. Take your time.

Fitz imagined he was in a limo cruising down the Mall, lofty and regal. Hello, Mechta. He'd finally fallen on his feet, as softly as a feather.

He turned a corner, following the large blue arrow pointing to Central.

Everything seemed to be so very, very easy.

Chapter Four
Conversations With the Enemy

A jolt. Rattling wheels and people shouting. The Doctor couldn't move. Why was the world blurring past? An effect of the sedative, perhaps. Uniformed men swarmed about frantically, reds and greys and blacks bleeding together under too-bright lights. He went over a bump. Someone else was driving, he didn't like it. Where were his friends? Where was...?

'They came down together.'

'Two in the same capsule? What is this?'

Excitement and fear and hate. 'They're from Haltiel. They have to be from Haltiel.'

'We should kill them now.'

The Doctor decided he'd better close his eyes again.

Jessen Kal leaned forward in her chair, the humming of the monitors and surveillance systems a soothing constant around her in the security suite. She'd seen Dam's car and the transport pull up in the hangar on the security screens, frowned as the two figures were stretchered out by a crowd of armed guards. Two of them?

She'd zoomed in on Dam, as she always did, trying to decipher her boss's mood from his appearance on arrival. His face always fell in a slightly hangdog expression, as if he was forever disappointed with whatever life brought him, so you had to look hard for the signs that something big was wrong. What was left of his thinning hair was standing up, which meant he was anxious and had been wiping the sweat from his pate. He was licking his lips a lot, too, and his face was even paler than usual. He'd have to report straight to Narkompros, she supposed. He wouldn't be back here for a while.

Jessen let Dam move out of view, and, rather than follow his progress through the corridors of the Facility, she closed her eyes and leaned back, savouring her solitude.

She could never understand how someone as apparently feckless as Dam had ever entered the security business, let alone how he had reached so high in his profession. He hated getting his hands dirty, hated guns, resented the use of force. But his record in government service was impeccable – she'd hacked into his files and seen for herself. His systems worked. He was clever, astute – and apparently incorruptible.

She wondered how many others like her he'd delegated the bad stuff to over his career. The brutality he signed away and authorised as part of the job if a project's integrity was compromised. She wondered what he must think of her now she was hardened to hurting people. Now that it was just part of her.

But she was just doing what she had to.

She could see the ghost of her reflection in the monitor screen, aspects of herself thrown into sharp relief by the spotlights in the ceiling. White-blonde hair like a ghostly crown. An arc of high cheekbone, a dark ring oppressing one eye.

Refocusing on the screen itself, Jessen punched in a different feed. The view of the hangar blurred to become an observation ward in Medical. She saw scientists in grey protective suits, flitting about like thin shadows against the sterile white of the walls and floor. The only colour came from the two prone bodies on the trolleys in the room's centre. One was dressed in green and grey, the other in pale blue. Then the scientists crowded round, obscuring her view.

'Whoever you two are,' she murmured to herself, 'you're going to be sorry when you wake up.'

'We're naked!'

Compassion had woken up groggy and sick. It had taken her some time to even question where she was. All around was metal. A machine of some kind? She had no memory of where she'd been, or what she was doing here now.

When she'd turned her head and seen the Doctor sitting nude and cross-legged on the floor, she'd decided she was dreaming. Then she'd looked at herself. Pressed her fingers into the floor.

. . . her fingernails turn white under the pressure. Felt her . . . thick in her mouth, and finally used it to articulate the obvious in alarm.

Now she stared in horror as the Doctor rushed over to calm her, his arms wide for a hug. She shrank away from him, instinctively covering herself.

'Get away from me!' she yelled. He stopped stock still. Compassion shut her eyes so she didn't have to look at him.

'Are you all right?' His voice was a bit sullen at her rejection.

'I expect so,' she muttered, turning on to her side away from him. 'Where are our clothes? My earpiece?'

'Impounded, I think,' said the Doctor. 'Now, take it easy. You've been sleeping. Deeply.'

'Where are we?'

'Nowhere very inspiring. Skale, I'd say, from the TARDIS records – a pinprick little planet orbiting a nowhere sun, all by itself. Shouldn't be surprised at our treatment I suppose. "Only planets" tend to grow up spoilt. Or not at all.' He paused. 'Would you like some water?'

Compassion stretched out an arm behind her and was handed a paper cup. She gulped the water down greedily. 'You got us off that space station, then?' she said.

'Yeah.'

'And Fitz?'

His long silence made her turn reluctantly back to look at him. 'I'm thinking of throwing one if we don't get some attention soon,' the Doctor said, eyes flashing a warning that she should keep quiet about their companion. She nodded her understanding. The cell was bound to be under observation, and she doubted their captors would take kindly to a third intruder possibly at large on their space station. As it was, the Doctor eventually answered her question with a forlorn, helpless shrug.

She glanced around. The entire room was bare. A thick glass window ran along the length of the wall her toes were pointing to. She couldn't see anything on the other side of the glass, it was too dark.

Compassion shivered. 'Why strip us?' she grumbled.

'Two reasons, I think,' said the Doctor, spinning back round with both hands over his eyes. 'We're in quarantine, for a start. Not that anyone told me directly. I get the impression they don't get many visitors here.'

'I see.' She gestured at the window. 'And the other reason is to humiliate us before an audience, do you think?'

The Doctor carefully peeked at the window through his fingers and smiled. 'Don't worry. Honour clothes the valiant. Besides, our stuff must've been covered in that gunk we were lying in. Perhaps we could enquire about their dry-cleaning service.'

Compassion ignored him. 'How long have we been here?'

'I don't know,' the Doctor said, knocking restlessly on the walls as if hoping to hit some secret exit mechanism. 'Could be any amount of time.'

'I need more water,' Compassion said.

'You've drunk all they've given us,' said the Doctor, without reproach. 'Let's ask for extra rations. I'm sure they must be watching us.'

Compassion nodded briefly and winced as the Doctor began calling out inane requests for glasses of lemonade and ginger beer. Her skull felt like it was splitting open. She'd been getting headaches for some weeks now, but this was the worst. She put it down to a consequence of the escape.

'Is your head hurting?' she asked the Doctor, trying to be casual.

He seemed pleased at her apparent concern. 'No. No, I'm fine, actually,' the Doctor went on. 'But thank you. Thank you for asking.'

His smile became a broad grin, and she snorted, though not unkindly. She'd met many idiots in her life, but the Doctor was at least the most likable.

They sat in silence, both facing the window, wondering what might happen next.

Dam burst into the security suite earlier than Jessen had anticipated, but she didn't jump. That was her: calm and professional, unfazed by anything.

'Singularity –'

He impatiently waved aside the traditional greeting. 'I brought back two unidentified people in that capsule.'

'I caught a glimpse of them,' Jessen said. 'How the hell did they get up there?'

'I don't know. It makes no sense.' Dam sounded bitter. 'We're to take the girl to a separate cell for questioning. Narkompros wants to talk to the man himself. We'd better get going. The old man wants answers from this pair immediately.' He rubbed his hand over his balding head. 'You know I almost find myself hoping they *won't* talk.'

Jessen looked puzzled.

'I don't think we're going to want to hear what they have to say.'

The Doctor jumped to his feet as a hissing noise filled the cell.

'Gas?' asked Compassion, scrambling up to join him.

'Airlock,' said the Doctor. 'They're coming for us. Stand behind me.'

Compassion shot him a look and stood by his side as four armed guards in grey hazard suits lumbered through a hidden door in the cell wall and surrounded them.

'What are you lot staring at?' the Doctor challenged. 'Never seen time-travelling naturists before? What?'

Two of the guards moved forward to grab Compassion. The Doctor stepped forward to block their path and was shoved out of the way. Compassion seized the distraction to run for the door, but she wasn't quick enough. A guard grabbed her clumsily by the hair, and she cried out, more in irritation than distress.

'Stop that!' the Doctor shouted. 'There's no need!'

Another guard took Compassion's arms and held them behind her back, then the pair of them forced her, struggling, through the door.

'Where are you taking her?' the Doctor demanded ineffectually, lunging forward to try to help her, but the remaining guards held him easily. 'Whatever you want to know, we'll tell you. There's no need for this unpleasantness.'

He'd barely finished the sentence before the guards sent him flying into the inspection wall. His face slammed against the glass, and he thought he was seeing stars until he realised the lights in the room beyond the glass had flickered on.

In the bright white light stood a thick-set man in his late fifties, dressed in some kind of military apparel, holding himself stiffly as if posing for a portrait. The look on the man's face painted a vivid picture itself, the Doctor decided. Here was a dour, hard-bitten, hostile character. The ruthless old man in charge, a sour inspiration to his people. A timeless icon.

'Thank you for dropping by at last,' the Doctor said. 'I'm so sorry to have made your day unexpectedly interesting. Where are you taking my friend Compassion?'

The man tilted his head back in an attempt at intimidation. His voice rattled out of hidden speakers in the cell walls. 'Your *accomplice*, like you, will tell us everything.'

The Doctor affected a taken-aback expression. 'What, *everything*? How much time do you have?' He felt the heavy rubber of the guards' protective gauntlets on his bare arms and shoulders and tensed himself. 'What I'd *love* to be able to tell you is why you've got hundreds of people orbiting this planet in suspended animation waiting to be launched into space, why some kind of cybernetically enhanced life form is watching over them and why everything seems to be going so terribly wrong up there…'

The military man wasn't looking very happy.

'And of course,' the Doctor added hastily, 'what I can do to help. But unfortunately I can't tell you anything of the sort. Not yet.' He clicked his fingers as if a brilliant idea had occurred to him. 'Hey! Perhaps you could tell me?'

The guards pulled and twisted the Doctor's arms, and forced him roughly to his knees. The sneering military man moved closer to the glass, and the Doctor smiled encouragingly. 'In your own time, of course…'

'Your name?'

Dam's eyes flicked between Jessen and the newcomer seated

behind the glass. She looked human. She sounded human. Why couldn't he shake the conviction she was something more than that?

'Compassion,' the woman said.

Jessen smirked. 'Pleading so soon? We haven't even warmed up yet.'

'My *name* is Compassion,' the woman said, rolling her eyes.

Jessen motioned one of the guards holding Compassion to strike her round the face. He did so with enthusiasm, and Dam tried not to wince. The noise of the blow sounded dull and heavy over the monitoring speakers, and their prisoner's breathing uncomfortably loud. Jessen had cranked up the speakers to maximum volume. She didn't want to miss a thing.

Dam hated interrogations.

'Compassion. That's a code name?' Jessen asked.

Compassion smiled and swept her hair back from her eyes. 'A man called Kode first called me by it, yes.'

Jessen stared hard at her. Compassion met her gaze with a look of weary insolence. It was a look she gave very well, Dam thought.

'What do you care about my name, anyway?' Compassion asked. 'It's my purpose in coming here you should be worried about.' She paused. 'Not that it's worrying in itself. We only came here because we had to.'

'You had to?' Jessen nodded with false sympathy.

Compassion shrugged. 'The space station we'd landed on became unstable.'

'You "landed" there?'

'That *is* what I said.'

'You're terrorists.'

'Tourists,' Compassion said simply. 'Accidental ones at that.'

Jessen leant back in her chair. 'Explain the device we found attached to your ear.'

'It's just decorative.'

'It's a receiver of some kind. Is that how you get your instructions?'

Compassion glanced up at the guard who'd hit her. 'Believe me, I don't take instructions from anyone. The Doctor and I have no agenda. We took that little craft because otherwise we'd have died.'

'The capsule was occupied.'

'Only by a corpse. And before you start, we didn't kill him.' Compassion looked straight at Dam now, as if he was more likely to believe her. 'It must've been the space station breaking down. The Doctor insisted we take one capsule together just so we *didn't* kill anyone else.'

'A number of capsules were launched as a result of your sabotage,' Jessen stated. 'Only your own deviated from its computed course to return here. How?'

Compassion blinked languidly while she seemed to take in this information. 'The Doctor steered us here. I'd imagine the launch co-ordinates are embedded in the navigational systems, aren't they?' She shrugged as well as she could with the guards' hands pressing down on her bare shoulders. 'I spent my sleep dreaming.'

'Dreaming?' Dam asked, surprised. 'Of what?'

'Why, are you offering to analyse it for me?'

Jessen was clearly about to get Compassion punished again, but Dam shook his head. 'Tell us. Tell us, or we'll have to really hurt you.' His voice sounded quiet in the room, which seemed filled with the sound of Compassion's amplified breathing.

'All right... Whatever. I dreamt I was standing somewhere, if you must know. Somewhere that felt like a platform overlooking... I don't know where. Everything. Whatever you wanted to see, I suppose.'

She seemed quite taken with her reminiscence, Dam observed; too taken, at least, to notice Jessen asking him with her eyes why they were indulging the prisoner like this.

'All I could see was grey, grey like smoke... Not really any one place at all. But that didn't matter. I remember wishing I didn't *know* it was a dream, wishing it could be real.' The woman suddenly seemed to realise where she was, looked away and said no more.

27

Dam considered her, sitting there, defiant again, bored-looking and aloof. Then he nodded to the guards and they marched Compassion, unprotesting, from the room.

'A waste of time,' Jessen said.

'Not at all. We know she's lying,' Dam said. 'She couldn't have dreamed like that in the gel – it's not possible.'

Jessen stood up and prowled the room, staring at the empty chamber on the other side of the glass as if their prisoner was still sitting there. Dam remembered when Jessen's entire body language had softened back to normal after an interrogation was over. Now he could barely detect a difference. He kept meaning to sit her down and talk things over with her, to see if there was anything wrong. But, as with so many things, he kept putting it off. There never seemed to be the right opportunity...

'Her whole story's a pack of lies,' Jessen said. 'That much is obvious.'

Dam pushed his fist to his mouth and considered. The hiss still sounding from the speakers accentuated his feeling that something had been left behind in the chamber, something unknown that they couldn't quantify.

He looked at Jessen. 'Nothing is obvious about any of this.'

The Doctor was leaning back against the far wall when Compassion was pushed through the sliding doors back into their cell. In a moment his pale eyes were sweeping over her, concerned.

'You're unharmed,' he noted.

'Not a scratch,' Compassion agreed, rubbing her face. It didn't seem to be bruising. 'They really don't know what they're doing round here. Amateurs.'

The Doctor looked at her a little sceptically, rubbing the back of his neck with feeling. She noticed red welts on his shoulders. 'I'm not so sure. This is only the start of it all,' he said.

'Obviously,' Compassion answered.

'It seems no extraterrestrial contact has yet been made on Skale,' said the Doctor, 'at least not by this power bloc. They're afraid of us. For now.' The Doctor pulled a scary monster face at her and waved his hands around like claws. 'How long do you think we can keep them that way?'

Compassion slumped down to the cold metal floor. 'Did you learn anything of use from them?'

'I discovered that we're spies! Isn't that exciting?' He grinned wildly at her. 'I had no idea! But they assumed we already knew that the Bastions – that's what they call those space stations in formation up above, apparently – were shielded from standard monitoring equipment and that no one on the planet even knows of their existence.' His smile became more controlled. 'Sharing their secrets with us already. How encouraging.'

'It doesn't suggest they intend to let us go free and spread them, does it?' Compassion said.

Chapter Five
Welcome to the Neighbourhood

You know how it is when you start somewhere new; whether it's school or a job or just moving to another neighbourhood, you have that horrible sense that you don't really belong for the first couple of weeks. You think over where you've been, and where you were happiest, and you resent your new surroundings; well, I always have, anyway. Travelling with the Doctor was just like being an Englishman abroad wherever we landed up, a tourist. You kept yourself pretty much to yourself. Now I find myself forced to be a Mechtan, doing as the Mechtans do, because the only other planet they know of is their own, a place they call, imaginatively enough, Homeplanet. It's a downer in a way; there are so many stories I could tell them about where I've been…

The time's flown by. That's possibly because the days are so short here; hasn't taken me long to adjust. I'm quite proud of myself; you can take me anywhere, it seems. And I'm not worried any more.

I've got a nice drum; well, same as anyone else's, but it's cool, really spacious. Like a villa or something – white walls and floors, raffia mats to break it up a bit. No music, which is a bit of a pain, I guess. No TV, either. It's like the old days – the way people amuse themselves round here is to talk to each other. To make an effort to get along with people, instead of ignoring them like they were rubbish blowing along the pavements, the way I used to back in London.

It's the littlest things that take the most adjusting to. Flimsy locks on the doors because no one's got anything that's worth nicking; you only use them if you don't want to be disturbed. It takes a while for it to sink in that people aren't out to get you. Believe me, I've been waiting for it all to go pear-shaped as usual, but… Well, I don't see how it can. It's not like the rat race back home. There's no one to feel resentful of for having more than you. There's no pressure to get a high-flying job and no corporate ladder to climb. I mean, I work as a carer in a kids' home. My mate Serjey serves in a bar, and Low Rez (his real name's Melores, we just call him that because he's the vaguest little sod you'll ever come across) cleans windows for his forty credits a week. And it's the same kind of stir for everyone: manual labour to occupy you and to involve you in the community. That's what we do here.

Of course, I've spun myself a bit of a back story, just for the hell of it, but there hasn't been much need even for that. The people here have forgotten most of their *own* stories. No one recalls that much of their lives back on Homeplanet, seems it's all a bit hazy. The old life getting fainter and fainter as time goes by. All part of the therapy.

That's not the case with me, though. My memory goes back a *long* way. It's kind of like *déjà vu* – you know, when you think you've seen something before? I can cast my mind back to going to San Francisco, or to the UN building, and find myself thinking it happened years and years ago. Like on wet Sunday afternoons, when you put on your old records and remember what you were doing when you first heard them – that feeling of nostalgia – except a thousand times stronger. Like I'm hundreds of years old, not twenty-nine. Or thirty. Whatever I am.

It bugs me a bit, all that, if I'm honest. Still, life goes on; I know it's all to do with the way the TARDIS pieced my mind back together again after… well, after what happened when I got caught up with the Remote. There's other little things I notice, too. My mind works in different ways; I can fill in a crossword much faster than I ever used to, and I've become a demon at anagrams. Something to be grateful to Compassion's lot for, I suppose.

COMPASSION
POISON SCAM
A COSMOS PIN

Funny, the way words suggest themselves to me now.

31

My dreams aren't the same any more, either: they make a bit too much sense... It's like something that's never actually dreamed itself is having a go at seeing what it might be like. I think the TARDIS was trying a bit too hard there. Full marks for effort, but... well, I used to love my dreams. Hated the way I couldn't remember them properly when I woke up, would lie in bed for hours trying to piece them together and work out the meaning. Not any more. For a time after I'd been a bit... Remote, shall we say, I used to feel scared every time I woke up, that I wasn't who I thought I was. The age-old thing – am I a Fitz dreaming he's a time traveller or a time traveller dreaming he's a Fitz?

But since I came to Mechta, there've been no dreams. *No one* dreams on Mechta, something in the air most probably: you have yourselves, and you have each other, but the only dreams are waking ones of what you might achieve when the time comes to go back home.

That won't be for a while, I hope.

So forgive me, dear makeshift diary, if I use you to scribble down my thoughts like this from time to time. It's stuff I can't talk to the others about. For my eyes only. If they ever found out the truth about me...

Well, I don't want to give anyone a setback, do I?

Chapter Six
Wrong Answers to Questions You Never Asked

'Alien visitors?' Narkompros stared at Dam, incredulous. 'And you believed her?'

'I've viewed the tape of your own interrogation of the male, Head Narkompros,' Dam said. 'I don't understand what either of them would gain from lying about such a thing.'

'A few more hours of existence before I put a bullet in their brains for espionage, perhaps,' sneered Narkompros.

Dam was unable to keep the wobble from his voice. 'Just suppose they *are*, though. Suppose they're so powerful they don't care *what* we do to them. Suppose this is just the start.'

'Of what? An invasion from space? Agents of Haltiel coming to get us, two at a time?' Narkompros snorted. 'Pull yourself together, man. Aliens are a long-term threat. They'll keep till we get out into space ourselves. Till we take the fight to them.'

Dam found himself turning on the old man. 'You actually believe that, don't you? You actually believe you've got *everyone* working to your own personal timetable!'

He regretted the words even as he said them. Until his contracted time was worked in full, his entire future could be decided for him by a single word from Narkompros. He took a deep breath and murmured his apologies.

'These are pressing times, Dam,' Narkompros stated after some deliberation, but Dam felt too humbled now to react to the patronising tone. 'Still, the ship of state must be kept afloat. A clear head is needed – and a respectful tongue.'

Dam couldn't look the old man in the eye. 'Of course, Head Narkompros. Singularity and strength in you.'

Narkompros waved the oath aside as he paced the room, thinking aloud. 'I can't believe they're working for any one Parallel…' He clapped his hands. 'A consortium of the Elite, perhaps. That could fit. Power-players with no allegiances, compiling information for the highest bidders.'

'Incredible lengths to go to simply to compile information,' Dam countered, warily. 'Surely knowledge of the Project's existence would be enough. Why get on board?'

'To see the proof for themselves. To see what other secrets they can sniff out. To find out about Mechta.'

'And breach our defences so effortlessly? And cause deliberate sabotage while they're up there – then come straight to us where the knowledge can only get them shot?'

Narkompros slammed his hand down on the table. 'Well if you've got so many damned questions, make *them* give you the answers!'

Your answers, you mean, Dam thought. Convenient, easy answers that won't trouble your sleep at night. That was why the old man hadn't blown up more at his insolence. He was as rattled as Dam was.

Dam cleared his throat. 'Indulge me, Head Narkompros. I want to be sure they really are as human as you and me. I want them scanned.'

'X-ray?'

'These people *wanted* to be discovered. If their technology can get them on board our Bastions...' Dam shook his head. 'I want a more... rigorous check.'

'Slice them open,' the old man snarled.

Dam half-smiled. 'I'm sure Jedkah would enjoy that enormously, but it's a little extreme at this stage, don't you think, Head Narkompros? I'm arranging to have our visitors sent through the scan module.'

'Each imaging costs a small fortune.'

'At least then we'll know what we're up against. Right down to gene level.' Dam took a deep breath. 'No doubt we'll find they're just as you say. Spies for some kind of consortium. Then we can interrogate them more... thoroughly.'

'It'll come from your budget,' Narkompros grumbled, stony-faced. 'Now, dismissed. Get this charade over with, then come back and tell me I was right.'

* * *

34

'That's it,' said Makkersvil, rubbing his eyes and rising to his feet. 'End of work-stretch. Good night, one and all.'

'Remain seated, Operator.'

Makkersvil's vision was crazy with spiralling black smudges from the pressure of his hands. He waited impatiently for Yve to come into focus.

'We've started getting fifty times more data from 634 than we can deal with right now,' she said. 'We need to know what that means.'

'We know what it means,' Makkersvil said casually. 'A glitch.'

'I can't afford to be a man down.'

'So find another man and get him up,' Makkersvil suggested. 'Shouldn't cause you too many problems.'

There she was, clearer now. That prim look of disgust on her face freezing into the cool little smile that always followed. How could she be so different but look exactly the same?

'I will only tolerate your insubordination so far,' Yve said quietly. 'Don't force me to make an example of you.'

'I've worked three twenty-hour stretches this week already,' Makkersvil said. 'I'm tired, Chief Supervisor Yve. I can barely focus on the screens.'

'You will do as I instruct,' Yve reminded him softly.

'Don't I always?'

Makkersvil slouched back to his station. One day he would let it all out. Make her see exactly what these last years had done to him, what watching her exulting in her position had put him through. It wouldn't make a scrap of difference, he knew, but the satisfaction, the release of just letting go and screaming at her in front of Terma, the other tech-heads, everyone…

And more. He'd finally learn the truth about her, about what she'd become, by what she'd do to him then. He'd have the proof – maybe not for long if she had a bullet put in his brain, but at least either way he could stop hanging on to that ridiculous, pathetic, demeaning little *hope* that someday she might realise…

He heard her wristcom start bleeping, and saw an amused expression spread over her face as she spoke to whoever was on the other end for a couple of minutes. Then she came over to him.

'I've decided to let you go after all. I've arranged for you to go on a special assignment,' she said, lending drama to the last two words. 'You were part of the team that rewired the body scanner, weren't you?'

'Yes, Chief Supervisor. You may recall I headed the project.'

'Such a promising career,' Yve said sweetly. 'Do please report to Security Head Dam in the observation suite immediately.'

She turned away. Makkersvil cursed at her back, then keyed in a secure message on his computer, barely checking the black letters that blurred as they burnt into the green screen, and hit SEND.

'Late night again. Sorry,' it would read when decrypted. 'Blame Yve.'

He imagined briefly the stack of evidence mounting against him if its recipient didn't delete these illicit messages as he did. Patterns repeating themselves... Sighing, he turned to go. He was so bad at this game.

And in the end, losing was as inevitable as discovery.

'I'm sick of being herded around like an animal,' Compassion said pointedly to the guard holding her. She didn't expect a reply. She didn't need her earpiece to pick up on the paranoia that buzzed around these people. Everyone spoke the right slogans to each other, trying to act like perfect media images of solidarity and strength in order to fit in. Outsiders were the enemy. An enemy within was unthinkable; which was why, Compassion reckoned, practically everyone on the planet thought about it so often.

That had to be the reason why they were about to be put through the machine.

Compassion felt afraid of it. Not because of its intimidating shape – it was all sharp points and hard edges, a deranged angular doodle of metal and wire and nozzles – but because of the weight it must carry in this insular society. The people here might be dreary, party-line-toeing fools, but machines like this were beyond all bias, all reason. They were impartial reporters whose conclusions would never be refuted.

Compassion didn't want it looking into her, it was as simple as that. She'd felt so different since travelling with the Doctor, felt sometimes that she barely knew herself any more. She didn't want some alien machine pinning down those fears under the piercing electric lights of this observation room, didn't want these faceless people to know her better than she knew herself. She wished she was back in the TARDIS.

The Doctor, ahead of her, was shoved towards the machine. She could discern men and women staring in at them through the observation wall. She squinted at them, barely aware of the naked Doctor berating the guard for being so heavy-handed.

With horrified fascination she watched the Doctor walk as directed into the lethal-looking innards of the machine. A low hum of power started up as wires cut the air around him, whipping around his body and twisting him into an unnatural posture. The equipment moved too fast to be properly observed, but gradually the Doctor's form disappeared under a mass of circuitry and probes, thick black snaking tubes vying for exposed flesh along with needles that must've been a half-metre long.

At least it was all over quickly enough. The Doctor was left standing with his arms open wide for a moment before he tottered forward on to his face with a single gasp. The guards stomped over and dragged his reddening body clear of the machine. Compassion saw him turn his head to look at her and wink. She felt the familiar frustration. He would never grasp that she didn't welcome those reassuring gestures from him in his pain. They only made her feel uncomfortable.

Two hearts, she thought. That'll do it. Maybe they won't bother with me, assume I'm the same. Unalike. This culture's not ready for proof of aliens sharing their galaxy. We'll both end up on a slab, cut open slice by slice as they search for something that'll convince them they're wrong.

'Body temperature suggests mild fever...' Compassion jumped and looked about her as a human voice rang out over the speakers, offering some kind of instant analysis. 'ID implant negative, no scar to suggest removal... Possible evidence of

surgical procedure in cardio-area, but hearts pumping strongly…'
Deliberation, then a measure of relief: 'Initial prognosis of subject normal. Awaiting genetic analysis…'

Terrific, thought Compassion, her heart sinking. The Doctor's ordinary here while I'm the freak. Heartless Compassion.

Her turn. The guard propelled her towards the machine. It stank of meat and engine oil, and her bare legs tingled with cramp as she stood before it, terrified to move closer.

The guard gestured with his gun for her to carry on. She looked at him dumbly.

'Compassion, it's all right,' she heard the Doctor say. 'Well, I mean, it's horrid, of course, but nothing you can't cope with.' He went on, trying to distract her with prattle. 'I'd imagine the hardware was originally intended for some kind of intuitive physiotherapeutic function – co-operate with it and it shouldn't hurt too badly.'

She turned to face him. His body looked a bit raw in places, but he was obviously fine. He nodded encouragingly at her, but seemed suddenly distant. Compassion's heart was pounding, a pressure building in her ears.

'You *mustn't* resist it, Compassion.'

It felt as if an abyss were separating the two of them.

Swearing, she stepped into it.

Security Chief Dam considered Compassion as she strode into the scan module. The snaking wires got a good grip of the woman's skin, and began pulling her in different directions, positioning different parts of the body for assessment. She was resisting it, stupid girl.

Dam glanced round at the small audience that had gathered here. He'd advised that the fewer staff who knew about their visitors, the better.

So here, then, was the elite team to deal with this situation and get them back on schedule. Jedkah, the stumpy little forensic analyst, was skulking in one corner. As ever, from the look on his face, it seemed his interest in their prisoners' bodies went beyond the purely professional. Makkersvil, a good-humoured young operator, had been sent over from Main to interpret the data as it came through from the scan module. Terma stood next to him looking worn out but stubbornly alert, fretting about the gibberish their malfunctioning Bastion had started sending down, no doubt. Perhaps he'd come here to take his mind off it.

He wished Jessen could be here with him for moral support, not this handful of faceless guards, but she was busy preparing the mindwalker for operation – the interrogator's favoured, and most costly, tool for teasing out the truth from its subjects. He was interested, as well as apprehensive, to know what results he'd get with this pair.

A throat cleared, irritably. Of course, Narkompros himself was here with them today, standing in front of the observation window, their glorious leader making a great show of taking a personal interest for the crowd. Dam could feel how desperate the old man was to turn to him and berate him for wasting all their time in this way.

Dam steepled his fingers as he watched Compassion twist and strain. Frankly, he would welcome any amount of personal punishment if it meant this pair checked out normal.

Irritated it should be taking so long, he turned back to Makkersvil, who was checking over the harvested data. The look of horror on the operator's face so startled him that he was still staring at the man when the scanning machine exploded.

Narkompros screamed and fell backwards as the glass in the window fractured. Dam glimpsed Compassion slump to the floor enmeshed in sparking wires before smoke billowed out into the room and he could only hear the people round him in their panic and confusion.

The Doctor tried to blink away the afterimage of the flash. The blast had knocked both him and his guard back against the wall. Checking first that the guard was only unconscious and not dead, the Doctor scrabbled forward into the dense smoke. 'Compassion!' he bellowed. 'Are you all right?'

Wading through the wreckage of the machine, he almost tripped over her. Her eyes were closed, her face screwed up like a petulant child's.

'Quickly, Compassion,' the Doctor whispered. 'Come on, we've got to get out of here!' Just as he began freeing her prone body from the melting wires, a bolt of yellow fire smacked into the floor in front of him.

'Back off!' the other guard instructed.

'Certainly,' said the Doctor, rolling backwards into the smoke and out of sight without another word.

Another blast of energy zipped past him. The guard was terrified, firing blind; he could hit Compassion. 'Over here!' the Doctor called, springing to his feet, and ducking as another bolt slammed into the glass behind him, distressing its weakened surface with a spaghetti junction of new cracks.

'Doctor?'

Coming round, Compassion spoke his name softly, but she still gave away her position. The Doctor heard the guard's blaster fire again, and a surprised yelp from the girl.

'Compassion?'

There was no response. Either she'd been hit or she didn't want to give away her position again. The Doctor knew he had to act quickly, that the place would be crawling with guards in another few moments.

'I've got your friend's gun!' the Doctor lied. 'Space people like me can see through smoke like it's air, so drop your weapon!'

He made out the shape of the guard coming towards him.

'Makes no difference,' the guard said, all bravado. 'Our gear's armoured.' He fired again, but wildly. He didn't know where the Doctor was.

'Heavily armoured?' the Doctor asked him, shrinking back further into the white fog.

The guard's only reply was another burst from the gun, closer this time. The Doctor ran forward and leapt into a flying jump kick, his bare feet hitting the guard in the stomach. The force lifted the man off his feet and sent him smashing through the damaged window.

'Well, you should be all right then, shouldn't you?' the Doctor muttered as he glimpsed the guard flailing around on his back. Someone grabbed his arm, and he turned to fight – then saw it was Compassion.

'What did I do?' she said, groggily.

'Later,' the Doctor said, grabbing her by the wrist and leading her through the window, his eyes watering with the smoke. 'It's time we made a point.'

Dam skittered backwards as the flying guard landed at his feet. His men out here had finally rallied themselves, ready to secure the observation bay, but a blurred glimpse of pink flesh in the corner of the room told him it was already way too late.

'Stop the prisoners!' he shouted. 'Left exit! They mustn't escape!'

Compassion struggled to keep up with the Doctor as he ran full pelt away from the chaos they had caused, zigzagging randomly through the base's corridors. Her body was tingling all over, and she could feel muscles twitch and spasm right along her spine.

A woman stepped out in front of them, and the Doctor waved his arms about like a madman. 'Unclean!' he wailed. 'Alien germs, unclean! Whooooo!' Terrified, the woman ducked back down the corridor she'd emerged from.

Compassion still felt dazed. She saw the Doctor perform an Egyptian sand-dance past another terrified member of the base personnel. 'Doctor, slow down a moment!'

'What?' said the Doctor, turning on one foot then jogging on the spot as he faced her.

'This is the most ridiculous and embarrassing escape you can ever have made.'

The Doctor stopped jogging and opened his mouth in pantomime surprise. 'You're probably right! I hadn't thought.'

He set off again, but this time Compassion ran faster and blocked his way. 'What happened back there, to the machine?'

'I don't know.' *Now* the Doctor looked embarrassed.

Compassion suddenly felt angry. 'You think I did it, don't you?'

'I… The machine could've been simply on the blink.' He looked down at her feet. 'Hiccuping on my triple-helixes. It wouldn't have liked those.'

'But it didn't just break, it blew apart!'

'It allowed us to escape,' the Doctor said, reaching for her hand. She snatched it away, just as a klaxon sounded. The lighting in the corridor turned a serene blue. 'Now we can sit down and wait.'

'What?'

The Doctor fell into the lotus position and beamed at her. 'I want to make that point I mentioned.'

Compassion stared at him. 'Point being that you're a fool? They'll catch us!'

The Doctor agreed amiably. 'We could make a good stab at escaping right now, that's just what they'll be expecting us to do. So we shan't. We'll wait here and give ourselves up like good little aliens.' He smiled and shrugged. 'They'll see we're actually terribly trustworthy after all and that they've been fussing about noth…'

Compassion realised the Doctor had apparently forsaken talking in favour of scrutinising her shoulders. She frowned at him. 'What are you staring at?'

'Is that right?' the Doctor whispered. 'For your skin to be so pale, I mean? Porcelain. Perfect.'

Compassion took a step away instinctively and covered herself with her arms. 'What's wrong with you? Stop it.'

He looked away, then looked horrified, as if suddenly aghast at his behaviour. 'Forgive me, I have such a dreadful attention span, don't I? It was just your skin. In this light, it's almost flawless, isn't it? Smooth as eggshell.'

She wouldn't humour him by looking herself. 'You're mad,' she said, feeling her anger growing.

'Look… Something's wrong, isn't it, Compassion?' the Doctor said softly, standing up. 'I've been worried about you for some time.'

She threw up her hands. 'I don't *need* worrying about, why can't you grasp that?'

'You can tell me, you know,' he said, advancing on her. 'Whatever it is.'

'I don't know what you're talking about,' Compassion said, starting to shake. Then she turned and ran, bare feet slapping against the polished metal floors. The Doctor called out her name, frantically begging her to stop, not to be silly, and then – realising it was no good – to take care.

She didn't look back. It was as if the smoke from the machine was inside her head now, and she had no idea who or where she was. The Doctor could've been calling for anyone.

Chapter Seven
Digging Holes for Yourself

Fitz opened the front door to find Anya waiting outside.

'You're early,' he told her.

'Nikol *left* early,' she replied, checking there was no one about to notice her slip inside.

Her voice made Fitz smile. It was deadpan, almost halting in its delivery. Her eyes were pale blue and flirtatious and her hair was brown and bushy. She had freckles all over her long nose and was skinny, almost painfully so. She was also about eight years older than he was and married.

So, naturally, he had started an affair with her within days of his arrival.

'Drink?' he asked her, gesturing at the dozens of full bottles lining his kitchen worktops.

'Sex,' she countered, lying back on the bed.

'You want ice with that?' he asked her innocently. By the time he'd fixed himself an Ethel – his terribly witty name for the only booze round here, a potent spirit called ethalol – she was already pulling off her clothes.

He sighed, not really in the mood. An affair had suited the pair of them, he guessed, first of all. Nikol, Anya's husband, who had to be twice Fitz's age, was a veteran of some war or other back on Homeplanet. The old guy couldn't remember it of course, but then he couldn't exactly forget it, either – he had only one arm to raise to the world, and a whole load of scars that no one could see cutting him up inside.

The couple had arrived here together, but Anya could now say with total impunity that she didn't know what she'd ever seen in Nikol; she cared about him, felt sorry for him, but really couldn't remember what more there had ever been to their relationship other than companionship. That had seemed justification enough for Fitz when they'd first met. She'd made him feel less lonely, and better about himself, in that slightly fraught time after his arrival. And she in turn got someone younger and prettier than her husband to make her feel attractive and vivacious.

Her undressing was a perfunctory act, nothing sexy, just a means to an end. As ever, Fitz thought, knocking back his drink, it was time to cut to the chase. 'You're not falling in love with me, are you?' she'd be whispering to him soon enough, as always. 'Only you must never fall in love with me.' As if the pyramids dotting the landscape were conjuring up the tomb of the pharaohs around them or something, like some dreadful curse might befall him if he ever developed deep feelings for her.

He felt as if he already had, if truth be told. She was a lovely woman, intelligent, sharp. She didn't want to own him, she said, which suited him; after all, how could she? She'd told him up front, she'd never leave Nikol. 'It just goes on until it stops' had sounded easy at first. Increasingly, though, when they were close, she would look in his eyes as if searching for some secret truth he could barely admit to himself. And he, in turn, was starting to resent her treating him like he was still some new boy in need of her care who didn't know any better.

I know what I'm doing, thought Fitz.

They did some talking that night. Fitz was stroking her hand as they lay back on the bed in the fading light, wondering how quickly Anya would have to leave to go back to her home in the block across the street, when he'd found himself tracing with his fingers the network of scars lining her palms. The time seemed right to ask her about them.

'They're there on my feet, too. On the soles.'

Fitz moved down the bed to investigate. The scars were white streaks against the pink of her skin, travelling all the way down from ball to heel.

'Nasty,' he said. 'What did you do?'

'I don't know. I think it was when I was a kid. You often do things to yourself when you're little, don't you? You know, experimenting.'

Fitz felt a little uncomfortable. Wounds as long as that would

45

take ages to heal; they'd keep opening back up, surely. Had she been a nutter or something?

'It doesn't really bother me, not remembering,' Anya went on. She wasn't looking at him now, she was staring into the distance. 'Our bodies aren't meant to hold on to extremes of emotion.'

Fitz forced a smile, sliding back up beside her. 'That's why we do things again and again...'

She laughed softly. 'But that's just it... We can feel the most extreme and incredible pleasure, but we can't hold it, or ever bring it back.'

This was getting a bit heavy. 'It takes someone else to bring it back for us. That's the point, isn't it? The point of being with other people?'

Anya ignored him, holding her own hand now as if it were someone else's and she wasn't sure what to do with it. 'It fades and we forget... If we didn't, we could never progress through life. Just lie and be lost in bliss, or in torment.'

'Takes longer to forget the torment, mind,' Fitz murmured.

'Not here,' Anya said, turning to him at last and kissing his face.

An hour later, with real life beckoning again, she left him on the bed, washed herself thoroughly in the bath and dressed, ready to return home to her husband.

'Where were you tonight?' Fitz wondered dryly.

Anya smiled. 'Out for a walk while Nikol concentrates on his campaign.'

He felt a twinge of guilt at her levity. 'What's he up to now?'

'The usual. Still convinced Homeplanet is trying to suppress us all here in some way, that they're up to something deep and dark and mysterious.'

Fitz smiled wryly. 'I don't notice a whole lot of suppression going on.'

'He's trying to get some pamphlets together, to try to get people on his side.'

'What's he doing, copying them out by hand?'

'I'm meant to be doing them for him. He's still not so good at writing with his left hand...'

Fitz felt suddenly embarrassed, mumbled an apology, but Anya waved it away. 'He's looking to raise awareness, get supporters… I feel a little dreadful for him that no one cares.' Anya came over to him. 'Do you think you could say *you're* interested?'

'What?' Fitz snorted. 'He gets to sleep with you every night, and I'm supposed to feel sorry for him?'

'It would mean we could spend more time together, stupid,' Anya said. 'It would take such a long time, copying out manifestoes, don't you think?'

'I don't know,' Fitz said. 'I don't want to get involved in any trouble.'

'What trouble could there be? He simply wants to arrange a demonstration outside Central, to try to force them into making their files on us public.' She shrugged. 'He wants to remember what he's been sent here to forget, that's all.'

Fitz remembered the receptionists at Central checking over the records for any sign of the Doctor and Compassion, finding nothing. 'It's enough just to know they're there, isn't it?'

Anya smiled wryly. 'For everyone except Nikol, it seems.' She stepped closer, brushing her nose against his. 'Listen. Just come round and meet him again, say you're interested.'

'That doesn't bother you? Me passing the time of day with your old man?'

'As long as you don't start an affair with *him*, of course it doesn't.' She kissed him again. 'He'll think he's getting somewhere at last. It'll keep him off my back and mean I've got more time to keep you on yours… We all come out winners.'

She turned and left without another word. Fitz stared after her as she walked away, and found himself a little unsettled. None of this seemed quite so carefree, any more.

That night, as he tried to get to sleep, he kept imagining a thick brown file with his name on it, faceless people poring over it for reasons he didn't understand.

He wasn't sure he really wanted to know the things they might have on him.

Chapter Eight
Strange Meeting

Every nerve on edge, Compassion swung herself round a corner and charged into a short corridor that ended in a red doorway marked LAUNCH BAY. She ran up to the door and tried it, but it wouldn't budge. A formidable-looking entry coder was mounted in the adjacent wall. She stared at it but the alarms were so loud they were stopping her thinking clearly. She hit some digits randomly, but nothing seemed to register. A single red light on its display screen winked mockingly at her.

Compassion was wondering what the light signified when, amazingly, the door clicked open. A woman in a blue tunic marked ENGINEERING emerged and gasped at the sight of her.

'You're staring,' Compassion said, and punched the woman hard in the face, back through the doorway.

The Doctor shook his head, alone in the blue corridor. 'Clumsy,' he told himself. He so wanted Compassion to change, to start caring, to appreciate the privilege of travelling the universe as he did… And yet she worried him. Not in the way Fitz worried him – whatever the problem, he knew he could help Fitz out. But Compassion seemed such a closed, self-centred person, riding his coat-tails like fare-dodgers ride a bus to get where they want to go on their own terms.

His demonstration useless now he was awaiting recapture alone, the Doctor sat down and rehearsed what he could say to appease his captors.

When the guards appeared round the corner seconds later he hadn't got very far. It didn't matter; they shot him the moment they saw him.

Compassion dragged the unconscious engineer by her feet along a concrete corridor. The droning of the klaxons faded as the corridor gave on to a vast hangar the size of a football pitch. Small spaceships, four or five streamlined, tubular affairs, were lined up in a row facing a wall of massive metal plates that clearly were designed to open up to allow the shuttles a shot at the sky.

One of the ships was damaged, a barrier of coloured tape stretched all round it. In its shadow, Compassion began to undress the woman, the slightest noise she made echoing accusingly back at her. The engineering tunic was way too small for her, but it was a relief to feel clothed again.

She was midway through scrabbling into the skinny woman's trousers when a guard emerged from the ship, practically bumping into her.

The unconscious woman at Compassion's feet had no weapon, nor anything that could be used as one. To buy time, Compassion dived behind the next ship.

'You scared the crap out of me!' the guard hissed.

Compassion frowned as she struggled to pull up the trousers.

'You must be the girl from Haltiel,' the guard continued, and Compassion could hear the smile in his voice. 'Not much of an invader, are you?'

He knew of her and the Doctor, but was joking about it. This was no guard: he had to be an impostor. Like her, he was somewhere he shouldn't be.

Perhaps he could be useful to her.

'What are you doing here?' Compassion asked, cautiously.

'Waiting till that engineer had finished checking the pipes back there.' He gestured to a far wall. 'Thanks for bringing her back again. Very helpful.'

Compassion stepped away from the cover of the craft. 'Do you have a way of getting out of here?'

'As it happens, I've just picked it up,' the guard said, flashing a couple of small plastic disks at her. Something in the way he spoke made the faceless helmet he wore look more like a carnival costume than an intimidating death mask. 'Right, then. I've got transport outside and I suppose I'd better take you with me. Leaving unconscious engineers lying around the place isn't going to aid my reputation as a superspy, is it? Come with me. Now.'

She chased after him as he ran across the hangar. 'So you *don't* think I'm an alien, then?'

The guard didn't slow down. 'To be honest,' he said, 'I'd hope for something a little more subtle from an extraterrestrial intelligence.'

Compassion thought briefly of the Doctor. 'I wouldn't get your hopes up,' she muttered.

The smoke in the obs suite was clearing at last. Dam felt almost sorry; nowhere to hide, now. There'd be hell to pay for this. He felt sick with anticipation.

He'd radioed Jessen and got her to secure all exits. They'd already caught the male with ease, just sitting there like an idiot. Now every guard that wasn't pursuing the woman was watching over the Doctor as he was prepared for the mindwalker. That should answer some questions – assuming the thing didn't simply give up and explode like the scanner.

Jedkah was carefully brushing broken glass from the groaning bulk of their fallen leader, squinting through his thick glasses. 'You're clear,' he said in his squeaky little voice.

Terma crouched by Narkompros's side to help him up. 'You should lie down in your quarters.'

Narkompros shrugged off his supportive grip. 'I'm going nowhere without an armed guard,' he muttered, his breath coming in reedy snatches. 'The male let himself be caught. He was stalling us so the woman could escape. She must have some kind of agenda.'

'She can't get far,' Dam said, licking his lips and hoping he sounded convincing. 'Not barefoot and naked.'

'Not without help, anyway,' Makkersvil suggested.

Dam glanced at the operator with irritation. 'What?'

'They're in league with someone here,' Narkompros said slowly. 'Yes, someone here, on the Facility.'

'Could be any one of us,' Makkersvil said quietly with a small smile.

'That's enough insolence,' Terma warned, stalking over to the operator. 'What caused the scanner to blow up like that?'

Makkersvil shrugged. His face was streaked with blood from a cut on his forehead, and a fresh trickle washed gorily into his eye as he frowned at the readouts on the console in front of him.

'Power surge,' he concluded.

'Caused by?' Terma asked.

'I've no idea.'

'Sabotage,' Narkompros said.

Dam turned to him. 'There was never an opportunity for them to do anything to the equipment.'

'They were *helped*,' Narkompros reiterated as if explaining to a child.

Terma nodded wearily. 'If this pair *are* working for another Parallel and have agents here among us...'

'Project security could be terminally compromised,' Narkompros concluded.

Dam felt himself withering before their combined gaze, and it was a real relief when Narkompros's guard escort arrived to rush the old man back to his quarters.

Now all Dam had to do was sort out this whole horrific mess.

'I wondered if you were the cause of those alarms,' Compassion's newfound accomplice said as they reached the shuttered opening of the launch bay. 'You nearly gave me a double coronary – till I realised every guard on this Facility would be rushing for the obs suite.' He punched in a precise sequence to another entry coder and a small door slid open in the wall of metal panels to reveal grey daylight. 'Should mean there'll be fewer guards to see you get in there.'

He gestured, and Compassion peered through the door to see a black, forbidding-looking vehicle parked thirty or so metres away. 'A guard transport?' she asked him.

'What did you expect? I'm a guard, aren't I?'

'No.'

'But I look the part, don't I? And so will you. There are spare uniforms in the back.'

Compassion stared at him. 'You really think they'll fall for this?'

The guard held up a small round datadisk. 'They'll fall for *this*. You'll see.'

'And then where will we go?' Compassion asked.

He didn't answer. He just ran across to the transport and slung the back doors open, gesturing she should get inside.

Once safely back in his room, Narkompros stood trembling, his eyes tightly shut, trying to push the nightmare journey over here from his mind. With every step, despite the guards, he'd expected that red-haired woman to drop on to his back with a knife or to press a gun against the back of his neck or...

He hugged himself, rocking on the balls of his feet. Glass. Glass all over him, and that smoke in his lungs – he could still feel it now. There was no telling how much damage it could've done to his insides.

Pulling off his tunic, he hurried over to Medik, then leaned against her cool silver surface as he tugged off his trousers. He hadn't let a human doctor examine him properly for years, not since he'd realised how dangerous that could be. If his enemies realised how fragile his health was they could use it against him – and there were always enemies, all around, outwardly respectful but secretly plotting to stab you in the back the moment you showed the slightest weakness. Besides, it was useless going to human doctors. He was too powerful to be told the truth. As Head of Facility, he could have the doctors shot if he didn't like the news they gave him.

He turned and shuffled forward to his salvation. Green lights winked on as he clambered inside the silver housing, and soon he could feel the warming rays of the laser scans, the tendrils of wire brushing over his skin, and tried to give himself over to the sensation that he was being well looked after.

'Report,' he instructed softly.

'Prognosis report: heightened blood pressure suggests state of mild shock,' came the synthesised female voice. There was a soft clatter as tablets were dispensed into a plastic beaker of water.

'This medication will help you feel better.'

'I… I fell, Medik,' Narkompros said, feeling wretched.

The warm caress of a lingering scan. 'Skin unbroken. Minor bruising to base of spine.' The soothing voice paused; then a further tablet was dispensed. 'This medication will help you feel better.'

Narkompros nodded and swallowed down the pills in one go, well used to the action. They tasted yeasty and bitter. Just that taste on his tongue made him feel stronger.

'So, I'm well?' he asked.

'You are well.'

The pay-off. He closed his eyes and smiled. The words were a token he waited trembling for, every time he gave himself to her embrace. He lived in fear of the day she would tell him something different.

Feeling a little more assured, he walked out from the metal alcove, wincing as his feet found the cold floor. He cast an appraising glance at Medik in her alcove as he pulled his trembling body under the bedclothes. Peace of mind was so hard to find these days.

Chapter Nine
Tram Scam, Mechtan Centreside

Picture the scene. I've been working all day at the Kids' Home, playing games and telling stories, carting the little beggars about and cleaning up after them, and I'm knackered. I'm there on the tram as it rattles and scrapes and bumps us workers along into town, feeling the tiniest bit blue. Homesick, you know, though I'm not sure what exactly I'm thinking of as home. The sun's in my eyes, making me squint. There's a breeze; someone's got a window open, and now and again I'm catching a whiff of ozone from the electric sparks overhead from this oversized dodgem car, squeaking on its merry way to the terminus Centreside.

There's a girl, sitting in front of me. Quite nice-looking. Redhead; redder than Compassion is. I watch her as she looks studiously out of the window, barely blinking as her wide hazel eyes take in the passing scenery: the fountain in the marketplace, the fat white statues lazing in the sunshine, crowds of people thronging the high walkways. And the dwelling places, of course, the pyramids rising over the skyline. Like a nice clean Egypt. Mystery. Power.

The girl yawns, it makes me smile. The pyramids are here to reassure, not to inspire. To the Homeplaneters, they're mundane, just the way dwellings are built. None of the resonances or associations they have for me are flitting through her mind, I can tell. She looks a bit fed up. Tasty, though. Hair curling to her shoulders. Thin red lips. Grey trouser suit, quite tight. Ankles wrapped in delicate chains. She lounges languidly on the plastic seat in a way that surely can't be comfortable, but she's too bloody-minded to shift her position now she's there. I like that.

The tram slopes away as it reaches a wide plaza, and the sun slides out from behind the ornate frame of the window. It's still all market stalls and cafeterias outside, browsers and boozers. Another fifteen minutes till we're at the terminus. I'm ready for a few Ethels. Like any other evening.

Suddenly, a man sits down beside her. There's plenty of seats elsewhere in the carriage, and she looks at him for a moment before retreating back to wherever her mind's been sitting.

'Excuse me,' the man says. 'Do you have a pen?'

She smiles. 'I think so, hold on.' A moment later she's got the pen and he's taken it from her.

'I just thought I'd write down my address for you. That way you can call round whenever you'd like,' the man says, smiling.

'That's what you thought, is it?' she says, snatching the pen back from him, looking seriously annoyed. 'Forget it. Would you mind leaving, please?'

He retreats, slouching off to another seat red-faced.

I, of course, can barely believe what I've just seen. I catch her scowling eye. 'Can you believe that jerk?' I ask her, the picture of sympathy. 'What was he thinking of?'

She smiles, relaxes a little. 'I know. What an idiot!'

'I guess you must have men coming up to you like that a fair bit, huh?'

She blushes and half-smiles – and we're off talking quite naturally. The conversation goes well – so well, in fact, that about thirteen minutes later I've got her address and an invitation to call round for a chat sometime. Once I've said goodbye, I spot the loser that made all this possible sidling along the crowded platform, and decide to thank him in person.

'Well done, Serjey,' I say to him. 'Worked like a charm.' Just as it always did on the tube back home.

'I still say it was your turn to act like the patsy,' Serjey said.

'Me, the patsy? With a girl like that?' I grinned. 'Know your place, my son. You know I can't bear waste…'

I called round that evening to Filippa's. There are no phones here on Mechta – the only way to communicate with someone is face to face. All part of the therapy, that's the catchphrase round here. Anyway, she seemed pleased to see me, and we went for a few drinks. Talked about all sorts of stuff. She works in a bank off Centreside. She's twenty-five. Quite a serious sort, doesn't like anything that's not good for her; well, except me, it seems. She said she gets quite down, sometimes. I, of course, immediately became the enigmatic broken-hearted type. Seemed to go down quite well.

She let me walk her back home. It was a lovely warm night as usual, and the stars were out. The skies were thick with them, like someone had kicked sand over the blackness. I told her I was desperate to know what the inside of her house was like, just to check that dwellings Centreside were the same as they are on my manor, down South. Surprise, surprise, it was exactly the same in every detail.

'Thanks for satisfying my curiosity,' I said, taking her hand.

'That's the only thing that's getting satisfied, tonight,' she said, taking it back again and leading me to the door. 'Good night, Fitz.'

The soft pressure of the kiss she'd pressed to my cheek seemed to stay with me a while. It was about halfway home, wishing she was facing me on the tram again, that I realised I was absolutely smitten.

There was a note from Anya waiting for me when I got back. I'd forgotten I was meant to be seeing her that evening. She seemed cool about it; the note said she understood that things sometimes came up unexpectedly, and that she'd see me at Nikol's strategy meeting the next day. The one I'd promised her I'd go to.

The thought of Anya makes me feel a bit sad, now. Meeting Filippa, it feels like something new is beginning.

I suppose that means that something else will have to end.

MADLY IN LOVE
NO MY LAD – EVIL!
MY NAIVE DOLL

Chapter Ten
A Walk in the City (Under Strict Scrutiny)

The Doctor woke up to find someone was gouging dirt from his fingernails. He tried to snatch his hand away but found he couldn't.

'Do you mind?' he asked the man politely.

'Be quiet. You're at our mercy.'

The Doctor pondered on this statement. 'Am I really?'

'Yes.' The man was short and wore thick glasses. He was scrutinising the lump of matter on the end of his spatula. 'Now, what will I find here, eh? Is dirt the same where you come from? Or will I have proof of your kind at last?'

'My kind?'

The man smiled knowingly. His voice was squeaky and high-pitched. 'Aliens. From Haltiel.'

'Ah. If I'm an alien from Haltiel, why aren't you wearing protective clothes?' the Doctor asked.

'You're out of quarantine,' the man said, distractedly, as he placed the dirt into a phial. 'The scanner did not detect any organisms inimical to us.'

'Was that before or after it blew up?' the Doctor said.

'There was a power surge. I don't think you caused it.'

'That's a relief,' the Doctor muttered. 'I was worried we'd have to pay for it.'

'You'll pay, all right.'

'Is this really the best way to cement good interplanetary relations?' The Doctor tried to look around, but found his head was held quite securely. He was clothed again, that was something; a baggy grey pressure suit was lashed to his body by a lattice of wires. But he felt an uncomfortable pressure in the small of his back and the back of his neck. The Doctor could see his reflection in the polished wall beside him when the man with the glasses moved aside. It was as if he was bound to a basic

57

anatomical representation of a human, a kind of bipedal simulacrum; its form moulded to his own in flexible alloy curves. He found to his frustration he couldn't move at all.

'What's all this in aid of?' the Doctor asked.

The little man shrugged. 'Some test they want to run on you. They think you're a spy.'

'The naïve fools, eh?'

'I'll show them,' the man whispered, tapping his phial and smiling craftily as the door began to open. A slim, balding, thoughtful-looking man came in, a blonde woman by his side. Both were flanked by red-uniformed guards.

'That will do, Jedkah,' the man said.

Jedkah didn't seem pleased to be found here. 'Security Head Dam, Administrator Jessen.' He nodded, a little sniffily. 'Singularity and strength in you both.'

'And in all 59,' Dam muttered. Jessen said nothing.

'What a lovely litany!' the Doctor said brightly. 'You should set it to music, something really stirring. I could help you if you like.'

'Your friend is still at large,' Dam said, keeping his distance.

'Don't worry, I'm sure she's all right,' said the Doctor. 'She's terribly good at looking after herself.' He attempted to lean forward confidentially but the wires bit into his neck. 'Ordinarily at this point you'd be well advised to threaten to kill me, or torture me, to bring her out into the open... but I'm really not sure that would count for a lot with Compassion.' He wished he could ask about Fitz's safety; but if he confessed to his companion's existence, who knew how these people might react; or what measures they might take to get rid of him? He needed information.

'Who is your ally here?' Jessen said quietly. 'Who is working with you?'

The Doctor flicked his wrist a fraction, indicating one of the guards. 'Him I think. No, no, the one next to him. Or is it both? Yes, that's right. I think they're in cahoots.' He grinned. 'Isn't that a wonderful word?'

He was almost amused to see the guards look at each other

uneasily as Jessen turned to regard them for a moment. These people were scared, *really* scared, no matter how hard they might pretend otherwise.

'You should take care of me a little better,' the Doctor said softly. 'For all you know, I'm an alien ambassador, and Compassion has transported herself back to our Haltien mother ship to get reinforcements. Is it Haltien? Or Haltielen?'

'You can't fool us,' Jessen said.

'The time for fooling is over,' the Doctor said in a spooky monotone, trying not to blink. No one seemed very impressed, so he flapped his hands weakly and reverted to his normal voice. 'You know, I'm really not very comfortable –'

'The mindwalker's not designed for your comfort,' Jessen said.

The Doctor smiled disarmingly. 'Mindwalker, eh? Well, all exercise is beneficial. But I meant I'm not very comfortable being so close to one of your machines. Look what happened to the last one.'

'You sabotaged it,' Dam suggested.

The Doctor looked at him coolly. 'Your friend Jedkah doesn't believe that and I don't think you do, either.'

Dam glared at Jedkah, then walked over to a small console. The wires lashing the Doctor to the framework snaked away into it.

'What do you use such intricate body-scanning equipment for around here, anyway?' the Doctor called. 'Something to do with those people in your Bastions? You're testing their bodies' reactions to long periods in space?'

Dam's only answer was to flick a switch. The Doctor felt the contraption holding him lurch into life. He gasped as it took a few steps forward, carrying him along helplessly. Pausing, it turned him slowly from left to right as if getting bearings.

Then it broke into a jerky run, heading straight for the wall.

The Doctor screwed up his eyes instinctively and felt a jolt of pain shock through him – but not from any impact. A sensation of being suddenly drunk, of being dragged along by someone determined to get you home when all you want to do is lie down and sleep, overwhelmed him.

When he opened his eyes he found he was somewhere else, in a busy street on an overcast day. People jostled past, heads down, apparently intent on going about their business with the bare minimum of human contact. The Doctor raised an arm, thoughtfully. He couldn't feel the metal pressure of the simulacrum against his body any more, and when he took a few steps forward it felt entirely of his own volition.

'Quite impressive,' he said out loud to no one in particular. 'Is this how you pass rainy days? Going for virtual strolls?'

No one took any notice. 'Playing with traffic?' he added, and strolled out into the road. Boxy articulated vehicles on six wheels swerved to avoid him, slewing to a halt, but one wasn't fast enough and drove straight through him. The Doctor raised his arms like a prize gymnast seeking glory from the crowd passing by, but they took no notice. Even so, a security guard in the familiar red uniform appeared by his side and moved him firmly back to the pavement.

Seeking further attention, the Doctor began limbering up like an athlete about to perform. He tried to dive into a forward roll, but found his body locked into a crouch before he could. It was as if some kind of invisible seatbelt held him solid.

Relaxing, the Doctor straightened back up. 'Well, that rather spoilt the illusion,' he said. 'What's the point of all this, anyway?'

He looked around him, drinking in these artificial sights. Clearly he was in some kind of city. Huge screens relayed propaganda films of how Parallel 59 was becoming wholly self-sufficient, how other Parallels were weak, desperate to negotiate trade deals. Parallel 59's splendid isolation was the envy of all Skale. The people around him didn't look particularly cheered by the news. Perhaps they'd heard it all before, the Doctor thought. Then again, this city looked so drab and lacking in imagination – all mouldering concrete pyramids and ziggurats – he decided it would be difficult to get enthused about much here.

The Doctor looked down and saw his clothes had changed. He was dressed, like those around him, in overalls in a dull shade of green. As he began walking along, following the flow of the crowd, he passed a dismal-looking alleyway. There was nothing even remotely inviting about it, so he wondered why he was strolling so confidently into its shadows.

Dam saw the alleyway through the Doctor's eyes on a bleary monitor screen. He turned away. The constant motion-jerking of the picture was making him feel a little sick.

'I don't think he'll fall for any of this,' Dam said. 'Nothing seems to faze him.'

'How can he be so confident?' Jessen wanted to know, her gaze flicking between the Doctor, moving puppet-like on the spot before them, and the sharp scribbles of the graphing monitor recording his double-heart rate. 'Why isn't he scared?'

Dam shrugged and rubbed his tired eyes. 'Maybe he's just not been here long enough yet for the fear to rub off on him.'

The Doctor found a door in the wall at the end of the alleyway, beyond which a staircase led up into darkness. He trotted lightly up the steps and waited for his eyes to grow accustomed to the gloom. They didn't. Another reminder that none of this was real, just as there was no change in the temperature now he was inside. But then, they weren't trying to fool him, he'd been awake from the outset. They wanted something else from him.

Of course, he thought, as he opened another door to find a room crowded with people and plastered with anti-59 propaganda posters. They wanted a reaction, for his hearts to leap at the recognition of comrades, confirmation of where his sympathies truly lay.

He glanced about glumly. The poor, paranoid dears, he thought as he pulled the door to and walked back down the stairs.

Jessen looked sullenly at the quivering ink needle. 'Not a flicker,' she said.

'So the machine thinks he's no enemy of the state,' Dam noted.

'Perhaps it's not functioning correctly. Like the scanner.'

'We could take the thing apart and put it back together again fifty times in a row, but Narkompros won't believe any answer it gives unless it's a damning one.'

Jessen looked at him, mildly affronted. 'And you would?'

The Doctor, in the grip of the mindwalker, floundered obliviously round the room. Jessen had to duck to avoid his arm swinging out as he pushed an imaginary door open and marched up and down on the spot.

Dam sighed. 'Configure Street 63,' he told an operator, 'and load in the personnel database for chance encounters. Then we'll run the newscast of imminent incursion and send the 27 sympathiser his way.' He glanced at the barely twitching needle. 'See if any of it means a thing to him.'

The Doctor moodily kicked another virtual stone along the pavement. Each one he tried travelled the same distance and bounced in the same way. He was sure the scenery was being recycled now, too, and he was irritated that the sky showed no sign of getting any darker. It was as if time had frozen at that moment when you're not sure whether you need your headlights on or not. A nagging wish that things were more definite.

Their attempts to identify what he was up to and with whom were not exactly subtle. He'd been stopped in the street by a bewildering number of people, only a couple of whom he recognised from his earlier jaunt round the Facility. He supposed he was being encouraged to embrace one of them as an old friend so as to reveal a shared guilt. He'd considered giving each a hug and a kiss, but couldn't be certain the powers-that-were wouldn't have everyone in the Facility executed as a result.

The Doctor found himself wondering how much of all he'd seen was an accurate representation of life in Parallel 59 and how much was just propaganda or misinformation. A holographic Skalen globe spinning atop a pyramidal tower had confirmed for him 59's geographical location, bisected by the 59th parallel. Judging by the number of people who had approached him for a spot of sabotage, while 59 was a relatively small landmass it was not short of enemies. Untold nameless territories were apparently poised to infiltrate by stealth. There were no differences in race, language or even accent that he could observe, none of the superficial physical differences that humanoid peoples so often targeted for abuse. Instead, he surmised, the hatreds had become focused on physical location. No reds under the beds, no vivid unquantifiables – just numerical certainties, seventy-eights and thirty-three-and-a-thirds, all at sixes and sevens. Degrees of paranoia.

Singularity, he remembered Jedkah saying; singularity and strength. He doubted any of these countries were so terribly different from each other in their dogma – parallels in every sense. Had things always been this way, or had some past catastrophe or war left scars too deep to heal, left insularity the safest option? Perhaps national nomenclature had been considered too emotive, had been sublimated by geographical accuracy to ensure a flat global parity. Or maybe these people simply had no imagination.

Having catalogued their planet so disingenuously, Skale now seemed to be fixing its sights on the heavens. A planetary space race was apparently in full swing, and the Doctor had no doubt that this Facility was playing some part in it all. Newscasts of 59's astronauts receiving honours played repeatedly on the enormous news screens. Billboards proclaimed the merits of space travel in harsh angular letters: SPACE BELONGS TO 59 – *LIVING* SPACE one read over a starry backdrop, while another showed a hand full of stars with the maxim 59 HOLDS THE FUTURE. But the most telling was one that said simply, REACH HALTIEL – BEFORE HALTIEL REACHES SKALE!

Here was what space travel meant to these people. The chance to stick flags into whatever planets they stumbled upon first, he supposed, pushing ahead blindly, pulling each other out of the way.

He saw no moon in the sky. Perhaps the architects of this place hadn't bothered rendering one, or perhaps Skale had no satellite. No helpful stopping-off point on the way to the stars, no means of getting such juvenile trophy-winning out of their systems. They'd do that out there on other people's property, he thought, gazing into the stubborn gloom of the sky.

'I'd like to go home now, thank you,' he called out. 'I really think I've seen enough.'

Jessen had got bored watching the output graph, had assigned an operator to take over. She was slumped in a chair next to Dam, tired and frustrated, hours overdue for her rest period. She'd had things to take care of tonight, which only made her more determined to strip away the mystery of this Doctor and his still-missing friend.

Suddenly Dam sat up. 'Get him out of there,' he barked at the startled operator. 'Come on, start powering down.'

Jessen stared at him and frowned. 'We should keep at it,' she argued. 'He'll have to tell us something in the end.'

Dam looked at her. 'Will he? Just suppose for a moment that he *has* come here from... from somewhere else. That he and his friend *are* –'

She sighed. 'From Haltiel?'

'Possibly, maybe, or in the employ of some other power...'

Jessen's mouth tightened but she tried to keep her tone light. 'We've been through this...'

Dam waved an arm at the mindwalker, and she saw how tired and drawn he looked. 'If he *was* sent here to gather intelligence, that thing's giving him a free guided tour!'

She looked at him, puzzled. 'Even if that's true, he's our prisoner, remember? He's going nowhere.'

Dam looked back at the Doctor, pirouetting in the embrace of the simulacrum, stamping more and more impatiently around the room.

Chapter Eleven
The First Raid on Central

'If Homeplanet truly care so much about us, why is no real treatment being administered for our apparent "conditions"?' Nikol demanded of the tiny crowd gathered in his front room. 'If we believe Central mean us nothing but good, we play into hands that may be taking who knows what away from us!'

Up the revolution, thought Fitz. He'd decided he'd go along to Nikol's little rally, and had persuaded Serjey and Low Rez to come along, too, for a bit of moral support. Anya didn't seem too pleased about that. She'd clearly wanted him to herself. She kept casting him catty little glances, but he just looked at her innocently. Buying himself time.

Low Rez wandered out for a leak halfway through Nikol's briefing and forgot to come back in again, diminishing their numbers by one-fifth. Nikol barely noticed, though, too busy preaching about how the wool was being pulled over their eyes. Why weren't they allowed to know the truth about what had put them here? He went on and on… like a cut-price Doctor attempting to rally the troops, but with none of the charm.

'Even at the weekly check-ups, the doctors never have our notes to hand,' Nikol pointed out, waving his arm expansively. 'It's as if we don't exist – or as if they want to keep our existence a secret, even from ourselves. And if we don't exist, what rights can we possibly have?'

So it had gone on, a paranoid rant about the freedom of the individual being assiduously removed piecemeal, leaving a city of well-behaved sheep. 'Baa!' coughed Serjey, and Fitz and he had been poised on the verge of a giggling fit, neither able to look at the other, while Nikol stormed on.

When the meeting was at an end, Serjey mumbled to Nikol that, yes, of course he would come again, and Fitz showed him out.

'This was meant to be a night off for me,' Serjey muttered darkly, polishing his glasses on his tunic. 'Thanks very much. When you said I should come over to check out a great arse this wasn't quite what I thought you meant.'

'Hey, come on,' Fitz protested, grinning. 'It was food for thought, wasn't it?'

'Baa-rely,' Serjey, said, and the two of them cracked up. Fitz noticed Anya hovering, watching them indulgently. 'I see what you mean about her,' Serjey said. 'Whatever will little Filippa say?'

'Nothing at all, since she's not going to find out,' Fitz hissed.

'Honesty is the best policy,' Serjey said, mock-solemn.

'There's less competition, I guess,' Fitz agreed. 'Anyway, like I said. I'm knocking all that on the head.'

''Course you are,' Serjey said, grinning broadly. 'Well, in the meantime, as recompense for inflicting this evening on my poor unsuspecting backside, you have to act as the fall guy on the next five tram scams.'

Fitz smiled like an angel. 'Fine. Now I've met Filippa, I don't give a toss.'

'You're very quiet,' Anya said to him later, as they copied out posters together.

'It's a sober business, overthrowing the state,' Fitz said, fully aware how brisk he was sounding.

'Are you tired?' she asked him, doubtfully.

'I think perhaps I am,' he said.

She put down her pen, smiled a little coolly. 'Time to call it a day, perhaps.'

Fitz looked down, pretending to study his poster in great detail. 'Perhaps,' he agreed.

Guilt, Fitz reflected, was a bugger. The better things were going with Filippa, the more he felt obliged to please Anya in the only way he could apart from sleeping with her: by getting in with her husband. A right royal mess in the making, he reflected. And he, as ever, was the master craftsman.

Nikol was a gruff old sod, but Fitz could tell he was quite

pathetically grateful that Fitz should even be listening to him. And in turn, Nikol would accept counsel from Fitz. It was Fitz's idea they should be here now, outside the giant concrete block that was Central, off on a reconnaissance. The posters and pamphlets hadn't got them very far; they had a grand total of zero new recruits, and someone was obviously pulling the posters down practically as fast as Anya could put them up. But if their numbers were small, Fitz pointed out, that meant they could more successfully steal into Central to attain the information they needed by stealth.

'The files are stored on the upper floors,' Fitz said. 'That's what the woman on the desk told me last time I was here, anyway.'

'The lives of six hundred thousand people stowed away in six hundred thousand files,' Nikol announced, as if addressing each and every one of them. 'The people of Mechta have a right to know what's being hidden from them.'

They also have the right not to care, thought Fitz, as they walked through the double doors and into the cool, marble reception.

'I wish to access my personal file,' Nikol said to the brunette at the desk, for what he later assured Fitz was at least the fiftieth time.

'That isn't possible,' the woman said simply, smiling with apologetic warmth.

Fair enough, bye, then, Fitz thought impatiently.

Nikol leaned forward. 'You insist on refusing me access?'

'Files may not be accessed by citizens without medical consent,' the woman replied, doubtless quoting from yet another secret file, one containing the etiquette of Mechta. The smile was still huge on her face.

'And no one is qualified in this place to grant such consent!' Nikol exploded.

Fitz edged away from them, making sure the woman didn't see him. An archway led to a corridor beyond with a right-angled turn; it was impossible to see where it led from the reception, and Fitz strode quickly along it. He reached the corner, and facing him were the big, brass doors of a lift. There was a black button set to one side, obviously for calling the lift down. There were no displays set above the doors to suggest the lift's position now.

He felt a sudden sense of unease, some faint alarm bell going off deep in his stomach.

Before he could consider why, a heavy hand came down on his shoulder, and he immediately felt like he'd been caught stealing or something, guilty, small, a child. He turned to see a tall man in a red suit, looking the very picture of the archetypal disappointed parent.

'You shouldn't be here,' the correctioner said. Just like the coppers back on Earth, there was always a correctioner about when you least wanted one. If you were doing something bad for your health – or for someone else's health – they came seemingly out of nowhere and *corrected* you, talked you into calling it a day and going back home.

Or occasionally, it seemed, they resorted to more blunt means. Without saying another word, the correctioner hauled Fitz back through reception and dumped him outside, where Nikol was already sprawled on the pavement, spluttering with indignation. Fitz wondered if having a heart attack might be the only way for Nikol to get medical consent to access his files.

'That was a bit off,' Fitz said, adjusting his tunic. 'Treating you like that.'

Nikol glared at him. 'Why? Because I'm a cripple?'

'An upstanding pillar of the community,' Fitz protested, offering Nikol a hand to make at least the upstanding part true. It was batted away.

'I can manage.'

Fitz shrugged. At least this whole charade hadn't taken too long. He was seeing Filippa tonight. She'd offered to show him some meditation techniques round at her place. Once he was in, he hoped to demonstrate one or two relaxation techniques of his own. After all, they'd been seeing each other a little while now.

'I'm telling you this,' Nikol blustered, 'that was the last time we play things their way.'

'They'll be quaking in their boots,' Fitz muttered.

Anya called round later that evening. Fitz was just about to leave his apartment when she arrived.

'What are you doing here?' His face affected happy surprise but the words still came out like an accusation.

Anya looked uncertainly at him. 'Nikol's lying down. He's worn out.' She smiled. 'Not like you, eh? Off out somewhere?'

'Yeah,' Fitz said awkwardly, still leaning against the door.

'I can't come in, then?' Anya said coyly. 'If it's the boys, they'll wait for you, surely…'

'No,' Fitz said, just a little too quickly. 'No, I'd best be off. Really.'

'Well, are you free then tomorrow night?'

'Can I let you know?' Fitz said. This was cutting him up, but he told himself he was acting for the best. An image of her scarred heel flashed into his mind. He identified with it.

'Of course.' Anya was still acting as if nothing was wrong. 'Just call round when you've got time.'

'I will,' Fitz assured her, and was just about to close the door when Anya stepped forward, pressing her palm against his chest. 'Who is she?'

He wanted to slump to the floor with guilt and relief. 'Her name's Filippa.'

Anya's eyes were like diamonds. 'Some slip of a thing, I suppose.'

'Not really. She's twenty-five.'

'Is she good?'

'Oh, for God's sake, Anya,' Fitz said, over-exaggerating his disgust.

Anya pushed past him through the door, shrugging off her dress, letting the hard façade fall with it. 'Don't leave me, Fitz.'

'Anya…' Fitz said warningly.

She took his hand and pressed it against her cheek. Her voice shook slightly. 'I'll do so much more than she will.' She pressed herself against him. 'I will.'

Fitz gently pushed her away. 'Please, Anya.' He took a deep breath, turned round as she silently dressed again. 'Look, I'll see you really soon, OK? Call round on you and Nikol. Maybe we can have a drink or something.'

Anya left the apartment with a brief nod of acknowledgement, appreciating the kind lie, hunched up as if cold despite the warmth of the descending night.

Chapter Twelve
Wouldn't You Like to Get Away?

Compassion sat up front with her rescuer in the guard transport. She was now clothed in matte-silver military coveralls and a gas mask. An angular insignia on the chest denoted she was now some upper rank or other. It was a relief not to be feeling so self-conscious and exposed, to be faceless and invisible. Empowered.

The transport rolled up to what Compassion guessed was the main gate, and she waited for guards to pour out and surround them. She wondered briefly if it was wise to leave the Doctor behind to meet whatever fate had been intended for them both, just to hook up with some other random element. Well, whoever this 'guard' was, he'd got in here on his own terms and was looking likely to get them out as easily, too. Exercising your freedom was better than meekly petitioning for it, as the Doctor seemed set on doing.

As it turned out, the checkpoint was deserted. Her companion had muttered he'd expected no less with the skeleton security staff operating here, then leaned out of the transport and inserted one of the disks he'd showed her into a featureless metal block. Presumably it was this that controlled the primitive-looking automated barrier blocking their path. There were no displays or winking lights in evidence, no way of knowing if the machine was even considering letting them leave. Compassion wondered first if it was broken, then if there was some kind of automatic shutdown in the case of such a security breach.

The two of them waited in an uncomfortable silence, until Compassion became aware of thumping footsteps getting gradually louder.

'Guards,' her companion said.

'Obviously,' Compassion replied, angling the wing mirror to frame a number of grey figures running towards them. Red uniforms for internal security, she guessed, and grey for the great outdoors.

'I'll handle this,' her nameless ally instructed, just as the first guard clattered to a halt at her window.

Ignoring him, Compassion swung open the door and jumped down to confront the squad. 'All right, we'll have to move fast,' she snapped, turning as she did so to address each person. 'We'll follow the track in the transport, you fan out around us,' she said, gesturing at the flat marshlands that stretched before them.

No one responded: they just stood there watching her, weapons trained.

'Credentials?' the guard nearest her said.

Compassion held herself stock-still as something whistled past her ear. The guard caught the disk thrown by her companion and slotted it easily into a wrist-mounted device. He scrutinised the display.

'You're part of Havdar's mob.' The guard, apparently satisfied, phrased it more as an observation than a question.

Compassion nodded. 'The visitor can't have got far – there's no cover out there.' She allowed her voice to become suitably withering. 'She shouldn't be hard to find. Bring her back.'

At first she thought the guards were still staring at her, but then she realised they'd been distracted by the barrier arm rising at last. It seemed to function as a final demonstration to the guards that everything here was above board.

The lead guard tossed the disk back. 'So how many of us should remain guarding the checkpoint as ordered?' he asked, clearly nervous now as to who to listen to.

'Your two best men,' Compassion ordered, climbing back up into the transport. 'The rest move out in our wake.'

The transport moved slowly forward, and Compassion's fellow escapee turned to her.

'I said I'd handle it,' he hissed, conscious of the men jogging alongside them. 'But I'm impressed.'

'I'm so pleased,' Compassion commented. Then she turned to the gas-masked head bobbing up and down by the window. 'We'll scout on ahead. Keep searching here,' she said. Taking his cue, her companion accelerated suddenly. The two of them bounced away over the rough terrain at ridiculous speed.

Not a shot was fired after them.

'Imbeciles,' she muttered, pulling off her helmet. 'No imagination.'

'The disks had all the right IDs. To that platoon leader I *had* to be part of Havdar's escort detail. End of story.' He paused. 'Shame the exit barrier held on to the other disk. Still, we should be well-enough covered.'

'You *do* have your sources, don't you?' Compassion said.

'Obviously,' her escort said, mimicking her voice. Keeping one hand on the wheel, he pulled off his helmet and wiped his fringe away from his forehead where it lay plastered to the skin with sweat. He had a giant grin on his face, but Compassion could tell that the man, who looked to be in his mid-thirties, had a face that would be considered to be generally quite jolly: chubby cheeks, twinkling brown eyes and bushy eyebrows.

'My name's Rojin,' he said. 'But that's top-secret, of course. All our names are. Tod wouldn't like me –'

'Tod?'

'Whoops, there I go again.' Rojin sighed, then chuckled. 'Hopeless. Tod's the ringleader of our little secret society.'

'We're on our way to meet him?'

Rojin nodded. 'At one of our many top-secret meeting points.'

'You *have* made sure this thing can't be traced, haven't you?' Compassion asked.

Rojin looked slighted. Then he pulled a pistol from a side pocket and blasted a hole in the instrumentation panel.

''Course I have,' he said.

She rolled her eyes. 'Well, anyway, I'm –'

'Compassion,' Rojin announced, grandly, as if her name was a dramatic secret. 'I know. Our special guest from up there.' He pointed up through the roof. 'Well, I don't know how they tried to get the truth out of you back there, but I'm sure *we* can be far more persuasive.'

'You're sure of that, are you?' Compassion said dryly. 'You and your "secret society"?' Rojin was keeping his tone light and unthreatening, but Compassion tensed herself for action just in case he tried anything.

'Oh, I reckon so,' Rojin said. 'Call it a pooling of information.' He winked at her. 'I reckon we can do a lot for each other.'

Compassion suddenly found the endless marshland through the window an arresting sight. 'Right,' she said.

He had no idea who he was, or who, for that matter, was cuffing him lightly round the face. Everything was a bright white, and there was a fizzing pain in his temples, getting wider and sharper.

He recalled a built-up street growing greyer and less substantial as it seemed to bend around him, cold concrete wrapping him up. He'd fallen to his knees, his body like lead, refusing to answer the fading, alien consciousness still trying to twitch his limbs into movement.

Just as he felt he couldn't take any more, he remembered he was the Doctor, that this sort of thing happened to him all the time and that he could cope. He felt another slap.

'Yes! Yes!' the Doctor shouted, causing Jessen to take a step back in surprise. 'No, don't stop, please,' he asked, apparently more injured by her stopping than by the blows.

She grabbed hold of his thick brown hair and pulled his head up.

'Oh, that's better, thank you!' The Doctor smiled in gratitude. 'Pain focuses the mind, helps me to shrug off the influence of whatever you have in that little console of yours.'

'That's why I'm hitting you.'

Jessen pulled harder on his hair but that only seemed to raise his eyebrows another notch. 'It's not an artificial intelligence, is it?' She slapped him round the face and he gasped, but only in a shock of realisation. 'You've got something organic functioning in this setup, haven't you? The traces of some living mind bridging the neural link? No wonder I could move this thing around without practice – and why your little ship was so easy to steer. That's what I *call* intuitive user interfaces…'

His face was starting to redden, his apparent enthusiasm turning to anger.

'That's enough,' Dam said curtly.

'Is it?' the Doctor challenged. 'How many living things have you butchered just to further your technology? I suppose you're proud of that travesty that used to be a man up on your space station –'

'Speak another word and I'll have you shot.'

The Doctor opened his mouth and Jessen saw Dam tense – then the Doctor closed it again. Dam took a step forward but stopped as the Doctor repeated the process, goading him.

Dam turned on his heel and walked out.

The Doctor closed his eyes and took a deep, shuddering breath.

'Release him from the mindwalker, then take him away,' Jessen told the guards. 'I'm going to get some rest.' She paused in the doorway, and looked back at her exhausted prisoner for a moment. 'There's so much we can do to you, Doctor,' she told him. 'This was just the start. Just the start.'

Chapter Thirteen
Night Thoughts

So me and Filippa are going steady. It's great. Well, it's mostly great. I haven't felt the need to write for a while, but…

I keep thinking about the Doctor. Any time now I can imagine him turning up, turning this place upside down looking for me. Sam once told me the Doctor traipsed halfway round the universe looking for her. Found her, too. So, assuming Compassion hasn't managed to talk him out of bothering to search for me, what do I do when he turns up?

I think I miss him; miss the effect he has on people. I've never been a brave man, but I could sometimes do brave things, with the Doctor around. The Doctor distracted me from whatever else might be going on in my life by giving me new ones. I've horseridden over the mountains with Barbarella. Conquered the Antarctic millions of years before any man set foot there. Become an undercover agent in exotic lands, befriended the natives, charmed the ladies, then got the hell out when it was time to move on. No ties, no tears… most of the time, anyway. In space, no one can sue you for alimony payments.

It's like remembering dreams the way I wanted to when I was little, and I want it to be real again in lots of ways, but what would I say to the people here? Explain to Filippa, Serjey, all my friends, that their Homeplanet is just a nothing-sized pinprick on the surface of the universe? That I'm from an alien world in a different time?

How to win friends and influence people.

I've knocked the Anya thing on the head, see. I'm making an honest go of things with Filippa; I think… Well, I *know* it's the right thing to do. I think. Oh, Christ…

You see, I can just imagine that wheezing groaning noise starting up just as me and Filippa are settling down to an early night. The Doctor poking his cheery little bonce out: 'What are you up to Fitz? Time we were going!'

What would I do then? Talk Filippa into coming with me? Tell the Doctor to sling his hook? Or maybe just do what the man did when he brought home a chicken: make a run for it. That's what I do best. Traditionally speaking.

See, I'd find all this stuff easier if I didn't know how quickly things can change round here. Low Rez just got Notification; that is to say, he got his marching orders from Mechta. He's 'taking a red car', as they say round here. It's like getting drafted, I guess, except you actually just go home – back to Homeplanet, I suppose. It could happen to any of us, at any time. What the hell would I do if I got sent there? I'd be rumbled in minutes. Anyway, you get eight days from Notification, then a taxi – only the red cars can travel outside the boundaries of Mechta – takes you to the spaceport to be ferried back to whatever presumably sent you running here in the first place.

And of course, no one knows exactly what that is. All in Nikol's famous files, isn't it?

One of those things, Serjey tells me. But I can tell he's upset, too. Low Rez is a clueless little bugger, and jumpy with it, like his mother's milk was taken in double cappuccinos from birth. Half the time he doesn't know where he is; or who the hell we are for that matter. I don't see *how* he can be well enough to go home.

So I talked to his doctor, who told me everything was fine, and there was no need for concern. Central had decided he was taking a red car, and that was it. I tried to press him for an opinion on Low Rez's health, but he insisted there was nothing to worry about. He said he was fine.

I don't believe him.

And that only makes things worse, because what am I supposed to *do* now I don't believe him? And does that make all other doctors here guilty by medical association?

In any case, two other serpents have wriggled into my concrete Eden.

There's this kid, right, one of the ones I look after in the home. Feelix. Funny-looking little boy, all freckles and fierce eyes... He wears these thick glasses, so it's like this psychotic Mr Magoo staring you out. When he speaks, his voice is soft, quiet. Not what you're expecting. Rencer, the guy I work with there, won't have Feelix in the same room as him. Says he gives him the creeps. Rencer's been there longer than me, I guess.

Feelix talks a lot. He's got no legs, poor little mite, so I think talking's his equivalent of running about. He goes on and on. I used to let most of it go in one ear and out the other, you know, as I got on with stuff and he wheeled himself about in his chair, following me around.

But he's been telling me about a place, lately. A place where no one can speak to anyone else without getting in trouble. Where people are locked up if they're naughty, and sometimes never get out again. In particular, he talks about a big building that's between the city and the sea, where old men sit around and decide how they're going to rule the world, and who they might kill, and how they might do it.

It's stupid, I know, but with those fierce eyes as he tells the story, and with me spooked anyway, I know what Rencer means. That poor little cripple's starting to scare the crap out of me. He told me how he wanted to leave here, how he kept seeing things from the corners of his eyes, but they were always gone when he looked round. And of course he can't run away from scary things, can he? Not with no legs.

I keep thinking of him, and then about what's happening to Low Rez. And in the middle of the night, when I'm straight and sober and it's dark outside, I know that if anything scary did happen, we'd all be just the same as Feelix. None of us can run anywhere.

And the worst of it is that… well, I think I'm starting to see the dark things from the corners of my eyes, too.

I told my doctor. He said I was fine.

Chapter Fourteen
Indiscretions

Makkersvil lay on his bunk in the darkness, pitifully tired but unable to sleep. His head was feeling better now he'd been stitched up, but the explosion in the obs suite had left a tedious ringing in his ears that refused to quieten down. Even though their mystery visitors had brought his shift to an earlier end than anticipated, he couldn't say he was too pleased to know that one of them at least was still on the loose. They posed too many questions; and while, fair enough, it wasn't his place to even try to answer them, their presence here disturbed the hell out of him.

He tried not to think about it, to close his eyes. But the little room was just too hot, and the rattle from his electric fan – such luxury! – too irritating for sleep to come. He *had* hoped for a more enjoyable way of staying awake tonight. Thank you, Yve.

Then there was a soft scraping at his door.

Makkersvil sat bolt upright, pressed his tongue nervously against the gap in his teeth as the door slowly opened. A torch beam shone in his face, and he raised an arm to shield his eyes. 'What is it? Who's there?' he hissed.

'Security check,' came a low voice. His heart leapt. 'What have been your movements over the last three hours, Operator Makkersvil?'

He relaxed, falling back on to his elbows. 'Rubbing the tears from my eyes, Security Administrator Jessen, in the forlorn belief you weren't turning up tonight.'

She lowered the torch and he could see her smile.

'You're sure it's safe?' he whispered.

Jessen answered him by switching off the torch and joining him on the bed.

Narkompros slept only fitfully. The incident in the obs room had shaken him badly. This wasn't supposed to be the front line: this was his unassailable fortress, from which he would oversee the first steps on the journey to make all space a province of 59. Now he felt more like he was locked inside its secret walls.

Narkompros had given orders that he was to be disturbed only in the direst emergency, so his hearts sank when the insistent buzzing of his pager woke him late at night. He listened to Dam's embarrassed report. Not only was the Doctor still proving a mystery, it now seemed the girl really had escaped the confines of the Facility, apparently with a member of Havdar's escort party, in one of his own transports. Air units could find no trace of where they might have gone.

Gritting his teeth, Narkompros resolved to keep calm as Dam reported his team's incompetence.

He lost the struggle about thirty seconds later.

The outburst sent him shuddering back to Medik, who prescribed a couple of pills but didn't seem to think any further action was necessary. That always made him feel uncomfortable. So he spent another twenty minutes in the diagnostics program, just in case anything had been missed.

He tried to relax under the warm scrutiny of the health check. He could picture himself months back signing off the security cuts as the budget got tighter, but remembered also the years of uninterrupted progress they'd enjoyed as the Project entered its final stages. Dam had been overresourced for so long; why couldn't this sabotage have happened then, when they'd have been able to do something about it?

That was exactly it, thought Narkompros. Someone had been waiting for him to drop his guard. Biding his time…

'So, will you believe me now?' Narkompros asked Dam, pacing round the briefing room in a state of agitation. It's almost dawn, he was thinking. I should be in bed; this is so bad for me.

Dam had summoned Havdar to the Facility from Great City to explain himself the moment the news of his involvement had come through. Narkompros waited hours for the man to arrive, only to hear Havdar deny all knowledge of the traitorous escort, even when confronted with the ID stats Yve pulled from the disk used in the getaway. Narkompros was going to order Havdar shot, but Dam, so relentlessly reasonable, insisted on checking with Central Records direct rather than using the Facility's own tap on the personnel database. Central confirmed the escort's name had been pulled from the official deceased list.

It was only the Facility's records that had him on file as being in active service.

'Proof positive,' Narkompros tried again as Dam hadn't answered him. 'They're enemy spies working with an agent here.'

'Painful though it is to report, and believe me, I've tried my utmost to convince myself, there is nothing to support that hypothesis, Head Narkompros,' Dam protested, rubbing his red-rimmed eyes. 'When you interrogated the Doctor he told us only that he was a traveller, an outcast of some kind and certainly nothing to do with Skalen society. He gave no quantifiable reaction to anything we presented to him using the mindwalker, and while the scan we ran was inconclusive in some respects –'

'He's well trained, that's all!' Narkompros bellowed, before remembering Medik's synthetic cooing to relax his way to better health. He took a couple of token deep breaths before continuing. 'Well trained and fortunate. You realise how much it will cost to fix that scanner?'

'Will further funding be diverted from security?' Dam enquired.

'If you troubled yourself more with your own duties, Dam, and allowed me to pursue Project administration without these... incidents, perhaps a traitor wouldn't be at large in the very heart of our enterprise.' Narkompros knew that the more he tried to impose calm on himself, the more verbose and loquacious he became. He wondered if others noticed and laughed at him behind his back because of it.

'I have the matter in hand,' Dam said, scowling but trying to make it appear he was deep in concentration. 'The disks with the access codes and user ID would both have to have been primed from a terminal here at the Facility. We're working to discover whose terminal it is, and should know very soon.'

'And what of the wilful sabotage of Bastion 634? No confession from the prisoner you've managed to hold on to?'

Dam steepled his fingers, clearly choosing his words carefully. 'I'm not convinced yet of the Doctor's motivation in all this. But one thing's certain – as the last person to set foot there he's the best placed to tell us what's happening.'

'He hasn't said much so far. Why should that change?'

'We'll be pointing a pistol at his head.'

'And why should we believe anything he says?'

Dam shrugged. 'Assemble all senior Project personnel and put him on parade. Any bluff he might try will have to get past all of them.'

Narkompros considered, still taking his deep breaths. 'I'm already calling a crisis meeting later this morning. The prisoner may attend.'

Dam nodded. 'Singularity and strength in you, Head Narkompros.'

Narkompros slumped down in his chair as the door closed behind Dam. 'Singularity and strength in me,' he parroted, unable to keep his eyes open a minute longer.

The Doctor was whistling a tune to himself in his cell to keep himself occupied. He wondered what it was for a moment, then remembered it was one of Fitz's compositions. A simple, plaintive little melody he'd written for Sam to practise on the guitar, what seemed like an age ago.

He felt bad about losing Fitz again. No, not losing him: Fitz was resourceful, he could usually watch out for himself. No, this was a feeling more of neglect. He shuddered when he thought of what he'd let the boy go through with the Remote... He'd tried his best to put the pieces back together but you could never be guaranteed a perfect match. People weren't like that. Even a machine so finely attuned to people as the TARDIS was couldn't hope to get everything right... and it shouldn't have to.

The Doctor drummed out the rhythm of the melody on the cell wall. He should've climbed into *Fitz's* casket, let Compassion please herself. But he'd put that right when he got out of here.

A shame there was no Sam about out there, ready to come to his rescue.

'Your dirt tells me nothing!' a throaty voice whispered through the cell door.

'I beg your pardon?' the Doctor asked frostily, although he was actually grateful for the distraction.

'The dirt from your fingernails!' It was Jedkah. 'Detritus from the shores of the Northern Waters.'

'What about my shoes?' suggested the Doctor. 'Have you examined them? Real leather, you know. They're Clarks, I think.'

Jedkah sniffed. 'I don't care who you took them from. They're clean.'

'I must've been dropped in the sea,' said the Doctor. 'You people really are terribly clumsy.'

'None of your clothing presents anything seriously anomalous,' Jedkah went on. 'I would *expect* a saboteur to wear untraceable garments.'

'Would you?' The Doctor yawned. 'I'd expect him to wear something that would help him infiltrate a place without arousing suspicion. Doesn't that make more sense?'

'The contents of your pockets, like your friend's earring, are unusual but not conclusively extraterrestrial...'

'You people really do take convincing, don't you.'

Jedkah paused. 'I know you're alien. If you let me prove it to Narkompros your treatment here could become very different.'

'But no more pleasant, I imagine.'

'If I could just take something from you...'

'What's all this about, anyway?' asked the Doctor, a little irritated now.

'I wouldn't need much... say, a toe or a finger joint?'

The Doctor sat up, wide-eyed with outrage. 'You can take *this* from me! Until I get some answers of my own I'm giving nothing away, got it?' He frowned. 'And especially not a finger!'

Jedkah was shushing him furiously from the other side of the door. 'If you're from Haltiel I need to know.'

'Why?'

'Since the ancients first detected Haltiel in our skies, theories as to its properties, its peoples, have proliferated. You're not what anyone would expect. You'd wreck every theory we hold true.'

'I'd try my best,' agreed the Doctor. 'What were you expecting, little green men?'

'Little grey men. They must live in the shadows.'

'It's possible they've invented the light bulb, you know.'

Jedkah paused. The Doctor imagined his fat little head turning left to right, terrified of his indiscretion being discovered. 'The findings of the two probes we flew by Haltiel suggest a high-gravity world with a noxious atmosphere. There are life signs, but no broadcast signals of any kind, which suggests a primitive people.'

'Depends how you define primitive,' the Doctor pointed out.

'Most scientific bodies are agreed that the Haltien people do not have space travel,' Jedkah said, more urgently. 'But there have always been sightings, unidentified objects in the sky.'

'You tried to shoot them down, I imagine?' the Doctor said.

'The sightings are always discredited. But now if I could prove conclusively to the scientific community that their views on alien life are so fundamentally wrong…'

'Ah, yes,' said the Doctor. 'Such infamy. Such prestige. Such a bore.'

'I would bring…' Jedkah was clearly searching for the right words. He didn't find them. '…a dignity to your study.'

The Doctor marched over to the door and slammed a fist against it. 'I told you. I want answers myself. What are those people in the space station waiting for? Where are those life capsules supposed to go?'

Jedkah paused. 'If you hadn't steered yourself here, you would've been on Mechta by now.'

'Mechta?'

Jedkah paused. His voice had become still quieter and the Doctor had to strain to hear him. 'That is where the capsules are designed to take their occupants.'

'But what *is* Mechta?' The Doctor pressed his face to the door. 'I need to know. I can't tell you why, but I *must* make contact with someone in charge there. Can you find out if there have been any new arrivals there? I'll tell you no end of interplanetary trivia, you can use any and all of it for your own advancement if you choose, but, please, you have to promise…' He trailed off, listening intently for any response, but there was nothing to hear. Perhaps Jedkah had been disturbed, or else was fearful he'd said too much.

But at least he'd learned something. If Fitz's capsule had launched, it hadn't followed them to Skale. Therefore, if Fitz wasn't still up on the Bastion, he *had* to be on Mechta.

Anything could be happening to him there.

The Doctor slumped despondently on the hard floor. I'll get us out of this, Fitz, he told himself. I will, I promise. Hold on. Just hold on.

Part Two
Getting Harder

Chapter Fifteen
A Gentler Pace of Life

'Do you know, I've been here for months and months and I've never, ever pulled?' Low Rez said mournfully, pouting at Fitz and Serjey.

'Not that you remember, anyway!' Serjey said. Fitz laughed raucously and clinked his glass against Serjey's own.

They were in a bar off Centreside. The three of them liked it because it had a generous ratio of women to men, and Fitz could go off to see Filippa after a couple of Ethels with the boys.

It seemed impossible that in another six days Low Rez would be gone from Mechta. He looked a bit like that little comic, Ronnie Corbett. Funnier, though. Not that he always meant to be.

'We can't let you leave here with a record like that,' Fitz told him. 'Criminal.'

'You're right,' Serjey said. 'So what're you going to do, Fitz? Speak nicely to Filippa, see if she'll help him out?'

'Oi!' Fitz slapped him round the head.

'Who's Filippa?' Low Rez asked.

Serjey groaned. 'You met her only last week! And Fitz has been rattling on and on about her for *ages*, don't you…?' He trailed off. 'You *are* joking, right, Low Rez?'

Low Rez looked a little confused, bushy eyebrows twitching as he smoothed his short dark hair off his forehead. 'Sorry?'

'I can't stand this, Low Rez,' Fitz said dramatically. 'Tomorrow, you're coming with me on the tram scam.'

Low Rez grinned, puzzled. 'The what?'

'And we'll sort you out with a bird so beautiful and bright you'll remember her for years after you leave this place.'

Low Rez looked suddenly downcast. 'Am I going somewhere, then?'

The night was warm as Fitz said goodbye to his friends and set off for Filippa's apartment. As ever, in Centreside, the streets seemed as busy with people as the sky was with stars. Fitz compared the scene with trudging back from East Finchley on a Thursday night in a London winter. Ridiculous. This was like being on holiday abroad, the sort of place his mum had always dreamed of visiting. He'd promised he'd take her one day, when he became part of the international jet set. 'A holiday's just what we need, Fitzie,' she'd always said. 'A real tonic!' She'd had to settle for a gin and tonic, of course, and to keep dreaming.

Mechta was perhaps a little further afield than Mum would've considered travelling to, but there was no doubt that while not exactly a holiday camp, it did a body good. Fitz had the feeling that whatever these people looked like, fat or thin or young or old, they'd never felt better about themselves, and it showed. Even in him.

When he'd first arrived he'd been stubbly and pasty-faced. Now, looking at himself in the glass of a shop front, he could see Mechta had gone to work on him as well. His hair felt finer, less straggly. His skin was well toned, smoother. And the feelings of fright, of depression, after all he'd been put through with the Doctor, had faded. He hadn't figured himself the type for a convalescence home. He smiled and shook his head.

This really wasn't like him. Sam had tried on occasion to get him into psychology and stuff, trying to tease little truths out of him in her own good-natured way, particularly after they'd been apart all that time in the 1960s. She kept calling him a prime case for counselling, saying that he should get a helping hand to find himself – but how could he take crap like that seriously? Others had claimed to want to help him in the past, when all they really wanted was to use him. They'd make him feel better about one part of his life, just to screw up another. The Red Army had 'helped' him. The Remote had 'helped' him. Even the TARDIS had added her tuppence worth… He'd been taken, a lump of Fitz-flavoured dough, kneaded and pulled apart and refashioned time and time again. Letting others make the choice for him.

It's in my DNA, he decided, crossing the street and walking down Filippa's street. My genes respond to manipulation, my body's programmed to lend itself to evil schemes. The Benelisans had a go, Faction Paradox got well stuck in...

He'd barely even noticed.

People back home reckoned he was cynical. How could he be? You had to know something about what's going on in a situation to be cynical about it, didn't you?

He looked at his healthy reflection again a little more thoughtfully, as if expecting the dark things to come creeping in from the corners of his eyes. But they didn't.

He whistled a little tune to himself as he picked up his pace, in a hurry to get to Filippa's now to distract himself from these morbid thoughts. After all, you couldn't live life assuming that *everyone* was out to get you.

Move on. Forgive your enemies. Especially the ones you can't beat.

He and Filippa had a nice, quiet evening. Sprawled on her bed, they talked about their day, and the conversation soon turned to Low Rez and his plight.

'I knew a girl who had to take a red car,' Filippa said. 'She couldn't wait to go.'

'Unpopular sort, was she?'

'Not at all. But it was funny: she'd just begun to feel ready again to face up to real life.'

Fitz snorted. 'What, without even remembering what real life was about?'

'When Notification came,' Filippa went on, 'it was like... well, like recognition of the way she was feeling. That she'd passed some test. Achieved something.'

'Who'd want to leave here?' Fitz said.

There was a moment of dreadful recognition in the following silence.

'Filippa?'

'We've been put here to get better. To look after ourselves – to live a life that's a little gentler than the one waiting for us back home, most probably.' She kissed him. 'It's just the way things are.

But don't hate me for wanting to feel that I'm strong enough to move on somewhere else.'

'What, so we're just killing time here?' Fitz argued, aware his voice was rising.

'Don't talk rubbish,' she said, squeezing his hand. 'You know we're all going to have to go home sometime.' She paused. 'You should feel happy for Low Rez. He's just ready to go home, that's all.'

'But, you've met him! He's not ready for anything...' Fitz sighed. 'Except maybe a frontal lobotomy.'

'There's not a lot any of us can do it about, is there?' Filippa said. 'We just have to make the most of the time we have.'

Fitz closed his eyes and held her a little closer. 'All good things come to an end, I suppose,' he reflected. 'Only the bad ones go on for ever.'

Another note from Anya was waiting for him when he got in early next morning. Apparently, Nikol wanted to meet up urgently to discuss the plight of Low Rez.

Fitz wondered if he'd done the right thing in telling the old man about his concerns. It had got Nikol all fired up, and seemed to have stoked up one or two feelings in Anya again, too, who probably thought he was making it all up for her benefit. The note said that Nikol wanted to call a meeting. That night.

Fitz decided he'd bring Serjey along, too. That way Anya needn't get any funny ideas.

It turned out that Low Rez was rubbish at the tram scam.

They'd met after work and let the *real* work commence straightaway. On the first run, Fitz had come along and done his bit and got blown out – the girl wasn't a fantastic looker, but then Low Rez wasn't exactly Elvis Presley – then hurried back to his seat like the proverbial scalded cat. And what had Low Rez done? Stared at the woman, mouth opening and closing as if there was something important he had to say to her but he didn't have the slightest clue what it was.

She'd moved to another compartment a minute or so later, clearly unnerved by this weird little man's goldfish impersonation. When pressed by Fitz, Low Rez had confessed he'd somewhat predictably forgotten what he was meant to be doing next.

'Just talk to her,' Fitz said, his voice calm and encouraging. 'Tell her what a prat I am, coming on to her like that, OK? Once the conversation gets going, you'll be well away.'

So Low Rez smiled knowingly at the second indignant woman twenty minutes later. 'That Fitz is a real prat for coming on to you like that,' he told her.

They took a break then for the red mark on Low Rez's face to go down before trying again. They didn't have much longer before they'd have to get off for the meeting, Fitz thought gloomily.

So for a third time, with a heavy heart, Fitz identified their most likely target. The only girl on the carriage with a vacant seat both beside her and opposite was an absolute belter – jet-black hair, green eyes, a cute little mole above her eyebrow.

'Practise,' Fitz told the stammering Low Rez. 'If you can hold a conversation with a goddess like that, you'll stand a better chance with the rank and file. Go on, sit down. Get ready to rock.'

So Low Rez did. The girl didn't notice, of course; she doubtless had so many people falling at her feet that one little feller salivating opposite was neither here nor there. He knew the type; there'd been a couple at Frontier Worlds. Ice-queens, beautiful but deadly; one cruel put-down could freeze you where you stood.

The knowledge made him, strangely, a bit more relaxed than usual about making a tit of himself.

'Do you have a pen?' he asked her.

She looked at him, momentarily surprised, then smiled. Her teeth were neat and white. She had the cutest dimples. 'Sure.'

'Only I need it to write down my address,' he went on easily, scribbling the details. 'So you can come up and see me sometime.'

He waited for the inevitable as she took the paper back from him. 'Hmm,' she said. 'You're a long way away, aren't you?'

'You're pretty far out yourself,' he found himself saying. Ouch.

'I don't go Southside,' she said, taking back the pen and writing on the reverse of Fitz's piece of paper. 'No time. But if you're passing northwards, drop in on this bar. I'm always there. My name's Denna.'

The tram creaked to a halt, and she bestowed another smile upon him as she pushed the paper into his hand. Fitz was too shocked to even look surprised as she led a flurry of passengers off the carriage.

'Beulah,' he muttered, 'peel me a grape.'

'What was that all about, then?' Low Rez asked him, frowning.

'Don't worry, mate.' Fitz was still staring at the name and address she'd given him, an incredulous grin widening on his face as the corners of his mouth apparently determined to grasp hold of both his ears. 'She wasn't your type, anyway.'

Fitz was still in a buoyant mood when he called round to Anya's and Nikol's. Anya was surprised and pleased to find Fitz so happy, no doubt getting all the wrong signals, but he was feeling too thrilled to really notice. Serjey, whose ear he had bent about the tram scam on the way over here, was looking significantly less happy. A bit green, in fact. Jealous, jealous, jealous.

'What about Filippa?' Serjey had said, not exactly disapproving; he was Fitz's mate, after all.

'Filippa's fantastic.'

'So you've told us often enough. So what's with Denna?'

'Denna's not a Filippa thing.'

'So what is a Denna thing?'

'It's a...' Fitz had had to think. Then he'd mimed the silhouette of Jane Russell. 'It's a phwoar! thing.'

'Right.'

'She doesn't have hips, she has hip-hip-hoorays.'

'Uh-huh. So you're going to call by and see her?'

'I'd be a fool to myself not to.'

'A fool to be risking Filippa, I'd have said. She's the one that makes your heart sing, remember?'

'So? It has to pause for breath sometimes, doesn't it? A heart with a sore throat's a bad thing.'

'Lame line, Fitz. Very poor.' Serjey had looked at him in a way that suggested Fitz's levity was slightly misplaced. 'Just be careful, eh?'

'Oh, I'm just mouthing off. It's flattering, you know. Probably won't see her anyway. No point, is there?'

'None. I know that. I bet even Low Rez knows that.'

'And *I* know that. So?'

Serjey shook his head, smiling faintly. 'So I can't imagine that stopping you for an instant.'

Jealous, jealous, jealous.

Fitz's mind was somewhere Northside while the big raid on Central was discussed, thinking of the lies he might get away with and the excuses he could make.

Chapter Sixteen
The Court, the King and his Fool

Yve surveyed the anxious faces gathered round the vast table in Strategy One. Some were colleagues, senior technicians and lead scientists. The ones she didn't recognise were probably government representatives – there could be some good contacts to be made over this; that was something, she supposed.

The others present were key faces from the Project's past, dragged out of their retirement dachas in the hope, presumably, that they could bring some elder-statesmen experience to bear on the situation. Some chance, Yve thought, looking at the sad collection of nervous relics twittering about the table. Narkompros was yet to arrive, and if he didn't present his crisis to the table for discussion soon she could imagine half these people keeling over dead from the stress of it all.

Disquieting rumours were spreading round the Facility. They couldn't go to Blue Alert and then just carry on as if nothing had happened. Makkersvil would know what had happened in the Obs suite, but he wasn't on duty again until that afternoon. Still, she could always call round beforehand. He'd get the wrong idea, of course, but that might prove an amusing diversion.

Just then, Yve caught a bloodshot glance from Terma, and automatically started shuffling the sheaf of papers she held into neat and relevant piles. She longed to get this meeting over and done with.

As if answering her silent prayer, the main doors opened inwards. While Narkompros's entrance was met with polite smiles and the nodding of heads, a sudden chorus of alarmed mutterings started up at the sight of the manacled man being frogmarched in by armed guards. He was quite tall but slight, his hair longer than Yve's own, staring idly about the room as if he was being treated to a guided tour.

He gave a small polite bow to the assembly, noticed her and

performed a neat curtsy. The guards shoved him forward before the smile had finished forming on his face, and he almost overtoppled, turning his momentum instead into a graceful twirl. He beamed at the crowded table and scowled at the guards. Taking in this bizarre display, Yve had the feeling that this performing little puppy dog could bite if provoked.

Security Chief Dam followed on into the room, and chose to lean against the wall rather than take a seat at the table. He gave a minimal gesture to the guards, who shepherded the stranger as he stepped daintily into a position just behind Yve.

Narkompros sat down carefully in his reserved place next to Terma directly opposite Yve, and raised his voice grandly over the astonished chatter about him. 'We'll do without the formal greetings. This meeting of the Senior Assembly has been convened in order to discuss and resolve several alarming developments in the Mechtan Project. As most of you will know, a life capsule from one of our Bastions came down in the Northern Waters yesterday morning.' A low murmuring came from those who'd missed shifts in Main yesterday. Narkompros used the pause to gesture disdainfully at the stranger. 'The capsule had been appropriated by this man.'

'I'm the Doctor. How do you do?' the stranger said, amid more concerned whisperings. Yve turned to look at him again. He made to shake her hand, then made a great show of realising his hands were cuffed. When the chains holding his wrists together made a jingling sound as he did so, he beamed around at his shocked audience and rattled them again for effect.

When Yve turned back round, utterly bemused by the prisoner's behaviour, she saw that Narkompros was looking dourly in her direction.

'Since then, a flood of… unusual data has been picked up from the Bastion,' he stated. 'Terma?'

'Yes…' Terma was caught in the middle of stretching, and struggled to regain his composure. 'No end of data and none of it welcome,' he said gruffly. 'It all points to the early stages of a complete systems failure.'

As Yve could've predicted, Narkompros was becoming increasingly impatient with the startled mutterings sweeping the table. 'There are more revelations to come, I would prefer them to be met with silence,' he snapped.

'No sense of the theatrical,' complained the Doctor in the quiet that immediately fell, then took in that everyone was staring at him. 'Oh, I do beg your pardon.'

Narkompros began to turn a shade of puce. 'Say another word, Doctor, and I'll have you shot.'

'Where?' the Doctor asked, politely.

'In the head.'

'No, sorry, I meant where *geographically* –'

'Doctor, you *will* be silent.'

The guards emphasised Dam's command by gripping the back of the Doctor's neck. He gasped in pain and nodded his understanding.

Yve noticed Dam was looking strained, but Terma continued pugnaciously as if nothing had happened. 'I believe the controller of the Bastion to be going off-line. If that happens we will have to act quickly to avoid a chain reaction upsetting the harmonic balance of the other Bastions.'

Yve heard a muffled noise behind her and chains jingling. She didn't need to look round to know the Doctor was waving his hands in the air for permission to speak. Terma looked at him more wearily than warily, while Narkompros turned to Dam.

'His information here could be useful,' Dam said simply.

The Doctor cleared his throat. 'Thank you,' he said, then turned to Terma. 'How many Bastions are there in your network?'

Dam smiled tightly. 'You're here to give *us* information, Doctor. This perhaps isn't the most opportune of times to display an interest in the finer details of our Project.'

'But I'm your helpless prisoner,' the Doctor protested. 'I can't use the information, can I?'

'There are two thousand Bastions in the network,' Terma said, becoming impatient.

The Doctor nodded. 'And do I take it that a Bastion "going off-line" is a euphemism for its controller dying?'

'You've seen the controller, then, I take it,' said Terma, meeting the Doctor's gaze unflinchingly.

'Then you can appreciate the genius of technology unique to this Parallel,' one old fossil piped up from the end of the table.

'I saw the pitiful remnants of a man grafted into a network of computer systems,' the Doctor said. 'That's not genius, it's simple cruelty.'

'It's dependency, whatever your viewpoint,' Terma stated. 'Neither man nor machine can survive without the other.'

The Doctor cocked his head. 'You mean...'

'The flesh-technology interface is maintained by a chemically enhanced sterile atmosphere. You disrupted it the moment you entered the Bastion.'

'Oh, goodness. I'm so terribly sorry,' the Doctor whispered. 'I'm afraid three people died as a result of our arrival. I know it's no excuse, but I promise you it was an accident.'

The assembly were looking at each other, uncertain and surprised. Yve didn't know what to make of the man. He was a spy and a saboteur, wasn't he? What was he making such a fuss about?

'At least three. And five other capsules launched with your own. It's extremely inconvenient,' Terma said, tartly.

'Inconvenient?' the Doctor echoed. 'My companion and I sealed ourselves off from the Bastion in a life capsule within about ten minutes of arrival.'

'The air-violation alarms had already triggered?'

'The bulkheads shut down, and we were cut off from our escape route. Certainly we'd have suffocated if we'd stayed much longer and we couldn't get back to our ship.'

'This ridiculous ship you claim brought you...' Narkompros rumbled.

But a thought seemed to have gripped the Doctor. 'You've got self-repair circuitry on each Bastion, surely?' he asked Terma, ignoring Narkompros. 'In case of accidents?'

'The damage appears to be ongoing. The circuits can't repair the Bastion quickly enough to keep up with the atmospheric decay.'

A wild-haired old scientist fidgeted impatiently to Yve's left. 'It's obvious to me these saboteurs deliberately left something on board to compromise the regulated atmosphere.'

'Impossible.' Terma nodded at the lead scientists to his left. 'Our figures show that for this scale of damage, the object would have to be far larger than anything they could smuggle on board themselves –'

The Doctor spoke very quietly, but he stopped the conversation dead. 'Oh dear,' he said. 'That'll be my mysterious ship, then. It landed us inside your Bastion.'

A light above them began to flicker, as if suddenly nervous.

'*Inside* it?' the wild-haired old man protested. 'You couldn't pilot a ship inside one of those Bastions, it's impossible!'

'Of course it's possible,' the Doctor insisted. 'Little boxes in big boxes is easy, it's the other way round that's the tricky bit. My TARDIS pulls it off admirably well, all things considered.'

'TARDIS?' the old man spluttered.

Again the Doctor targeted Terma. 'It's a box of *this* mass,' he said, grabbing a sheet of paper and a pen from Yve and scribbling furiously on the back of it. 'Run your tests, taking these figures into account, and you'll find the ratio of the contamination to the shortfall in the correction circuits *will* tally…'

'It does, you're right,' Yve blurted out, taking in the scrawled figures. 'We'd be looking at an object of that same mass.' The look from both Terma and Narkompros made her wish she'd kept her mouth shut, but the government reps were watching her intently – she couldn't back down now. 'All we can do is try to localise the damage, work 634 outside the harmonic equation. But that will take time. From my figures here, too much time.'

One of the government reps spoke now, a sour-faced, suited man, clearly in charge of the delegation: '*Why* will it take so much time?'

Yve was careful not to make eye contact with Narkompros. She looked up instead at the flickering light and shrugged a little sadly. 'We have insufficient resources.'

'That will do, Chief Supervisor Yve,' Narkompros said heavily.

Terma supported his old comrade, of course. Doubtless he knew they stood or fell together. 'In any case, the damage will soon be spreading throughout the network.'

'You've no fail-safes on board?' The Doctor was incredulous.

'Masses of them,' Terma said simply. 'All externally triggered.'

'We didn't allow for theoretical absurdities like solid structures forming themselves inside out of thin air,' the wild-haired old duffer said dryly.

'Insufficient resources again, I'll be bound,' the Doctor said innocently, smiling at Yve.

Narkompros attempted to recover his dignity, smiling at the sour-faced man reassuringly. 'The fail-safe triggers, naturally, were among the first things to go off-line when the saboteur had done his work – but reactivating them by radio signal is our number-one priority.' He looked pointedly at Yve. 'We're confident of success, aren't we, Chief Supervisor Yve?'

Yve chose her words carefully. 'We're certainly more confident of that than of re-establishing network stasis before 634 compromises the entire Project,' she said, favouring the rep with her report, then turning to Narkompros with a brave smile. 'But my team won't give up until we have an answer.'

'I'm co-ordinating Chief Supervisor Yve's activities while also running diagnostics on every system used in the Project's development,' Terma said, re-establishing his own importance to the proceedings with a suitable degree of ostentation. 'We'll make sure no possible route to success is overlooked,' he told Narkompros, who in turn nodded benignly at the rep.

Sour-Face didn't respond. 'I have to report this to the committee. Keep me informed, Head Narkompros.' He paused. 'Singularity and strength in you.'

Yve heard the Doctor quietly shake his manacles along to the litany, and to the time-honoured response Narkompros delivered in turn. The moment the door closed, Yve saw both Terma's and Narkompros's eyes were fixed on her. She returned their looks innocently, but was relieved when the prisoner cleared his throat. She realised he must've been peering over her shoulder at the equations she'd revealed under the top sheet.

'You know,' he said, apparently deep in concentration, 'these calculations are a little long-winded. I think I can improve on the timings quite significantly.'

Now it was Yve's turn to be hostile. 'You can tell that from glancing at these papers, can you?'

'Yes,' agreed the Doctor.

Yve couldn't believe what she was hearing. 'But you caused this mess in the first place!'

'So allow me to tidy up after myself, please!' the Doctor implored. 'Under the strictest military and scientific supervision, Head Narkompros, naturally.'

Outraged mutterings started up round the table again, particularly from the lead scientists, but Terma held up a hand, dry amusement on his face. 'You can demonstrate this miracle solution, naturally.'

'Naturally,' the Doctor said, apparently offended. He started scribbling again on the top sheet. Yve looked plaintively at Narkompros, while the frail old men, the initial architects of the Project, looked like they were about to spontaneously combust. But their leader merely watched and waited. Yve realised she'd managed to alienate him to the extent he now seemed ready to listen to their mysterious saboteur if results could be guaranteed.

Yve held her breath as the Doctor passed his sheet of scribbles to Terma. 'I don't understand the purpose of this network of yours, and I'd need to see the exact equations you have in operation, but I'd say you could strike a line through several pages of these figures. A nip and a tuck, and a stitch in time saves six hundred and thirty-four.'

Terma stared at the paper with a reluctant fascination. Narkompros watched him closely, then nodded to himself and turned to address the bewildered figures around the table.

'I'm calling an end to this meeting,' he said. 'Terma and I need to discuss the situation in the light of these new revelations. A full debrief will follow. Staff, return to your posts; visitors, my aide will assist you with transportation away from here. Singularity and strength in you all.'

The response was muted, barely audible over the scraping of chairs and the grumblings of old men dragged all this way for nothing.

Jessen, slumped in her chair in the security suite, surveyed the progress reports from the hunt squads chasing Compassion and her accomplice. With no visual clue from any of the air units or the spy sats, the guards had no choice other than to search the entire wilderness around them systematically. Even with the several platoons Narkompros had co-opted from Havdar's command – Havdar was leading one of them himself at his own behest – it could still take weeks to track down the escapees.

If Dam hadn't located that forged disk with the exit authorisation, she reflected, Narkompros would probably have had both of them shot as incompetents by now. The computer was still running a trace on the terminal that had originated the instructions, assessing subroutines and command processes through the Facility's server. She'd had no idea the computers here could do that. Still, like so much round here, it was taking an inordinately long time.

So began another perfect shift at the Facility.

Jessen yawned, luxuriating in the feeling for a couple of moments, then smiled. Grabbing those few hours with Makkersvil had been risky but rewarding. She'd decided, years ago, you had to take what pleasures you could in life – though really, Makkersvil was too accommodating for his own good. She'd warned him that if even a whisper of their affair got out, she would make sure none of the grief landed on her, whatever that took. Perhaps it was taking advantage of his romantic streak, but she couldn't be blamed; he'd agreed quickly enough. She suspected he would quite enjoy playing the martyr.

Jessen sent out a signal to the hunt squad, advising them of a change of tactic. A circular movement would perhaps bring more results, she suggested, a change of focus. Peering at the virtual map on the main screen, she selected some co-ordinates and fed them in.

Yve rose from her chair to follow the rest of the Assembly filing away.

'Please remain seated, Chief Supervisor Yve,' Narkompros said. 'You stay, too, Dam, and your men.'

'Well?' the Doctor asked Terma, looking at him hopefully like a dog eager to go for his walk.

'I can see how this *might* work,' Terma said, guardedly. 'In principle.'

'I'm a man of the highest principles, I assure you,' the Doctor said. 'Give me twenty minutes and access to your operating systems.'

'You can't be serious!' Yve exploded.

'I'm not trying to step on anybody's toes, I assure you,' the Doctor said. 'Point as many guns at my head while I'm at it as you like, I work well under pressure.'

'If word of this got out, we'd be a laughing stock,' Narkompros muttered, glancing at Dam.

'I'm also terribly good at keeping secrets,' said the Doctor. Dam looked slightly embarrassed. 'Alternatively, you could send me up to 634 in one of your life capsules and I'll take my ship off the Bastion myself!' the Doctor added, beaming. 'Everyone's problems solved!'

Yve snorted. 'Absurd.'

The Doctor's face fell. 'Even under armed escort?'

'Anything larger than a life capsule launched from here would attract too much attention from spy satellites,' Terma explained. 'Even if we sent a party up to our legitimate space interests, the Primeira stations, they're out of alignment with 634 right now, unable to launch repair ships for another forty-eight hours.'

'Legitimate interests?' the Doctor blinked. 'Ah. Your mysterious network of Bastions is a sleeping tiger-in-hiding, is it? Shielded? Forbidden by any number of global treaties regulating the exploitation of space, hmm?'

Narkompros stroked his chin. 'With every deduction you make, Doctor, your demise within these walls becomes more painful.'

'You can't afford to kill me yet, Head Narkompros. You need results.' The Doctor placed his manacled hands on the table and leaned forward. 'I'm well aware you consider me a thorn in your flesh, but consider the situation. I've got... property, shall we say, aboard that Bastion. I'd be a lot happier and far more co-operative if I thought it was safe and sound. So I have a vested interest, don't I?'

'You want to make some kind of deal?' Narkompros said, sceptically. 'Forget it.'

'Wait till you see results,' the Doctor said, evenly. 'Perhaps we can talk then.'

'All right, here's what we do. Terma, change shifts on Main. Put on a skeleton crew, your best people, right away.'

'Splendid! There's no time to lose!' the Doctor said.

Yve shook her head. 'You're granting a spy access to our most secure systems?'

'I'd share your concerns if these computations could betray anything of the actual nature of the Project,' Terma conceded. 'As it is they might as well be an exercise in mathematical abstraction.'

The Doctor started jogging on the spot. 'I love exercise, it's terribly good for you, you know.'

Narkompros ignored him. 'Get straight on to it, Terma.'

Terma nodded and left the room.

'Security Head Dam,' said Narkompros, 'please ensure you have enough men to blow a thousand holes in this man at the first sign of trouble.'

'Trouble?' The Doctor seemed aghast. 'Me?'

Yve narrowed her eyes as Dam and his guards led the Doctor from the room.

'Now, then, Chief Supervisor Yve,' Narkompros said, shaking his head and tutting. 'What am I to do with you?'

'Head Narkompros?' Yve asked, wide-eyed.

The old man looked at her with disapproval. 'Your rising through the ranks here has been quite meteoric. Do take care you don't tumble back down to the ground with a bang.'

Corny old fool, she thought. 'Indeed, Head Narkompros.'

He kept on looking at her as if considering some niggling problem. 'I want you to ready one of the relief ships.'

Yve looked blankly at him. 'Head Narkompros?'

'If all this clever computer talk comes to nothing, I want us primed and ready for physical action. It's a risk, I know, but we can't sit back and let my –' he paused, smiled coldly – 'let thirty years of work come to nothing. Not without trying everything at our disposal.'

'Of course, Head Narkompros.'

'You're to attend the launch bay and run diagnostics on 59'1. I want it readied for immediate take-off. If you find anything amiss, you rectify it personally. Do you understand?'

I understand this is a taste of what I can expect my duties to involve if I upset you again, you old hypocrite, she thought.

'Perfectly, Head Narkompros,' she said.

The Doctor whistled Fitz's little tune as he was bundled along the corridor by his duo of armed guards. Dam, who was radioing ahead for an armed guard to meet them in Main Control, flashed him an irked look.

'You're an intelligent fellow, Dam. Surely you can see I've been telling the truth all along?'

'A convenient version of it, perhaps,' Dam said. 'Your accomplice escaped from this Facility with well-organised help from someone here – and yet you claim you know no one.'

'I don't know how she did it,' the Doctor admitted, then sighed. 'She's a resourceful girl, but somewhat wayward. We're really not as close as you might think, I'm sad to say.'

'She's managed to evade all our patrols, so far. It's as if she's dropped off the face of the Parallel. But make no mistake, we'll bring her in.'

'Good luck,' muttered the Doctor.

'I suppose I'm wasting my time asking if you've some alternative means of travel hidden somewhere here?' Dam asked, keeping up his dry act. 'Some means of getting off-world?'

'To Mechta?' the Doctor enquired quietly.

Dam skidded to a halt. 'How do you know of Mechta?'

'I'm an alien spy, remember?' the Doctor whispered, the corners of his mouth curling upwards.

Dam set his party moving again. The Doctor noticed him looking a bit wobbly. 'Look, why's it such a big secret? It's a planetary body, isn't it, surely? You can't claim a monopoly on it.'

Dam came to a halt outside doors marked MAIN CONTROL and stared at him.

'Or can you?' the Doctor pondered. 'I suppose you've shielded Mechta from observation, too?'

'Naturally,' Dam said. His fingers danced a pattern on the entry coder outside and the large doors opened. He led the Doctor and the two guards inside.

'Is that why you're storing so many people in space for so long before sending them away? For secrecy's sake?'

'Their places must be readied.' Dam smiled faintly. 'You could call Mechta the great dream of our people. The key to securing safe, interstellar travel. To guaranteeing protection from outside attack.'

'For 59, of course.'

Dam said nothing.

'Interesting. So what exactly is it, then? Some minor planetoid or a checkpoint? Some kind of strategic refuelling outpost?' The Doctor clicked his fingers. 'Are these people colonising it, paving the way for all those who will follow?' He clicked his fingers twice more. 'No, not just a colony in space – a bridgehead! Building your forces for an assault on Haltiel…?' Still Dam said nothing, but the Doctor smiled grimly. 'I'm getting warm, aren't I?'

'That'll be air con gone down again,' Dam said wryly. 'Wait here and shut up until we're ready for you.'

'Just tell me one more thing,' the Doctor said urgently, grabbing hold of Dam's arm. 'On Mechta… the people there *are* all right, aren't they?'

Dam freed his arm carefully from the Doctor's grip, and didn't answer.

Chapter Seventeen
The Second Raid on Central

It was typically warm and quiet tonight as Serjey, Nikol, Low Rez, me and Anya made our way to Central, our cars whining softly along the deserted streets. No thunder gathering for dramatic emphasis. No storm approaching. Just starlight and streetlamps above us.

I was quite grateful for the thoughts of Denna still dancing about in my head, they took my mind off what we were going to do. Ordinarily I'd have had a bit of Dutch courage to loosen me up, but the cars here don't start if the sensors pick up you've been on the sauce.

I found myself wondering about Filippa. I feel a lot for her, more than I've felt for Maddy or Alura in my other lives... But the Denna thing has just reinforced for me the whole idea that me and Filippa aren't about real commitment. What did Filippa say? We're all going to have to go home sometime. There's a recognition there, right, that this is just a transitory thing? People clinging together until they have to part. All part of the therapy, yeah, yeah.

But the Denna thing's also made me realise that even though I care about Filippa, I still want to see Denna. I'll still do whatever she'll allow me to get away with. It's like I'm so bloody flattered she could think me all right, I have to go through with whatever's on offer. Rude not to, almost. Oh, what a martyr.

And yet, as I drove along, I knew Filippa wasn't thinking of anyone else. She definitely wasn't casual in her commitment to me, but I told myself: if Low Rez can go any time and he's a jumpy little wreck, how long can someone as sound and sorted as Filippa stick around?

Notification could come through for any one of us next.

Maybe we'd find out some of the answers tonight, I figured. That gave me a small reassurance we were doing what was right here. That the Doctor would approve, wherever he was. Wherever he is.

Before I knew it, Central was rising up in front of me, white and sheer like a vast paper cut-out against the indigo sky.

The first thing we realised about Central was that all the lights had been left on. Perhaps they just liked to give the impression that people were working all through the night, like Mussolini used to do in his pad, I thought. That led on to a discussion that none of us actually knew anyone who worked in Central. We'd seen people trooping in in the mornings and trooping back out again in the evenings, but none of us actually *knew* any of them. Doesn't sound like much of a big deal, I know, but when you're all keyed up and ready for a break-in, the little details tend to take on a significance you wouldn't normally give them.

Like the dark shapes I *still* keep on glimpsing from time to time. Just as I've convinced myself they're nothing at all, I catch another shadow with nothing about to cast it.

Perhaps I'm just the most paranoid person in Mechta.

Anyway, I've had a bit of practice in undercover stuff, sedition, infiltration missions, all that gubbins. I was the best man for this job, I figured. It was quite funny when I started telling them how they should go about getting in, and they were all listening. It's the sort of attention I'd never get if the Doctor was around.

I told them we needed to stage some kind of distraction that would bring out the night shift – from our previous recces we knew there'd be no more than two of them on the front desk – preferably before any correctioners appeared on the scene.

So Nikol and Low Rez, not really well suited for any rough-and-tumble stuff, got busy. Low Rez started scrawling rubbish on the concrete plaza outside, in big letters, while Nikol pretended to be upset and agitated by this.

He banged on the double doors. 'There's a man out here vandalising your property!'

There was no reply. Old Nikol kept it up, though, until the doors slid open – just as a pair of correctioners turned up in their bright-red uniforms and started having a quiet word with Low Rez. Anya, Serjey and me ducked inside behind Nikol as he strode up to the desk and started haranguing the man and the woman sitting behind it.

'The man out there is clearly unwell. He's claiming he's being red-carred in five days, when one has only to look at him to know how utterly unsuitable he is for…'

While the big old windbag gradually let his reactionary air out, Anya shuffled past him on her hands and knees so the receptionists wouldn't see.

'What is his name?' the man said.

'Melores, Arden Melores.'

'Notification would not have been sent to Arden Melores unless he was a fit subject for reintegration into society,' the woman informed him.

'You're not even going to check your files?' Nikol stamped his foot in self-righteous fury – my cue to get going on all fours to join Anya, shuffling round the corner.

'There is no need to check records. Notification is not given without full medical approval.'

I saw Nikol lean forward over the desk. 'There's clearly been some kind of mix-up, a mistake.'

'There is no mistake.'

That was a new voice. I glimpsed the blood-red of a correctioner's outfit come through the door just as I slid round the corner of the reception desk. Low Rez had done a pretty good job keeping them busy, but now the correctioners had come for Nikol. And they'd caught Serjey, too, of course, worst luck, before he could follow us on.

Just me and Anya, then. She looked at me and smiled, and I remembered what I'd seen in her despite the age thing, despite the complications. Or because of them, Christ, I don't know.

We made it on all fours to the kink in the corridor, then scrambled up as we saw the lift. The doors were wide open, and I felt my heart leap as we dived inside and Anya hit the switch that closed them. Soundlessly, our view of the corridor began to vanish behind the polished metal. No one came into sight to discover us there. We'd done it.

It was the perfect opportunity to find out what exactly the deal was with the files here, and when I came to think of it, that realisation filled me with dread. Suddenly I didn't want to know whatever was going on here. I turned to Anya and was actually going to ask her to open the doors again.

She had her back turned to me, staring at the wall. I came over and joined her, and that's when I realised my wish had been granted.

There wasn't even a way to get out again. The only control in the whole lift was the one that closed the doors.

There were no buttons to choose floors, no emergency phone in case the thing got stuck, no hatch in the ceiling for a brave and daring getaway in the event of some kind of lift disaster, nothing.

'Well,' Anya said. 'What do you make of that?'

'Maybe it can only be operated from outside,' I reasoned. 'From the front desk.' I was relieved to see Anya was nodding. 'To stop the staff knocking off before home time.'

'Must be pretty security-conscious. I didn't see a stairwell, did you?'

I shook my head. What if there was ever a fire or something? It seemed crazy.

'So,' Anya said at length, smiling. 'You and me. Stuck in a lift.' That lovely halting voice of hers.

'Good thing it's a large lift, isn't it?' I said. It was almost a relief she was flirting with me. Reassuring. Familiar ground found on an unfamiliar ground floor.

Nothing happened between us, though, as it turned out. We just talked: Filippa was a conversational corpse we buried quite quickly, and we kept the chatter light and jolly after that. I felt closer to her than I ever had, and she fell asleep in my lap. I kept waking her accidentally on purpose through the night, to talk a bit more. Didn't want to feel I was alone.

In the morning, the lift doors slid open. I braced myself for the worst. Two people in dark suits, employees, confronted us. They didn't say anything; they didn't have to. The man on the front desk from the night before rounded the corner, looking mightily cheesed off, and shepherded us out. The woman at the desk gave us a filthy look; I thought they might do something, but a correctioner appeared in time to take over and escort us out. He told us – warned us? – not to come back again. Ever.

Serjey and Low Rez had crashed round my place and had fallen asleep waiting for me to turn up. I told them the score. Serjey reckons that maybe the upper levels of Central are automated, that only robots can be trusted with the records. That the people taking the lift are just caretakers or whatever.

So why leave the lights on all night? And just what's kept on these bloody files? What's so secret that none of us are ever allowed to see? It sets your mind racing. Your heart, too.

And what's worse, I can't help feeling now that this will mark me in some way. Like I've become in some way a problem, that whoever's in charge here will want to do something about me now. Send me away to Christ knows where, shut me up for good, all because they think I might know something. What if I can't convince them otherwise? I know nothing, for God's sake!

And to be honest, I really don't want to know. Serjey and Anya don't want to know either, and even Low Rez isn't that bothered – he'd have forgotten the details anyway by the time you'd finished telling him. So I'm all for letting it lie; it's probably nothing anyway. Never put down to conspiracy what can be explained away by stupidity, as the man said. But Nikol's like a dog with a bone, he won't let it go, and he's not about to let me off the hook, either. He's determined. He has to have answers.

Who died and made him the Doctor?

Maybe I shouldn't dwell on that.

Chapter Eighteen
Compassion, Meet . . .

Compassion looked pointedly at Rojin. 'As secret bases go, it's a little on the small side isn't it?'

'Ha, ha,' Rojin said dryly, passing her a torch. 'This is just the way in.'

He'd driven the stolen transport into a camouflaged hide, deep in the marshland. Apparently, the cell he belonged to owned many such hides scattered all round the area. They certainly seemed better organised than the fools at the Facility, but then she guessed they needed to be. There were no government funds or back-up for this bunch. They had only themselves to rely on.

At the back of the hide, obscured by a filthy tarpaulin, was the opening to a small tunnel.

'You go on,' Rojin told her with a cheery smile. 'I'll cover our tracks and join you in a moment.'

Switching on the torch, Compassion shrugged and went inside. She found the tunnel dipped down steeply before leading on to a larger passageway, hollowed out from the stone. A metal track ran off into the darkness, and a kind of battered metal carriage sat ominously waiting for anyone stupid enough to get inside.

Compassion turned at a scrabbling behind her. Her torch beam revealed Rojin, the smile still large on his face, carrying some lights. 'Are we seriously meant to ride in this thing?' she enquired.

He coughed apologetically. 'I know it's not as comfy as the guard transport, but if it was good enough for the miners…'

Compassion looked sullenly at the skip on wheels. 'I take it this part of the mine is disused, then?'

'It's all disused,' Rojin replied as he clamped the lights to the front of the skip. 'Antiquated and abandoned. All minerals round this part of 59 were used up a century ago.'

Rojin flicked a switch and an eerie light spilled into the cold darkness of the tunnel ahead. He clambered inside the skip, then looked at Compassion expectantly and held out his hand.

'No ticket required,' he said.

Compassion smoothed damp hair from her forehead, feeling her blistered hands tingling as the sweat stung them. She was boiling hot despite the chill of the tunnel. This base, assuming it actually existed and Rojin wasn't just some maniac in a world of his own, was extremely well hidden.

They'd used metal beams like bargepoles, pushing the ends into the rocky ground and propelling the skip along the tracks. This, Compassion suspected, was the real reason Rojin had decided to take her along from the Facility. The journey was exhausting enough with two people putting their backs into it, although neither of them could ever be as tired as the jokes Rojin kept cracking.

Obviously, he'd wanted to know about how Compassion had come to be on the Facility in the first place. Appreciating this was a paranoid culture, she'd decided it would be best to make out the two of them were on the same side, that she held the same aims as Rojin's cell: the terrorist overthrow of the Mechtan Project, whatever that was. He'd become terribly excited when she'd told him she and the Doctor had breached one of the Bastions. Luckily, he thought her reasons for being vague about the actual logistics involved in that breaching were those of wariness with strangers yet to earn her full trust; not because she was part of a ramshackle band of time-travelling aliens.

Eventually the tunnel seemed to come to a dead end.

'Oh no,' said Rojin. 'We've come the wrong way. I don't *believe* this!'

'Neither do I,' said Compassion flatly. 'These tracks wouldn't be so well maintained if you hadn't had to use them before. So get on with whatever you have to do now, I'm not in the mood for games.'

For a moment, Rojin seemed duly chastised; then his infuriating grin returned. 'Touchy,' he said, as if cautioning her, and got on with delivering a series of knocks on the mouldering stonework with his metal bar.

Compassion was grudgingly impressed when a camouflaged sheet of metal in the ground was pulled back by whoever was on the other side of the wall, revealing the entrance to a short tunnel that would lead them inside the secret base. She'd been expecting a concealed door in the wall, or an entrance hidden holographically; something actually a lot more obvious.

'This place would be hell to find if you didn't know what you were looking for,' she observed.

'You're not wrong there,' said Rojin. 'We'd be a lot more effective as an espionage unit if half our members weren't wandering around lost in these tunnels.'

He gestured at the hole in the ground and Compassion impatiently climbed down, squeezing under the wall and into a dark, musty chamber the other side.

'Don't move.'

At the sound of this new voice, Compassion looked up warily and saw a boy who could barely be out of his teens. He had spiky white hair and was staring dispassionately down at her, pointing a gun at her head. Rojin didn't react as he came through behind her and slid the covering back in place, so she guessed she must be safe enough.

'This is our alien spy, is it?' the boy enquired, laconically. 'Come to swell our ranks?'

'Dunno about swelling our ranks; she'll take charge of the lot of us if she gets the chance, I reckon,' Rojin smirked, peeling off his sweaty guard's uniform and rubbing a filthy white towel over his body.

'She *won't* get the chance.'

Rojin chuckled to himself. 'Hey, where are the others?'

'I sent them on to bolthole six,' the boy said, tucking the gun back inside his jet-black tunic. 'We'll join them later. This girl's a possible risk to our security. I wanted to check her out myself.' He took something from Rojin and furtively activated a portable computer, his body shielding whatever he was up to from her.

Compassion was sitting on the floor; she couldn't be bothered to get up after their long journey. She looked about and tutted to herself. The place was filthy, a great oval stone room littered with debris and a few grubby boxes of supplies.

'You're Compassion,' the young man said at length, powering down the computer.

'And you must be Tod,' Compassion answered, getting to her feet. He looked startled. 'It's OK, Rojin told me,' she added.

Tod marched angrily over to the older, taller man. 'How many times do you need telling – no names!'

'I know, I know,' Rojin protested. 'Look, she's OK. She's been on board, Tod! She's been inside one of the Bastions!'

'I wouldn't believe it to look at her, if I didn't know it was true,' Tod remarked. His skin was milky-pale, as if he'd lived underground here all his life, and he was skinny. His eyes were dark and penetrating, but his jug-ears, even with chunky earrings, somewhat spoilt his moody white-trash image. 'How did your cell do it, spacegirl?'

Spacegirl? Compassion gave him a withering look. 'By not hanging around in dives like this, for a start.'

'This was once the recreation room for the miners stationed here. These used to be the largest pits in the Parallel,' Tod said. 'Besides, you can't move freely above ground for much of the area. Not unless you want to go up in smoke.'

'Really.'

Tod was warming to his theme, and clearly enjoying the sound of his own voice. 'Great tracts of minefield have surrounded the city for two hundred years; testament to a better time, before advances in technology made war an impossibility – at least down here.' He kicked a rock across the floor petulantly. 'So now the whole world scrabbles for the stars just to raise the stakes a little higher.'

Compassion interrupted him before he got too worked up. 'You hanker after the good old days of the ground forces, do you? What are you, some kind of technophobe or something?'

'Not at all,' Tod answered, suddenly earnest. 'But my cell believes there are problems closer to home our people should be dealing with, not committing fresh atrocities out in space.'

A well-rehearsed little piece, thought Compassion. Probably just getting started. But since she was pretending to be from a similar cell herself, she supposed she should at least show an interest. 'How many of you are there?' she asked.

'Enough.'

'And does this cell of yours have a name?' She found herself unable to think of a more interesting question.

Tod smiled, a little self-consciously. 'No names,' he said.

'Oh.' Compassion mentally rolled her eyes. 'Obviously.'

Chapter Nineteen
Confession/Crime

The day after their fruitless raid on Central, unable to keep his concerns to himself any more, Fitz confided in Filippa round at her place. She was surprised; and a little upset, he suspected, that he'd said nothing sooner.

'What is this, then, some kind of secret society you belong to?'

'No! No, it's nothing like that. Just this bitter old crackpot out to stir up trouble.'

'You joined up with him readily enough.'

Fitz decided that 'Yeah, but only 'cause I was after his missus' wasn't much of an answer. He thought quickly. 'I was new here, wasn't I? Love thy neighbour and all that. I wanted to fit in.' He waved the thought away. 'Anyway, I didn't think any of this would happen.'

'And you didn't think any of it was worth telling me sooner?'

'I so nearly did, so often,' Fitz said quite truthfully. 'But... well, I guess I didn't want to worry you.'

'What do you take me for, Fitz?'

'My little heart's desire?' She wasn't smiling, so he tried another tack. 'You're my best friend on top of whatever else,' he said, more softly. 'I didn't want you involved –'

'But if this Nikol is just a crackpot...?'

'OK, so I think maybe he's on to something.' Fitz shrugged. 'I hope he's not, but I can't help thinking it. So that's why I've told you, now.' He took her hand and squeezed it. 'I couldn't go on keeping things from you. Your trust is one of the things I value most.'

That did the trick. 'Well, you have that.' She gave him a sympathetic smile. 'You poor thing, stuck on your own in a lift all night.'

Fitz nodded ruefully.

'You must've had so much on your mind lately. No wonder you couldn't get into that meditation we tried.' She seemed to reach a sudden decision. 'When are you seeing Nikol next?'

'I told you. I don't know whether I want to see him at all.'

'Of course you do. And I'm going to come with you.'

Fitz's face dropped. 'What?'

'What's the problem? You said you thought he had a point, you've been in with him so far –'

'I don't want to be. I don't want *you* to be.'

'I just want to talk to this Nikol and find out more about what he thinks is going on.'

'But he's a crackpot.'

'A crackpot who maybe has a point, you said so.'

'Yeah, but…'

It went on, the gentle disagreement escalating into a full-blown, unreasoning row. He tried to talk her out of it, the image of Anya stalking over to the pair of them and dropping him in it motivating every discouragement, every warning; eventually, every bare-faced lie.

His insistence that she should never come round to Nikol's despite his apartment being so close to Fitz's own became so unreasonable and illogical, the only thing he could do in the end was simply walk out on her. He slammed the door behind him, jumped in a car and hit the ignition, but trundling along at ten miles an hour was hardly giving vent to his frustration.

Abandoning the vehicle, Fitz angrily pulled the piece of paper that Denna had given him from his pocket, and strode off to catch the nearest tram going Northside.

The bar was the same as any other, made unfamiliar with strangers. Fitz had started to calm down a bit, but that had only left him with a familiar ache in his gut. His anger was turning inward, and he needed to defocus it.

The answer was Ethel, of course, as it so often was, and so he stood, anonymous in the crowd, and started drinking.

He deliberately didn't look for Denna for the first couple of drinks. He didn't want the disappointment of finding she wasn't here, that she *never* came here, that she'd been joking at his expense; and equally he didn't want to be faced with the decision of whether or not to go for it if she *was* here. He simply stared very carefully at his glass, and kept drinking.

Midway through drink number three, he couldn't help spotting her. So many girls in the bar were wearing their green metallic dresses, but no one looked the way Denna did in hers. What was he even doing here? She was surrounded by blokes, she had her pick. Back off, he told himself, don't bother. In Archway, the only thing he'd had the pick of was his nose – why should his luck be any different here?

He got to his feet a little unsteadily, and worked out his best route to approach her. She wouldn't recognise him, of that he was sure. She'd stare at him like he was dirt, and she'd be quite right. 'You mean you fell for that?' she'd say, and all her friends would laugh, or start pushing him around. Yeah, and then they'd kick the hell out of him, and serve him right, too, for being such a stupid, idiotic, unfaithful little –

She was in front of him sooner than he should've been; he hadn't finished beating himself up. Well, let her mates, already staring at him suspiciously, save him the bother.

'Hi, Denna,' Fitz began quietly. 'Do you want a drink, or would you just like the money?'

She looked at him for a moment that seemed to last as long as the journey here had taken him from Centreside. Then, recognising him, she smiled, all teeth and dimples. 'I think I'll take the drink, thanks, since you ask.'

Fitz gave her a small bow. 'Ice and a gentleman's company with that?'

'A gentleman!' Denna said, and laughed throatily like a sink draining. 'I'm charmed.' The remarkable noise kind of detracted from her overall perfection, but Fitz figured he could live with it for a night. As the men around her looked on disgruntled, Denna took Fitz firmly by the arm and led him back over to the bar.

Chapter Twenty
What Happened to Yve

Yve warily opened the door on to the launch bay. This was the last place the Doctor's accomplice had been sighted after she'd savagely attacked an engineer, and the area had been closed off while Jedkah and his forensics team had been poking about.

She slammed on the main lighting.

The arc of the spotlights above her threw the shadows of the ships into stark relief. There was no one about now. The vessels looked almost sinister grounded here, sleek housings which were half polished silver, half darkness.

Berthed on the far side of the hangar was 59'1. As Yve moved towards it, listening to the echo of her footsteps, she caught a snatch of some electronic report, a brief, weird signal.

She froze. She couldn't hear anything now, but it had come from the ship sealed off with warning tape, she was sure of it.

'Who's there?' she asked, but nothing answered, no matter how many times the echoes repeated her question.

What if the Doctor's accomplice had returned? There might be a chance here to redeem herself in the old fool's eyes.

Steeling herself, Yve ducked under the tape and moved towards the cockpit door.

The Doctor, hemmed in at a computer terminal by twelve guards, raised his hands and waggled his fingers. Soon he was sending streams of data scrolling across the green monitor.

He decided it should prove fairly simple to temporarily stabilise 634's decaying resonances by siphoning minute amounts of power from the other two thousand or so Bastions. What worried him a little was that he'd noticed some subtleties in the power equations. They suggested that this network, whatever it really was, had been experiencing tiny fluctuations in energy even before the TARDIS had arrived; and *that* suggested he'd merely exacerbated an existing inherent fault in the system, not that anyone would ever believe him. He'd just have to patch things up as best he could and hope that would win enough of these people's trust to find Compassion and recover Fitz.

An unfeasibly large number of digits flashed on to the screen, and the Doctor wondered if the figure was a representation of the odds against him.

Narkompros was alone in his quarters, sweating not just with the heat. He was hunched over his personal comms unit.

'I assure you, the Project is still progressing well within acceptable parameters,' he said, 'despite the near-disasters we have recently experienced.'

He winced, regretting his choice of words as soon as he had uttered them. Sure enough, the voice at the other end crackled accusingly over the comlink. He was tired, probably coming down with something dreadful, but he couldn't afford sloppiness, not now.

'Things *are* in hand. I assure you I have the situation well under control,' Narkompros said smoothly. 'Perhaps *difficulties* would be a better word – but in any case, they've been dealt with successfully. Target will be reached, and all will go ahead as planned.'

The radio link cut dead, and Narkompros rose shakily to his feet. He glanced at his reflection in the mirror. It was a good thing he had no visual link-up here, he decided. He looked as bad as he felt. Pale, sweating… Surely he *must* have some kind of fever?

He was just stepping inside Medik for another scan when his comms unit spat into life again. 'Government on-line, Head Narkompros,' came the respectful voice of his aide over the speakers.

'Patch them through,' said Narkompros, feeling tension squeezing at his shoulders. He took some deep breaths, then sat down and spoke brightly into the comms unit.

'Singularity and strength… Yes, of course, sir, sorry. I quite understand.' He closed his eyes, willing himself to be strong. 'I assure you, the Project is still progressing well within acceptable parameters,' he said. 'Despite the... *difficulties* we have recently experienced...'

Yve climbed cautiously inside the cockpit of the supply ship. It was empty, and she breathed out heavily with relief, leaning on the control panel. Then she snatched her hand away.

Part of the control panel was warm, as if recently used.

She heard a scraping sound from outside. Suddenly terrified, she cowered into the scant shadows the tiny control room afforded her as a hiding place.

The Doctor tapped out a set of computer codes in a jazzy little rhythm, then paused for a moment. Dam had informed him that Terma was monitoring his actions from an ancillary control room with a team of operators, which was useful information. Sparing a smile for the security chief, watching him from just the other side of the terminal, the Doctor directed a highly complex, self-calculating algorithm that should temporarily snarl up all terminals other than his own.

He was soon uncovering the exact co-ordinates of Bastion 634, then instigating a background search for the co-ordinates of Mechta.

'Alert,' announced the computer's calm, synthetic voice in the empty security suite. 'Alert.'

Jessen came back in with a drink of water, heard the announcement, and punched the respond button. 'Search on illegal file origination completed,' the computer voice went on. 'Enter password for result details.'

Jessen turned to consider the flashing cursor on the monitor screen, and shook her head. 'You should have been more careful,' she muttered.

Yve had been crouched down under the little console for what felt like an age. There'd been a scraping at the hull for a few moments, some quiet footsteps, the sound of the lights shutting off, then nothing for some time.

As quietly as she could, she got up, wincing at the cramp in her legs. Slowly, softly, she moved over to the doorway and looked out into the darkness.

A flash of sparks went up, and pain burnt a clumsy path through her body. Screaming, Yve toppled backwards. She crashed heavily against the ship's control panel and slid to the floor.

The fire broke out in the cockpit a few moments later.

Chapter Twenty-One
The Send-Off

The morning after in every sense, Fitz was spending his rest day standing sullenly in a meandering line of well-wishers trailing round the Southside Departure Area.

Low Rez was saying his goodbyes, and everyone who knew him had come to wave him off, including Filippa. She and Fitz hadn't spoken since their argument the night before; he watched her, waiting opposite him with some of her workmates. Anya was nearby, a bit too close for comfort, standing between Nikol and Serjey. Behind them, a few blocks away, Central loomed up, bright in the sunshine, casting a cooling shadow over the bustling streets.

Fitz realised that part of him actually wished he was leaving today as well, to escape this whole sorry mess. Denna had proved great company – as vivacious as she was vacuous, an unchallenging bundle of curves, as opposed to the tempestuous bag of hormones that was Filippa. He watched as Filippa hugged Low Rez, speaking words of encouragement to the little man and making him smile, and felt rotten as hell. She deserved better. Here she was giving herself away freely, while he was collecting girls like badges.

This situation just didn't feel right; in the past, he'd always felt the pursuit of the girl was probably better than actually winning her... that the first kiss was always the beginning of the end. 'You're a loner,' he'd told himself. 'You weren't designed for other people.' It had always seemed a fair excuse, before he'd realised there were creatures out there that had their own designs on him. That he could never be entirely sure exactly *what* he was. And before Alura had died back on Drebnar.

Travelling with the Doctor, so many things ended up chasing after you that your first instinct was always to run away, which had suited him fine. You could run away from practically everything. But the Doctor wasn't around and, like Feelix, the little boy with no legs, Fitz wasn't going anywhere. So face up, Fitz, he told himself. Who'd have thought running could be so lazy?

Suddenly Low Rez was in front of him. Fitz felt a helpless pang of regret at the sight of the little man squinting up at his chest.

'I don't want to go, Fitz.'

'You silly old bugger, you should've hidden or something.'

'I did, kind of,' Low Rez said defensively.

Fitz smiled and shook his head. 'You forgot you were even meant to be leaving, didn't you?'

'The correctioners came round,' Low Rez complained. 'Thought I was trying to get out of it. Marched me down here all the way.'

Fitz scrutinised his friend. 'And you've not even packed a toothbrush?'

'Hey!' Low Rez shook Fitz's hand. 'You can't blame me for everything. We're *supposed* to forget our baggage here, aren't we?'

Fitz awkwardly slapped him on the shoulder and propelled him on his way along the line. 'Just watch out for yourself, OK?'

Low Rez nodded, solemnly. Filippa must've seen Fitz was getting choked because she smiled sympathetically over at him. You wouldn't if you knew where I was last night, he thought. But not again. No way.

A few minutes later, a pair of correctioners announced Low Rez had to board his taxi. It was a lot flashier than the rest of the transport here, Fitz observed. Racing-car red, gleaming in the sun. A send-off with style. Low Rez clambered into the back of it, and Nikol barged up to the driver. Curious, Fitz took a step closer himself. Unlike any blue car, the red taxi had a roof. Why, when it never rained on Mechta? And the front windows were frosted, you couldn't see the driver inside.

'Where are you taking this man?' Nikol demanded, rapping smartly on the window with his knuckles. 'I wish to travel with him to ensure his safe arrival.' There was no response. The correctioners approached.

'Please move away, sir,' one said. There was something about the way they firmly manhandled Nikol back to the pavement that gave Fitz the creeps. Their movements were extremely precise, effective. Could they be robots or something? They seemed so lifelike…

The roar of the red car's engine reminded him that his imagination wasn't the only thing ready to race off. He focused on the taxi. It certainly had more power than the blue cars; maybe that was why it was designed with a roof, to stop people falling out if they went over a bump. Nikol had told Fitz he'd tried to follow a red taxi once but that the exercise was pointless: he'd been left for dead at the end of the street.

Low Rez made a pathetic sight as he was driven away, waving at them all through the rear window, confused. Then, the red car turned the corner and the noise of its engine faded away.

Filippa came over and slipped an arm round Fitz. 'Are you OK?' She looked at him slightly oddly as he froze, feeling Anya's eyes on his back.

'I'm… I'm sorry,' he said, awkwardly returning the embrace.

'You're really cut up over this, aren't you?' she said, her round face seemingly spun from worry lines.

Fitz nodded. 'Well… Low Rez was a mate, wasn't he?'

'He was a man distinctly unfit to be taken out of convalescence,' Nikol added, walking over. 'If they have nothing to hide, why do they cower behind frosted glass?'

'Maybe the taxis are automated,' Anya said, walking over to join them.

'Could be,' Nikol said doubtfully, leaving them to try to pressure some of Low Rez's other acquaintances into joining his group before they could drift away from the departure area.

Fitz swallowed as Anya smiled at Filippa, then turned back to him.

'After all, that lift that you were in was automated, wasn't it, Fitz?' Anya enquired innocently.

Bitch. 'It was. Good point,' Fitz agreed coolly.

Filippa introduced herself, apparently fed up with waiting for Fitz to do the honours. Anya beamed and shook her hand.

'You're Fitz's girlfriend,' she said with apparent delight. 'How lovely to meet you at last. He's been keeping you a secret for far too long.'

Filippa glanced at him, but Serjey came up to them all, smiling. 'You can't blame him, Anya. If I had a girl like Filippa I'd keep her to myself as well!'

Filippa blushed slightly, while Anya's smile remained picture perfect on her face. Fitz felt a drop of sweat from the back of his neck rush along his spine as the conversation lurched onwards with exaggerated politeness.

'I'm calling a meeting of the group,' Nikol announced, soon tiring of the frivolity of small talk.

'I'd like to come,' Filippa said.

'You're not a member.' Fitz winced inwardly at how crap he sounded.

Nikol, of course, was delighted. 'Don't be ridiculous, Fitz, she can become a member without further delay.'

'I'd like that,' she said resolutely. 'I'd like to understand more about the running of this place.'

'But you told me that we're just not meant to worry about the details,' Fitz protested.

'Not having second thoughts, are you, Fitz?' Anya said, peering at him with a look of faint amusement. 'You've always seemed so committed.'

'I know what he means,' Serjey said loyally. 'We could be red-carred any time, any one of us. Maybe it's best just to get on with things.'

'How can there be harm in us knowing a few simple truths?' Filippa said, and Nikol slapped her heartily on the back.

A few simple truths, Fitz reflected, acknowledging Serjey's helpless shrug in his direction.

Chapter Twenty-Two
What to Do in Case of Fire

The Doctor blinked indignantly as the computers failed for a second time to find him any information on Mechta whatsoever. The reaction was the largest he dare risk with this many guns on him. Heaven help him if he sneezed or something.

With more time he was sure he could ferret out *some* information, but he recognised these people's patience was something he couldn't presume upon. As if to confirm this, a piercing siren started up, different from the klaxon he'd heard when pretending to escape.

'What's that?'

'Fire alarm,' Dam said. 'We'd better move.'

'Oh well. I've just about finished, anyway,' the Doctor announced, tapping a few more keys.

Dam looked at him suspiciously. 'You've stabilised the network?'

'I've done all I can,' the Doctor answered, nodding.

Dam's communicator bleeped at him, audible even over the din. 'Jessen?' he answered.

The Doctor saw Dam's frown grow still deeper. 'All right. Locate and apprehend immediately – this fire may be some kind of diversion. Keep me advised. I'm heading for the launch bay now. Out.'

The Doctor sighed. 'Things seldom run smoothly, do they?'

'I might need these guards,' Dam said. 'Come on. You're coming with us.'

'What a treat,' remarked the Doctor.

Makkersvil knew there had to be better ways of taking advantage of an unscheduled rest-stretch. All he could be bothered to do was lie on his bunk. He was slightly perturbed by the temporary shutdown of Main Control for 'emergency maintenance', and fully expected to have to waste half his next stretch undoing whatever the so-called experts had set up for double the money *he* earned.

As he was lying there, half listening to the hourly news bulletin, wondering not for the first time who was paid to make it all up and for how much, there was a harsh rapping at his door.

He clicked off the radio. 'Who is it?'

The muffled voice set his hearts racing all over again. 'Security Administrator Jessen.'

He trotted over to the door, lethargy forgotten, and threw it open. He grinned to see her standing there.

Then he saw the gun she was pointing at his chest, and the two guards standing behind her.

She held up a disk with her free hand. 'Stupid, Operator Makkersvil,' she said. Her voice was so cold, so angry, it barely sounded like her. 'Really *very* stupid.'

Dam threw open the doors to the launch bay and a thick cloud of smoke engulfed him. He was caught by surprise – stupid of him, there was a fire here, what had he expected? – and fell back reeling. Someone grabbed him and helped steer him away. Eyes streaming, he realised it was the Doctor. He pulled himself free, choking.

'Are you all right?' the Doctor asked, concerned.

Dam swore. 'Where are the fire operatives? Damn these cutbacks.'

'We'd better get to work ourselves then,' said the Doctor. 'Someone in there may be hurt. Come on!' Before anyone could stop him, he had dashed into the smoke and vanished from sight.

The guards immediately gave chase, Dam bringing up the rear.

The smoke wasn't so bad once you were through the access corridor. It shrouded the roof of the hangar in poisonous clouds, and when Dam switched on the lighting it was like a spiteful evening sky hanging over them.

Dam spun around, wildly, looking for the Doctor more than for the cause of the fire. If he'd lost his only other prisoner, too... No. No, there he was, framed in the doorway of the damaged ship, holding something – someone – in his arms.

'Hold your fire,' Dam ordered his men. 'Get hold of some extinguishers, move!'

Coughing, the Doctor sadly set down a charred bundle at Dam's feet. Dam stooped to inspect the body through the smoke as a team of fire operatives rushed into the room. It was Yve. She looked as if she'd been dipped in tar, black and glistening.

'She needs medical attention, immediately,' the Doctor snapped. 'Use that wrist thing of yours, quick.'

Dam nodded and turned away, the image of Yve's smoking body lingering in his vision even when he closed his eyes. He arranged a medical pick-up, then rounded angrily on the fire chief.

'What took you so long?' he demanded. 'You call that a response time?'

The fire chief didn't turn round, overseeing his team as they doused the hull of the flaming ship with chemical foam. 'You know we've had to relocate to premises in the east storage bay. Had to run the length of the Facility.'

Dam looked down at the Doctor as he stooped over Yve and gently took her hand. Yve was trying to open her eyes, but melted skin had caked them over. 'Communications circuits...' she croaked. 'Still warm... Went up in my face...'

Dam saw with relief the ambulance buggy trundle into the launch bay, and behind it Jessen with a couple more guards. He relaxed a little. The situation would soon be back under control.

Jessen looked at Yve's body in horror. 'What was she doing here? What's happened to her?'

Dam shrugged, rubbed sweat and dirt from his face. 'I don't know. Not yet.'

Two medics moved Yve carefully and professionally away. The Doctor stood up, wiping the soot from his eyes. Then, as the fire team began aiming their foam spray inside the still-smoking cockpit, the Doctor dashed suddenly towards them. 'No! No, don't do that!' he cried, his flapping arms beating a path through the smoke.

'Bring him back!' Jessen ordered her guards, then turned to Dam in outrage as the Doctor squeezed past a fireman and pushed himself into the cockpit. 'That's a spy and a saboteur, not some child on an outing! Are you going to let him run amok all over the Facility?'

Dam stared at her, momentarily lost for words. He checked to see if his own guards had heard her outburst. They were watching him, impassively.

'If you have a criticism to make concerning my handling of this investigation...' Dam tailed off. He'd kept his voice cold and clipped but knew he was hopeless at hiding the hurt in his eyes.

He turned round instead to see the Doctor being dragged struggling from the wrecked spaceship's interior, the bright-red uniforms of the guards like fresh flames among the smoke. Jessen pressed a hand against Dam's back. He turned to her and saw she was sorry.

'Forgive me,' she said, softly. 'I've just had to make an... unpleasant arrest.'

'The traitor?'

She nodded. 'Operator Makkersvil.'

Dam frowned. 'Makkersvil? He's been here longer than I have.'

'It fits,' Jessen said grimly. 'He was operating the body scanner when it blew, wasn't he? He helped assemble the thing, knew its workings backwards.'

'But he was assigned at the last minute, by –' Dam broke off, suddenly wide-eyed. 'By Chief Supervisor Yve...'

Jessen flashed him a look that said *What the hell is going on here?*, then let her face harden as the Doctor was dragged over to them.

'Look,' the Doctor said, extricating a hand from one of the guards and holding out a few scraps of what looked like silver foil. 'I found these on the hull, by the doorway.'

'What are they meant to prove?' Jessen said scornfully.

'At least see what they are,' the Doctor chided her, turning over one of the larger pieces and holding it up to Dam's nose. 'There.'

Dam lowered the Doctor's hand to examine the fragment properly. 'What are those lines?'

'Hairline circuitry,' the Doctor explained. 'The device must be designed to reduce down as it operates, leaving no evidence. Clever.'

Jessen studied the fragment briefly. 'Very convenient,' she said, turning to Dam. 'He's wasting our time.'

'No, I'm not,' the Doctor retorted. 'I think it must've been generating some kind of electromagnetic distortion, enough to scramble the drives of every one of these ships. Must've attached it to the damaged craft so natural ion leakage from the fuel systems would make a more likely explanation than…' He paused dramatically, then threw the silver scraps up in the air. 'Sabotage! Each one of these ships would have to be junked and replaced, if poor old Yve hadn't managed to get herself in the way.'

'Could she have set this device herself?' Dam mooted.

'I doubt it,' said the Doctor. 'She must've been inside the ship when the device was set outside it, and shorted out the thermal balance with her body heat when she tried to leave.' He shrugged. 'Whatever she was doing in there in the first place.'

'You expect us to believe any of this?' Jessen stared at him as if he was mad.

'It's how the fire started.' The Doctor was beginning to sound like a teacher surrounded by idiot children. 'Look, I'm sure your experts will tell you something similar. Perhaps you'll accept it from them.'

Dam looked sternly at him. 'You're very well informed, Doctor.'

'I'm trying to help,' the Doctor said wearily.

'Your accomplice, Compassion, was last seen in this area,' Jessen said.

'The whole place has been gone over by security and forensics since then,' Dam pointed out. 'Which leaves us with Makkersvil.'

Jessen nodded. 'It has to be him. Shut out of Main, on an enforced rest-stretch, he'd have had the perfect opportunity. I'll check the cameras, and have him questioned.'

'The cameras haven't functioned in here for weeks,' Dam said sourly. 'Remember? Not a priority, Narkompros said. Well I'm getting them fixed after this, and damn him.'

'Of course,' the Doctor said brightly, 'if Yve recovers, perhaps *she* can tell us the name of the saboteur herself, without anyone having to go through the tedium of an interrogation.'

Jessen looked pointedly at him. 'Makkersvil will soon tell us who he's working for.'

'Good. I'll soon be in the clear, then.'

'Who *all of you* are working for,' Jessen said flatly.

'This conspiracy seems to be more wide-reaching than you first thought, doesn't it?' the Doctor noted, wryly. 'I wonder how far up it goes. Don't you?'

Chapter Twenty-Three
Shadow

'This is stupid,' Fitz grumbled under his breath for the hundredth time in as many minutes, keeping careful tabs on the wild goose he was chasing.

At least the job was made easier now the crowds were thinning out on the Northside streets, filtering off into bars and homes and vending alleys. Relaxing, uncaring, unthinking. Lucky swines.

Nikol's latest plan had been as simple as it was pointless: wait until the hapless staff started flowing out of Central, then each of the group to pick one at random and follow them to see what they did and where they went. Fitz had a suspicion Nikol was hoping the trail would lead to some satanic bunker or other where their targets would all rendezvous and eat babies or something. Personally, he had his doubts; the pasty-faced man he'd trailed halfway across Mechta might be lean and sour-faced, but the most sinister thing he'd done so far was push past a woman to take the last seat in a tram carriage.

Now, as the sun was just starting to think about going down in the pale-blue sky, Fitz was tempted to jack it all in and just say he'd lost sight of his target. Even pretending to be a private eye, narrating his every action aloud, couldn't rescue this particular enterprise. He wondered if Serjey was having any more excitement than he was; the older man had gone along with Nikol only on sufferance as a favour to Fitz, to begin with, anyway. Now Filippa was a member, too, Fitz didn't want to risk looking a berk by managing to lose a quarry at slow-walking pace on an emptying street, while Serjey got the plaudits for a mission accomplished. He had his pride, somewhere, after all.

The lean man turned a corner, and Fitz quickened his pace. A dwelling pyramid rose up like a concrete volcano from the end of the street, and Fitz hurried after the man as he disappeared inside it.

Up the stairs to the first floor… and in. Now he could act like a friendly neighbour just arrived and use his charm and guile to tease out the answers to a few of Nikol's more innocuous questions. Then go home again, job done and the armless old git kept happy.

Fitz knocked on the door, and mused over what sort of voice to use on this poor sop. The Mechtan accent he'd adopted on arrival was so dull, not so different from a flat Home Counties brogue. He was dying to try something a bit wackier.

He knocked again. Something exuberant, pally; American tourist, perhaps. Or maybe something meek and restrained would better suit. The meek shall inherit the Earth, his mum had always told him. Well, they'd hardly have the brass neck to refuse it, would they?

Five minutes later, still waiting, ignored outside in the empty corridor, he began to realise any voice he tried would be falling on deaf ears.

He went out and crossed over to a building the other side of the street, an admin building like the one Filippa worked in. They'd closed up, but once the cleaner had opened the door Fitz was able to rush in apologetically, claiming (in a very meek and restrained manner so as not to waste his earlier preparation) that he'd left a bag upstairs and would only take a minute to fetch it.

Peering across at the dwelling pyramid, Fitz could see his quarry's blinds were pulled down, despite the fall of dusk being a good hour or so away.

Clearly, the man had no intention of being disturbed by anything.

Fitz had no such luxury.

He caught sight of something in the corner of his eye, turned with a smile expecting the cleaner, and screamed at what he saw. Something deformed, bleeding and black was shivering by the entrance, like a cancer carried on air. It had slipped through the door and was now slumped against the wall, an ill-defined shadow flecked with grey stars, hugging the paintwork.

Fitz cowered back, shouting in alarm, knowing it couldn't be real and that it had to go away if he only stared at it enough. Then it did, but he couldn't believe it had really gone, and was afraid even to blink in case it returned while his eyes were shut. He shouted at the cleaner, making the man touch the wall where the thing had vanished, making him *slap* the wall to prove it was solid, shouting at him for playing tricks. Then he was pushing past the man, running angrily down the stairs.

The warm world outside was no comfort; Fitz was rushing snow-blown into the sunlight, shivering.

Chapter Twenty-Four
The Heat Is Rising, Slowly

The fire alarm had jolted through Narkompros, waking him from a terrible nightmare of shadows falling from the sky, tearing down the stars and burying him beneath them. Shaking in his bed, sharp stabbing pains shooting through him, he found himself short of breath. It was his hearts, it had to be. An attack of some kind.

Forcing himself heroically to his feet, not daring to let his critical condition be common knowledge – what would that do for morale? – Narkompros had staggered unaided to the hospital unit, step after dizzying step.

Now, as he lay on the forbidding mattress of a sickbed, Chief Clinician Tonfran was trying to tell him nothing was wrong.

'You think I'm imagining these pains?' he demanded, tugging feverishly at his collar.

'Not at all,' Tonfran assured him, a little awkwardly. 'Your blood pressures *are* quite high. I'll give you something to bring them back down.'

'My medicomputer can do that for me, woman,' Narkompros snapped. He'd only come here because he'd been in such pain he imagined surgery would be necessary. A sudden beeping started up from a comms unit on the wall.

'They're bringing the casualty in,' she muttered.

'*I'm* a casualty!' Narkompros complained softly. 'Please. I insist on a full diagnostic.'

'You know the body scanner is out of commission,' Tonfran said, her tone insufferably reasonable, her thick-rimmed glasses sliding down her pointed nose. 'It'll take weeks to be put right.' She must've noticed the dissatisfaction in his eyes. 'However, I'm very glad you've come to us, Head Narkompros. I assure you, your health is our number-one priority. We can't allow anything to happen to *you*, now, can we? We'll run some more checks to be sure there's nothing going on we've overlooked.'

'Thank you,' he said, feeling a little better already, just as something on a gurney was shoved through the sickbay door behind Tonfran.

'But you can help yourself, you know,' she went on, 'by trying to relax a little –'

'Yve?' Narkompros could barely recognise the bundle in the blanket as his chief supervisor. He pushed himself up from the sickbed. 'What's going on?'

The young orderly pushing Yve was clearly torn between doing his duty and addressing the Head of Facility. Tonfran took the matter out of his hands. 'Where was she brought in from, orderly?'

'Launch bay,' the orderly said, heaving the gurney through to Critical Theatre. 'Fire there,' he grunted.

'Where *exactly*?' Narkompros said, starting to follow them into Critical.

'Please, Head Narkompros,' Tonfran said, trying to block him from entering, 'you should really remain lying down until –'

'Where was the fire?' Narkompros exploded.

Tonfran pushed her glasses back up her nose. 'Please, Head Narkompros, you mustn't upset yourself.' She turned to the orderly. 'I'll start cleaning her up. Tell him as quickly as you can – you're all the support I have, this shift.'

Narkompros looked urgently at the orderly. 'It was ship 59'1?'

The boy flushed scarlet, looking at the ground. 'I don't know the serial codes, Head Narkompros,' he admitted. 'I think the ship they found her in was already damaged, awaiting repair.'

Narkompros slumped heavily down on the sickbed. 'The ship was destroyed?' he asked hoarsely.

'I'm not sure, Head Narkompros,' the orderly said. He took a tentative step forward. 'Forgive me, but you look a little unwell.'

Narkompros had the ludicrous urge to grab hold of the boy, to hold him and to be held and to blurt out everything that was hanging over his head. To feel close to someone, just for a few moments, to tell them what an old fool he had become.

'It's nothing,' he said stiffly. 'When will I be able to question Chief Supervisor Yve about what occurred?'

'She looks bad, Head Narkompros,' the orderly said, non-committally. Then he excused himself and scuttled back into Critical.

Narkompros sat down heavily on the bed, massaging his temples with cold fingers. A few minutes passed, then his communicator started buzzing urgently, a coded signature. 'Yes, Terma, what is it?' he snapped.

'I'm reopening Main, Narkompros,' Terma said, with little trace of pleasure. 'The Doctor has succeeded in stabilising the Bastion without removing it from the network. We might stand a chance of bypassing 634's controller before it decays entirely and placing those aboard under different guidance.'

'*Might* stand a chance?'

Terma paused. 'Power is still seeping out from the network faster than our calculations suggest it should.'

'More sabotage from the Doctor?'

'Can't be. My team were monitoring him the whole time,' Terma said.

'Well, what then?'

'It might simply mean the damage already done is irreparable.'

Narkompros closed his eyes. 'And have you heard about Yve?'

'No. What?'

Narkompros glowered at the doorway to Critical. He'd have to pull himself together, get back down to Strategy One, arrange a debriefing from Dam and for Engineering to fix the damage. As ever, it was down to him alone to make things happen.

'It seems there's been an incident in the launch bay…'

Compassion now found herself with the others in Tod's cell, in a similarly grotty hole in the ground a few kilometres from the first one. It had been another long walk, some of it above ground over a carefully marked course to avoid unexploded mines since the tunnel didn't extend this far. Tod claimed he'd wanted to meet her and Rojin alone in case it was some kind of trap. The two men had spent much of the journey conferring alone, but apparently she was now considered at least trustworthy enough to meet the others.

They were a fairly motley lot, Compassion decided. Karron was Rojin's girlfriend, a black-clad beanpole with big hair. Rojin apparently hadn't seen her for some time by the way he was mauling her about in the corner. Still, thought Compassion, at least it meant she'd be spared any more of his clumsy flirting. Amman and Kurd were a couple of computer geeks, brilliant with programming languages, not so good at speaking their own. They seemed to be using their tongues right now chiefly to salivate in her direction – Compassion supposed they didn't get out very often. Lastly, there was Slatin, a quiet, rotund girl sitting cross-legged on the floor who was, Tod had explained, 'a great thinker'. Tod, even though he led this little band, was the youngest person here by some way.

'These are just my active agents,' Tod explained, a little tetchy since Rojin had once again forgotten the no-names policy and gone ahead and introduced her to everyone.

'I see,' Compassion said, uncertainly. Slatin in particular didn't seem to exactly embody the active life. 'There are more of you?'

'You might call them freelancers. Back at Main Base I've had entire tech teams hidden away at times.' Tod smiled smugly. 'Big plans.'

Compassion decided she might as well know sooner rather than later if this group would be of any help to her at all in reaching the TARDIS. 'And do any of them involve reaching and boarding one of the Project's space stations?'

Amman and Kurd looked goofily at each other. Even Slatin cocked her head. Rojin and Karron actually broke off for air. Quite a reaction, Compassion concluded.

'Come on,' she said. 'You must be planning something to do with the Bastions, or why else would you be sending Rojin to the Facility to meet with your mysterious source?'

'That was just reconnaissance,' Rojin protested. 'I wasn't meeting with anyone. Just making the pick-up.'

'Oh, I see. So that was another disk you handed Tod when we arrived, your source's way of bringing you up to speed.'

Rojin looked guiltily at Tod, who was shaking his head with an

'I-don't-know-why-I-bother' expression on his face.

'Bit of a risk picking it up in person, wasn't it?' Compassion went on.

Karron was looking dreamily at Rojin now. 'Not really,' he said, a little embarrassed, glancing at his watch.

'Illicit communications from top-secret facilities tend to get picked up,' Tod pointed out. 'Anyway, our source swung the security angle. Rojin was never in any real danger.'

Rojin snorted. 'Till Compassion started running wild.'

Then Slatin piped up. 'How were you able to get on board a Bastion, Compassion?' she asked, her voice quiet and mousy but alive with interest.

Compassion smiled. 'By having even bigger plans than you do?'

Tod shook his head. 'Didn't do you much good, though, did they?'

'You don't know the damage we achieved up there,' Compassion said. 'The damage we could go *on* to do if we could get back to our... ship.'

'Ship?' Amman echoed.

'My... group developed and constructed an experimental craft,' Compassion said. 'Something specially designed to infiltrate the Bastions.' The group was hanging on her every word. 'We did it too – but we had to bail out in a life capsule when the emergency shutters came down.'

'Awesome,' whispered Kurd, his eyes alight.

'And your ship's still up there?' Tod asked.

'On board number 634,' Compassion confirmed.

'Say we *could* reach it,' Tod said. 'If we could get our hands on that...' He looked at her sharply. 'We could use it to gain access to the other Bastions?'

'Oh, easily,' Compassion lied blithely. 'Each and every one, if you wanted, no problem.' Tod was glancing at his watch and fidgeting. 'Am I boring you?' she asked.

Tod looked up. If anything, he seemed nervous rather than bored. 'Not just now, you're not,' he said, wandering over to the far side of the room. 'So. How many would this vessel hold, then?'

'Well...' Compassion began.

The brilliant flash of an explosion in the doorway left the question unanswered. Smoking darts of burning wood flew through the air, and Compassion dived for cover behind some empty crates. Cautiously raising her head once the air had cleared a little, she saw armed guards start swarming into the room.

Tod produced his gun and shot two men dead before shrieking, 'Fall back!' He kicked open a side door. 'Move!'

Compassion saw Slatin lumber to her feet, following Amman and Kurd as they squeezed through the doorway both at once, like a comedy duo caught hopelessly out of place. Tod fired again, and another guard tottered backwards, not that it made much difference – there had to be a whole platoon on its way down here. Karron was screaming, apparently rooted to the spot, while Rojin was lying sprawled on the floor, dazed by the blast.

The crates were kicked aside, and Compassion rolled herself backwards into a standing position. A guard came at her; she kicked him hard in the groin and threw herself forward to avoid another lunging clumsily in her direction, landing at Rojin's side. He didn't seem to want to get up, so almost without thinking, she grabbed hold of his sleeve and started dragging him towards the door.

'No!' Rojin yelled, struggling to free himself as they saw Karron knocked to the floor by a guard's rifle butt. 'Let go of me, you stupid bitch!'

'Charming,' Compassion remarked, hauling him up, spinning him round and booting him through the doorway. She heard more gunfire – Tod? No, it was the guards: they were opening fire on them now. The wall by her head erupted in a cloud of plaster as the bullets hit and she slammed the door shut after her.

'That won't hold them,' Compassion said, falling back against the wall. 'Come on.'

'It's all gone wrong!' Rojin yelled.

'It's too late now,' Tod shouted, placing a small black sphere hurriedly in front of the doorway. 'Get back!'

He ushered the rest of his terrified 'active service' along the tunnel. Compassion, leading the way though she had no idea where to, heard the booming of the guards' guns slamming against the wooden door, then the thunderclap of a tremendous explosion that threatened to throw her off her feet. It was a fate Slatin did not escape; not exactly designed for speed, she tripped up Rojin as she fell.

Rojin stayed lying down, panting for breath, and Tod ordered them all to wait while he checked the tunnel was blocked.

'Grenade,' he explained helpfully when he rejoined them. 'They won't be coming after us now.'

'What about Karron!' Rojin insisted, livid with anger.

'She'll be fine. They've been ordered not to kill us.'

'They were firing at us!' Amman whimpered.

'Not *much*,' Tod said derisively. 'It had to look good, didn't it?'

Compassion strode over to confront Tod. 'So I take it you two knew all this was coming?' she said, prodding Rojin with her foot. 'Checking your watches, getting ready for the big event?'

'You set us up?' Slatin accused Tod softly, still on her knees.

'We set *them* up!' Tod said, his voice an octave or so higher in his indignation that she could think such a thing. 'It was all arranged with our source, Rojin picked up the details – discovering one of our bases gives them a result, keeps the heat off them *and* us.'

'But they've taken Karron,' Kurd said.

'They were supposed to take me,' Rojin muttered.

'Supposed?' Compassion queried.

'OK, so not everything went to plan,' Tod conceded reluctantly. 'But Karron will be fine, just like Rojin would've been.'

'I don't know, Tod,' Amman said in his wheedling voice. 'She's not exactly fearless, is she?'

Tod gestured furiously that Amman should shut up, and then turned to Slatin and Kurd. 'The raid was need-to-know stuff. I didn't want to scare you.'

'How sweet of you,' Compassion observed. 'So why *did* you arrange for Rojin to get caught, beaten up and tortured, then? Apart from the obvious reasons, I mean.'

'Messenger, get it?' Tod said. 'I told you, transmissions can be traced, and our source won't take too many risks. But while Karron's locked up safe and sound in a nice little prison cell somewhere, our source can put the co-ordinates of Mechta right in her sweet little hands. And then...' He drew his gun with a flourish – *such* a poseur – and smiled like the heart-throb he clearly felt himself to be. 'When we launch our *totally* unexpected surprise attack to rescue her – at the prearranged time, of course – we get two precious commodities back safe and sound for the price of one. Don't we?'

Compassion surveyed the rest of the miserable little crowd as they reacted to the news. It was, she decided, a good job Tod seemed zealous enough for all of them.

'Whatever else may happen, I'm glad I'm not either of those two,' Dam said to Jessen, closing the door to Strategy One. They'd left Narkompros and Terma inside to agonise over which straw to grasp at next to keep the Project on-line.

Jessen agreed. 'Hardened partyliners like them... They'll be crucified by the Government if all this screws up.' Dam was sure he'd caught a twinkle in her eye. 'I feel happier knowing Yve was supposed to be in the hangar, anyway.'

'Suppose so.' Dam shrugged. 'Doesn't explain what she was doing on board the wrong ship, though. Particularly a decommissioned one.' He sighed. 'We'll just have to hope she regains consciousness soon.'

'In the meantime, do you want me to talk to Makkersvil?'

Dam looked at her. 'If that's all right with you.'

Jessen nodded. 'I reckon he's the one person in this Facility who would swap places with Yve gladly.'

Makkersvil still couldn't believe any of this was happening to him. To the casual eye, he supposed it might appear he had simply traded one sweaty bed in a stuffy little room for another, but to have the woman that had been sharing that bed now locking him up and pointing a gun at his head...

He'd been set up. They seemed to think he'd been running off illicit IDs, that he was allied to the intruders, to saboteurs everywhere. It was a witch hunt, and the fingers all pointed at him. He'd dropped himself right in it with his big mouth back at the body scan when Narkompros had first mooted there was a saboteur in their midst. 'Could be any one of us,' he'd announced. Nice work, Makkersvil. Clever.

Typically, he found one of his biggest regrets to be that if they shot him here and now for treachery to the great Project, he'd never get to finally have things out with Yve. He supposed it only proved you got what you deserved if you went through the motions. If there was a next world, he decided, he'd spend less time thinking and more time doing. Doing things differently, too.

Jessen, only his second in what he suspected would've been a long line of thrillingly illicit, but ultimately pointless, affairs with powerful women who had the power to ruin both him *and* his career, had been the one to break the pattern before it could become ingrained – by having him arrested. When it came down to it, she'd acted just as she'd always said she would if there was trouble – as if there was nothing between them.

Who was he kidding? This was always his problem. There *was* nothing between them.

The door opened. There she was. He didn't get up.

'Well, well… Jessen Kal, ice queen of fair and frozen 59.'

'Hello, Makkersvil,' she said.

'Visiting time, is it? Or are you here to beat a confession out of me?'

'You're really wallowing in this bitterness, aren't you?' she said.

'What do you know about it?'

'I know everything that's on Yve's confidential bar graph,' Jessen said, the hint of a sneer on her face.

He froze. 'And what's that old bitch got to do with anything?'

'We're investigating her as we are you,' Jessen went on. 'Our report suggests she's screwed you over for promotion several times – for no very good reason other than to keep you on her personal staff.'

Makkersvil felt his guts twist. 'Perhaps she just likes my face,' he said.

'You really *are* in love with her, aren't you?' Jessen said, as if receiving confirmation of something she'd known all along. The faintest trace of that sneer returned. 'Always have been, always will be.'

Makkersvil turned away. 'I don't know what you're talking about, Security Administrator Jessen,' he said. 'Mind getting to the point?'

'I've watched you, you know,' she said softly. 'In Main. On the security cams. Seen the way you look at her.'

He got up from the bunk, unsettled. 'What's this all about? Some kind of jealousy thing?'

Jessen laughed. 'Dream on. You're a spy, my lovely Makkersvil, it's cut and dried. In a few days, you'll be going to the same place Yve's heading for.'

'What do you mean?'

'Since the fire that burnt half her face off,' Jessen confided with mock concern, 'she's not been looking quite so attractive.'

Makkersvil stared at her. 'What?'

'She's just lying there now, in Critical… like an oversized roasted joint.' Jessen smiled. 'Like you, she's so easy to abuse.' Jessen sauntered across to the other side of the cell.

He had a clear run at the door.

'Helpless, crippled thing. But compared to what's coming for you, I'd say she was the lucky one.'

Makkersvil stopped seeing things so clearly, then. He was aware of pushing easily past Jessen, then of knocking into the guard blocking the cell doorway, of the energy bolt sizzling into his stomach, kicking him back against the wall, of struggling for breath, wondering why his legs weren't holding him up, where all that blood was coming from.

Jessen picked herself up and looked down at Makkersvil, checked for a pulse, and cursed silently to herself.

'I'll call the hospital unit,' the guard said, clearly shaken, already fumbling for his wrist communicator.

It was a good try, Jessen told herself. She'd known exactly which buttons to press with Makkersvil. She'd stationed the guard in the doorway because she'd thought a stun burst at point-blank range would be enough to kill. But while Makkersvil's stomach was quite a mess, he was still alive.

'I meant it, you know. I wanted to spare you what is to come,' she whispered to his prone body. 'You poor, sweet little bastard.'

Chapter Twenty-Five
You Do It to Yourself

I imagined that blackness in the room, of course, I must've done. Or I had a funny turn of some kind – I'm not my mother's son for nothing. Or it could've been some kind of trick – maybe even some kind of warning from the man I followed, I don't know. But it wasn't real. I *must've* imagined it.

I was shaken, whatever, and having legged it down the street I ran into the nearest bar I could find. It was the company of people that was the real draw, actually, not the Ethels. That surprised me. It became a kind of wry surprise, though, as I realised I was in Denna's haunt again, despite the million resolutions I'd made to stay well away.

And I felt better pretty quickly, too. It's funny how we end up ignoring anything we can't explain. We worry at first, but its importance fades because it doesn't make sense; we just reject it. Especially if there's something else happening that we *can* understand to take our minds off it. And I didn't have to be back until midnight for the group meeting to compare our reports. And I didn't want to think about what I'd tell them of the thing in that building. You know, I actually nursed the pathetic hope that the cleaner *was* having me on, and that Filippa would tell me every admin block had a black thing hovering about. Kind of Mechtan shredding machines, or something.

The bar seemed a bit rowdier than it had been the night before, so I asked the barman what was the occasion.

'Double red-car party,' he answered. 'Two Notifications through on the same day. It's rare, is that. Almost unheard of.'

It was probably unheard of over the noise, I decided. The party was rocking, people yelling and singing and dancing. Weird songs; maybe they would've been better with music. To my ears it sounded like no one in the place could carry a tune in a bucket, they were all over the shop. I guess I was seeing it all as an outsider; what clue did I have about their culture? I felt lonely again, the loneliness of the long-distance runner, maybe. Gone to seed. Gone to ground.

Then I heard a familiar voice yell my name, and my throat tightened as Denna threw her arms around me and spun me around.

'Come to play again so soon,' she said, licking her lips needlessly – it was her eyes that were eating me up. 'Thought you didn't like coming out North.'

'I don't,' I told her, which on reflection is about the only honest thing I've ever said to her apart from 'You look fantastic'.

She took a seat by me, and I realised that the longer I stayed the trickier it would be to tear myself away, but she was just what I needed: light and bright and breezy, cooling me down as the evening hotted up. More and more people seemed to be getting their Notification orders, she told me, but when I asked if she was bothered by this, or if it made her nervous, she just laughed.

'There'll be time enough to be bothered in the real world,' she said. 'While we're here, we work, but we don't need the money. We can fall in love like we've never been hurt...' Just then she gave me the most wonderful, dangerous grin I have ever seen. 'And dance like there's nobody watching.'

She laughed like a drain again and sprang to her feet, beginning to move to a rhythm she clapped herself. *Everyone* was watching, but true to her word, she didn't care one bit. The onlookers started taking up the rhythm as well, banging glasses, stamping feet, starting up an off-key chorus to accompany her movements.

I found myself standing on a table, cheering her on; then we all were. The noise was deafening, and she looked wanton in the applause she got when she'd finished, basking, the spotlight her sun.

It was a good night, but I kept my eye on the clock and left like a good boy in plenty of time to go home and freshen up before the late-night meeting. Denna waved me off, and I promised I'd come to see her again soon. When she kissed me it was like every girl I'd ever dreamed about was joining in. But even after only a few minutes into my long journey home I found I couldn't recall

147

the feeling of her lips on mine, and the night seemed just a little too bruised and dark outside the rattling tram.

I got home, and found Filippa on my bed. Her eyes looked red and straight through me.

'You all right, babe?' I asked her; it was a stupid question but as good an opener as any. 'What's up?'

'My designated Central employee led me Northside way,' Filippa said very carefully. I was transfixed by the way she let the tears roll down her face; they always itch the hell out of me if I don't wipe them.

'Northside?' I was stupid. As soon as she said the words I could only think of my stain-thing, that the floating tumour had to be what had upset her and that it was real and there were more of them...

'You didn't... *see* something, did you?'

'Yes, I saw something, you scrawny bastard coward,' she shouted, eyes like lasers now. 'I saw you in a bar with your hands all over some little slut.'

'She's not a slut,' I said automatically. Stupid again, I meant to say she was no one, a nothing, not even worthy of tart status but it sounded like I was defending her. I tried to tell Filippa about the stain I'd seen but it was useless now, like another lie to change the subject, and I was telling her I'd been scared and I'd been frightened and I needed to talk to people, to have people round me and she said yeah, and all over you, too, I noticed... And I got upset as well because I realised exactly how much seeing that thing had scared the hell out of me and *still* scared the hell out of me and now Filippa wouldn't listen to a single word I tried to say.

'It makes things easier, in a way,' Filippa said, with a seriousness in her voice that managed to scare me more than anything else.

'What do you mean?'

'The news I got today.' She looked at me, dry-eyed now. 'I got Notification. I'm taking a red car in eight days.'

It was one of those stupid, idiot moments where your jaw flaps open as if you're trying to fit the enormity of someone else's lightly spoken words into your own mouth. But how could I even attempt to take it in, when I was about six inches tall, transparent, no room in me for anything but myself?

Surprisingly, Serjey could still see me when he came into my apartment an hour or so later, wondering why I hadn't come to the meeting. Filippa had left by then, saying she needed time to think about things; she didn't listen when I told her she didn't have *time* to take her time. She just left me.

Good old Serjey. He's been like a brother to me here, like the older brother I'd always wanted. We talked for hours... We shouted a lot, too – blood's thicker than water and all that but I guess it boils a lot faster, too. He didn't mince words about what a moron he thought I was, and when was I going to grow up and all that... It was good though. I feel a bit better for it today. Less good about the other stuff he told me. Stuff from the meeting.

Seems it was the same for everyone we followed – our wild geese led us all around Mechta, went into their apartments and stayed there, not answering the door or coming to the windows, not making a sound. And there had been an unprecedented number of Notifications city wide. I told him about Filippa's news; well, when I could get the words out, anyway, and he hugged me and told me that if either of us got Notification we'd burn it and we'd hide out somewhere and take on the correctioners and anyone else who might try to have a go... I doubt either of us really believed it, but just to be making our own plans felt good.

'Do you think it could be us?' Serjey asked, about to go home to his own bed as the sun started to rise. 'Could we have got too close to something?'

That set me off all over again, of course, had me reaching for pen and paper the minute he'd gone to write all this down... because what if it's me? I don't belong here, I shouldn't be part of this world. I'm a cuckoo. Everything was OK here until I arrived. It's the Doctor's gift of jinx, I'm sure of it. When the TARDIS did to me what all the king's men and horses couldn't do, it probably passed on to me the precious gift of shagging up every place I might ever visit.

And there's no one in this whole city I can possibly tell.

CAN'T TELL A SOUL
CALLOUS TALENT

Chapter Twenty-Six
Power and How to Wield It

The world came back to confront Karron's aching eyes with the image of a row of boots on a filthy metal floor. She was in the back of a vehicle, surrounded by armed men. She had to keep quiet, and still. Play dead, so they'd pay her no attention. She'd be OK. If she kept her wits about her like Rojin –

The sob wrenched itself from her body before she could do anything to stop it. One of the boots flipped her over. She saw a dozen men staring at her.

'Nice sleep, was it?' one of them said, pouring a drink over her face. 'There's a little shower for you.'

The men were laughing. The air in the transport was hot and stank of sweat and mud. The liquid stung as it ran over her cheek, and she remembered being hit round the face by the gun butt when the guards had rushed in. She touched the wound – it felt enormous. Karron felt sick at the thought of a scar, of her pale skin being ruined. Of never looking normal again.

Someone else poured a hot drink over her. 'Three of our boys your friends took out, you little scrubber,' a voice said, but she'd closed her eyes and could only imagine the anger in the face that went with it.

'Oh, she's trying to get back to sleep,' another voice jeered. She felt the boots pushing against her body, rocking her this way and that.

'Won't be much sleep where you're going, darling,' said yet another, and there was more laughter.

She covered her face with her hands and the prods and the kicks kept coming. What had happened to Rojin, to the others? She moaned with fear. Already she wanted to stand up and scream that she'd tell them everything they wanted to know.

The Doctor was snoozing in his cell, trying to keep calm and focused instead of raging like a mad thing against the walls that held him, when he heard a quiet *snip*.

Jedkah was hovering over him, brandishing a small pair of scissors in one hand and a lock of hair in the other.

'Hey!' the Doctor yelled, snatching for the hair. 'That's stealing!'

'You're a prisoner, aren't you, eh?' Jedkah said, trying to hold his little body with dignity. 'You have no rights.'

The Doctor studied him. 'And you have no right to do this, do you?' he said. 'You should be taking that launch bay apart trying to find indisputable evidence of your traitor's identity, right now, shouldn't you? Not giving me a haircut!'

Jedkah held up the lock of hair. '*This* is evidence of your true extraterrestrial origin!' he hissed.

'Oh dear. Back here again, are we?' The Doctor got up. He was between Jedkah and the door, a fact that was not lost on the stumpy little man judging by the nervous quiver of his hands.

'Don't... don't get any ideas,' Jedkah stammered. 'I bribed the guard to let me in, but he's not far away!'

'Why didn't you bribe him last night?' the Doctor asked, puzzled.

Jedkah looked scandalised. 'On what they pay me here?'

'In any case, a dangerous move in a climate such as this, I'd have thought,' the Doctor said, slowly advancing on him. 'Especially at the moment. There are rules about that sort of thing, aren't there?'

The little man smiled craftily. 'Oh, they know old Jedkah, you know.'

The Doctor tried not to grimace. 'I'm sure. Now, listen to me. That hair won't tell you anything very much...' He came to a halt and sucked thoughtfully on a finger. 'But just say that I relented, that I aided your... *dignified* study a little, that I demonstrated how my evolution has cheated all expectations for a high-gravity world with a noxious atmosphere like Haltiel...'

'Yes?' The excitement on Jedkah's face would've been quite endearing under different circumstances.

'I would expect, in exchange, a little local knowledge.'

'Mechta, again, eh?' Jedkah said, impatiently.

'I want a precise locational fix. And I want co-ordinates and approach trajectories for Bastion 634.'

Jedkah smirked. 'That information's restricted.'

The Doctor tutted. 'So's this cell, but that hasn't stopped you so far.'

'What good could the information possibly be to you?'

'It'll satisfy my curiosity.'

'Even assuming you could ever get out of here, Mechta's not somewhere you'd like to go, you know. Right now, least of all.'

'The dissolution of the Project has been affecting Mechta directly?' the Doctor asked.

'I'm saying nothing more,' Jedkah said, skittering past the Doctor in a wide circle. 'Not until you give me something more conclusive on your true origins.'

'Everyone seems to have their own opinion on that one,' the Doctor sighed. 'It's such a bore.'

'Keep my little visit to yourself,' Jedkah said, cautiously opening the door a crack and squeezing through.

'It's not the sort of thing I'd brag about.'

'I'll be back later.' Jedkah paused. 'With a scalpel.'

The Doctor sighed as the door locked behind the little man. He'd had to fight back the urge to nobble Jedkah and take his chances on a *serious* escape attempt. But without more exact information, how could he even start looking to rescue his friends? Soon, he decided. When Jedkah came back with the info. Then the waiting would be over and the game would be afoot. Provided, of course, Jedkah didn't manage to exact a foot as payment for his data.

It was time to go on the offensive.

Chapter Twenty-Seven
Rabble-Rousing

Fitz didn't see Filippa at all the next day; he called for her but she was either out or else doing her best impression of a Central clerk. He only saw her the next day at Nikol's for the emergency meeting, and the circumstances weren't as intimate as he'd have liked.

In contrast to every other assembly of the old man's group, the apartment was teeming with people from all over the area. There was an atmosphere of general bemusement as so many had been given Notification, and nothing like this had ever happened before. Nikol was taking full advantage of this new Mechtan vibe of vague concern by harnessing it to his personal crusade. He was promising answers for everyone – and knew he had to be quite quick about it. Nikol's own Notification had come through that morning.

'It'll be perfect for us,' Anya had said to Fitz, wearing next to nothing at his front door. 'With Filippa and Nikol both safely back on Homeplanet, there'll be nothing and no one in the way.' Fitz had closed the door in her face. She'd banged on the windows and sworn, but not too loudly. Nikol hadn't gone yet. She still didn't want to make a scene.

Now Fitz was feeling sick with worry. How many people would be left in Mechta if red-carring carried on at this rate?

Filippa had made a discovery herself, and Fitz watched her tell the room full of inquisitive people, just one more troubled face in the crowd. She'd tapped into records at her work, and cited some strange examples of the patterns occurring – like the bar on Centreside where twenty regulars had been red-carred on the same day – and a barman notified the day after. The correlation held at a number of places – Filippa mentioned a nursing home had lost ten patients to the taxis, and a carer shortly after. The numbers were being kept nicely in proportion.

Nikol called it a cull.

'There are many of us now,' he announced. 'Central will have no alternative but to listen to us – and then to tell us everything we wish to know!'

'What we're going home to,' someone said.

'Why we're here at all,' Fitz joined in, hoping his voice might attract Filippa's attention, but no. She just stared straight ahead.

'When do we go?' a woman asked.

Nikol raised his one good arm like a fat spear. 'We go now!'

Chapter Twenty-Eight
Desperation Takes Hold

Terma dismally surveyed the strat-screen. Everything they tried met with failure. The Bastion was barely responding to radio signals at all, now. The others were still compensating for the moment, but he could think of nothing feasible that could be causing 634 to act like this. This was beyond any problem with the flesh-technology interfacing. The controller was initiating subroutines that threatened to destabilise the entire Project. It would be... What would Narkompros say? 'Terminally compromised.' Thirty years of secret funding, the heaviest public taxing ever known, billions upon billions spent... all to generate two thousand dead lights in the sky that no one would ever see.

And now with both Yve and Makkersvil hospitalised... though he'd never cared much for either of them personally, he could recognise he'd lost two good minds to help him reason the problem out. Short of finding a stick long enough to prod the Bastion into life from here, he could think of little more to do.

He slumped in front of the screen and closed his eyes. Like Narkompros, he had invested so much of his life in this Project, had formed so many plans of what he might do when it was operational at last. Now, like Narkompros, all he could do was wait and hope for either the Doctor or this latest saboteur they'd found to shed some new light on the situation.

Too much was at stake for all those stored up there in the blackness to drop out of the dream now.

Rough hands shoved Karron into the tiny cell. She felt almost relieved. Her body ached all over from being kicked about, she was soaking and sticky with whatever the guards had been pouring over her, and her face felt like it was cracking open. Her eyes were swollen and stinging with tears. At least here, locked up, they might leave her alone for a bit.

Suddenly she slipped on something wet and fell heavily to the metal floor. She realised she was lying in a dark puddle of someone's blood.

'Sorry,' the blonde woman called from the doorway. 'We haven't got round to cleaning up after the last person here. Staff shortages.'

The door slammed shut as Karron started screaming again.

The fluorescents were turned down low in Strategy One now Terma had gone. Narkompros was staring at motes of dust sailing aimlessly in the weak light.

There was a knock at the door. Embarrassed, Narkompros slid the lights back up to full strength just as someone entered. Impatient with his eyes for taking so long to adjust, he squinted into the new brightness. 'Well?'

'You asked to be kept abreast of all developments, Head Narkompros.' Dam, dutiful and deferential as ever. 'I have mixed news. Makkersvil's been shot trying to escape.'

Narkompros clenched his fists. His sight was returning but the effort of concentration was making him feel queasy. 'Is he dead?'

'No,' Dam said. 'He should pull through all right. He's out of Critical now – we should be able to question him fully before too long.'

'How long?' Narkompros demanded. 'With Yve's condition unchanged, it seems no one we need answers from can utter a word –' He broke off as he felt something bite at his guts, and let out an involuntary groan. Dam took a step closer, apparently concerned.

'Are you all right?'

As with the orderly earlier, Narkompros got the sudden urge to let everything spill out, every ache and pain, every itch and guilty secret. So many years of keeping so much to himself… and with the prize slipping away now he was in sight of reaping the rewards…

'Just stomach cramps,' he said, dismissively. 'Tension, I suppose, nothing serious.'

'There *is* some better news,' Dam said. 'We've captured one of the saboteurs. She's safely in a cell now.'

Narkompros felt a surge of hope. 'The Doctor's woman?'

'No. Someone else's little girl, by the sound of her wailing.'

'I take it we can question *her* straightaway?' Narkompros enquired, and Dam nodded. 'Excellent. We'll put her with the Doctor, play one against the other. I'll attend in person. We *have* to uncover what they've done, Dam, and what they're doing. Terma *has* to be able to undo it.'

'Of course, Head Narkompros. I'll arrange it right away.'

'By the way, Dam. Engineering have informed me they've pretty much fixed up the ships in the launch bay. We can risk a launch within twenty-four hours if we have to!' Narkompros was aware he was being exaggeratedly jovial. 'We're not beaten yet, eh, Dam?'

Dam smiled politely. 'Not yet, Head Narkompros,' he said, closing the door again behind him.

Tod had led his subdued gaggle of active agents to further underground quarters. Now they were supposed to get some sleep before attacking at dawn the next day, as their source had arranged. Compassion hadn't much fancied the filthy hammocks, nor the grubby mattresses strewn around the room, but the others had obediently lain down. She wondered what lives they'd all known before Tod had taken charge of them.

He was lying on the biggest mattress, an overturned table acting as a screen to shield him from the rank and file. After a couple of hours, she prowled over to join him. There were things she needed to know.

'I wondered if you'd be joining me,' Tod said quietly as she sat down beside him.

Compassion heard a click as a dull lamp flickered on next to Tod's hand. The shadows it cast on his face suddenly made him look a lot older.

'Wondered or hoped?' she said.

Tod smiled. She noticed he'd removed his top. His body was white and skinny, like his head. 'Rojin hopes we can join forces,'

158

he said. 'My lot with your lot. For greater security.'

'What did he do before he became your right-hand man, sell pensions?'

'He's a scientist, like me,' Tod said. He noticed her surprise, and enjoyed it. 'We were working for a government psych-firm, cutting-edge stuff, the programs we were developing. You should've seen some of the tricks we made monkey brains do.' He chuckled at the reminiscence. 'Jump-start the right bits and you get some lethal accuracy…'

Compassion kept up the pretence she was at all interested. 'So you left it all behind for this?'

'Government shut us down, didn't they? They'd decided to put the money they'd save directly into the people we were supplying. Into Facility One.'

'I take it you weren't meant to discover anything about that – or their Project?'

'We put our week's notice to pretty good use.' He grinned again, smugly. 'Dangerous, leaving jaded tech-heads around all those computers.'

'I'm sure. So how did you win over this bunch? You've got them well trained.'

'I'm just brighter than them,' Tod said, with an honesty Compassion could relate to. 'I'm an organiser, I know what's needed, and I know how to come by… finance.' He smirked. 'I hacked into the Great Bank's payroll once, gave Slatin a director's wage. They didn't notice for six months.'

'So why didn't you all just lie back and enjoy the money? I mean, how old are you, Tod… twenty? Twenty-one?'

'I'm twenty-four, actually,' Tod said, a little put out. 'I *was* like that, just looking out for myself. Until I found out what the Project was really about. What went in to making Mechta. You and your friends must feel the same, surely?'

Compassion nodded, wondering how he'd react if she told him she really didn't know what he was talking about. Shoot her for the spy in his camp she was, probably. The Doctor's spy, she realised. She wasn't just gathering information to get back to the

TARDIS: she was doing it for *him*, too. Like the way she'd taken the time to help Rojin to safety back in the ambush. She'd obviously been picking up TARDIS vibes for too long – it was trying to make her into an 'old girl', too.

Still, why not? It used to be the case that signals were all that mattered back in the Remote. There was no rhyme or no reason, there didn't need to be. But then principles had been introduced to impose their stupid illogical order on their lives. Her people had been meant to learn from them.

She supposed that no one embodied the principle of imposing an illogical order more than the Doctor. It was just what he did, his way of making things better. She didn't see him as a friend – Compassion didn't think she could *ever* properly grasp the concept of 'having friends' in the way that Fitz or the Doctor or even Tod could – she saw him more as a *function*. A function of the universe she found she could respond to. Maybe that was why she'd been feeling like so much was changing inside her. It scared her, scared her quite badly. Something she felt but couldn't quite put a name to was liberating itself.

She realised Tod was still talking, all about his struggle to recruit for his nameless cell, his visions for a better future, his dreams, all of that. She knew, though, it wasn't important that she actually hear him speak. She had only to be *seen* to be listening.

He reached out and placed a slightly trembling hand on her arm. 'We find the right people who feel the same as we do… and we get together to do something about it. Big plans.' Compassion allowed the hand to remain but did nothing to encourage it. As she'd expected, it rapidly withdrew. 'You should see the scale of the project we've been working on.'

This was more like it, thought Compassion. 'I'd like to.'

He was looking intently at her. 'What about you, though? How'd you learn about the Project?'

'We just kind of stumbled upon it,' Compassion said, coolly, moving a little closer. 'I don't think we're as well funded as you, though. All our money's gone into this one prototype ship.'

'Impressive, though,' Tod said generously, clearly wondering if he should risk his hand again. 'Got the whole Facility up in arms.'

On the word 'arms' he took the risk and held her wrists by way of demonstration. She stroked one finger against his skin in response.

'Can I trust you?' he whispered.

'Actually, you can,' Compassion said.

Tod fell silent for a moment. She could hear one of the others snoring gently under his softly spoken words. 'We've got our own launching bay. And two mineships. Each loaded with megatonnes of fissile material.' She imagined he'd be gratified by a degree of astonishment so she widened her eyes. 'We're going to fire them at a strategic point in the middle of the Bastion network.'

'I thought the Bastions were impregnable.'

'Practically. Our source has the co-ordinates for a strategic point in the network. There's a forty-five-per-cent chance the explosion will trigger a chain reaction.' His eyes were gleaming in the dim light from the lamp. 'The network can survive losing one, two, maybe even three Bastions temporarily. Knock out more than that... You've got a thousand billion's worth of floating space junk.'

'And not very good odds.'

'We figured it was our only shot.' He smiled. 'Then you came along, spacegirl.'

Compassion tried to smile as if his corn was a compliment, but her lips wouldn't quite oblige. She started speaking instead. 'You said it yourself back at bolthole six. If we can use your mineships to get to my craft, we can pilot it to any number of Bastions.'

'But things went wrong,' Tod pointed out. 'You had to jump ship.'

She slid closer, freed her hand and placed it gently against his mouth to silence him. 'I don't make the same mistakes twice,' she said. 'Are you with me?'

She felt his lips quivering against her palm. Eating out of my hand, she thought.

Yet another bunk, yet another boxy little room, thought Makkersvil. Except this time I get to savour the feeling of plastic tubes snaking up my nose and into my wrist.

Clinician Tonfran had clearly done a good job, Makkersvil decided, not that he could remember any of it. He couldn't even feel his stomach now, just a numbness.

Pretty much everything felt numb, come to think of it.

The wound was buried deep beneath a pile of wadding. I'd have a silhouette like Narkompros if I could get up now, he thought, then tried to, and realised he was going nowhere. He was helpless. They'd wait for him to get a bit better, then they'd kill him anyway trying to make him talk.

Melancholy, he guessed Yve must be nearby somewhere. Well, hadn't they always been close? Makkersvil looked at the blocks and graphs glowing on the diagnostic computer's viewscreen, and wondered what pattern Yve's burnt-up body was generating. It was ridiculous, pathetic, but he still wanted to see her more than anything else right now.

A thought struck him. He was pretty trained up on these self-diagnostics. It had been a while, but anyone could tweak the insides of a medicomputer if they knew vaguely what they were doing. If he could rig the basic settings so it placed him at death's door...

'This is the inevitable speaking,' he croaked aloud. 'We are experiencing some minor delays to our schedule this afternoon...'

Stiffly, he reached for the access panel.

Karron sat curled up in a ball in the corner of the cell, shivering, eyes tightly closed. If only she could give up hope perhaps the fear would go. But part of her refused to give up on the thought of Rojin rushing in to her rescue. He'd been here before after all, a few times. Knew how to get in undetected. Knew his way all over the Facility, he'd said so.

When the door quietly opened she didn't dare risk a look to see who had come for her. Part of her so desperately wanted it to be him she knew she couldn't bear to be disappointed. Footsteps padded nearer, and then she was being pulled roughly to her feet.

A sudden strike of pain burnt her chest, forcing her eyes to bulge open of their own accord. But staring down, Karron saw only the hilt of the knife sticking out from her ribcage before collapsing into blackness.

Chapter Twenty-Nine
The Final Raid on Central

Keeping his band together on the trek to Central wasn't easy for Nikol. He tried to keep them focused by chanting slogans, but the correctioners turned up pretty quickly, and inevitably a number of people melted away from the crowd, anxious to avoid confrontation. Fitz had argued they were just singing, hoping again for some kind of acknowledgement from Filippa, but while she glanced at him and smiled briefly she wouldn't talk to him, choosing instead to confer quietly with Nikol.

When they finally reached Central, Fitz's heart rising a little closer to his mouth with every step he took, two men ran up and he tensed himself for trouble. Bizarrely, the men tried to convince them all that something suspicious was going on with Central's running of Mechta, and that the spate of recent Notifications was to prevent people finding out the truth. These men had set up a demonstration only that morning, but it had been disbanded; now they were urging everyone who passed by to listen to them and to take action.

Correctioners soon appeared, but by then Nikol had gripped one of the men in a clumsy embrace and shouted to his band that they weren't alone.

'You see?' Nikol yelled over the correctioners' polite invitation to move along. 'All over Mechta it's the same! People treated like cattle, herded into neat configurations, working to unknown agendas. You *must've* wondered why you're here…'

There were mutterings of 'All part of the treatment', a mantra that the correctioners took up, still trying to bustle Nikol away. The two men tried to pull the correctioners away, but more appeared, red bees buzzing round grey flowers.

'Understanding the treatment we're receiving here won't make it any less effective. How can it?' Nikol struggled with renewed vigour as a hand clamped over his mouth, shutting him up, and

Fitz's eyes widened in alarm as Filippa tried to stand on a low wall to continue the tirade.

'Filippa, no!'

'Why should we be afraid of asking questions?' she yelled. The rising panic was rushing through the crowd now like a living thing. 'All we want are simple answers to –'

Fitz shouted Filippa's name as she was knocked backwards off the wall by a flailing limb. She'll be trampled, was all he could think of. He had to assume responsibility like the Doctor would. Do something. Lead this crowd away.

Grasping hold of Serjey's sleeve, Fitz pulled his friend after him. 'Inside!' he screamed. 'The answers are inside!'

The correctioners were too far away and too tangled up in the various limbs of Nikol and his new recruits to stop Fitz and Serjey flinging open the double doors. It was as if a spell had been broken; Fitz's command echoed round the square, and the sight of the open doorway seemed to sting the crowd into angry action. Suddenly, the assembled men and women were surging forward after the two men, yelling assent.

Fitz and Serjey sprinted past the astonished receptionists, Anya leading the throng behind them.

'Make them take the lift up,' Fitz ordered her, his voice a higher pitch than he would've liked. 'We're going to find out exactly what those records say!'

The crowd pushed Anya's scrawny body against the desk, unthinking. She cried out, but the sound was lost in the clamour of the mob. The people were blocking the entrance hall, preventing the correctioners from getting through. Anya tried to scramble over the desk, but the receptionist grabbed her by the throat and tried to push her back. Someone hit the receptionist in the face and Anya was able to break the woman's grip. At last, she slid behind the desk and grabbed her by the hair. Even now, the receptionist's assistant was being hauled to the floor by others in the baying crowd.

'Now or never,' Serjey said to Fitz, his face flushed.

They sprinted down the corridor, and Fitz slipped as they

rounded the sharp corner, slamming his shoulder against the wall. The great brass doors of the lift gleamed dully in the electric light like gold. Serjey slapped his palm against the call button.

The doors slid silently open.

Inside the lift were scores of people in the dark business suits of all Central employees, crammed into the metal box in silence. Their eyes were open but unseeing, their bodies twisted unnaturally with the compression, like corpses in a mass grave. The dead staff of Central, waiting for home time to come.

Fitz finally remembered how to scream, just as the correctioners finally caught up with him and Serjey.

The lift doors softly closed again.

Chapter Thirty
Resurrection

The Doctor had no real idea how much time had passed, but finally, a scuffling at the door alerted him to the fact that Jedkah was here.

'I've got what you wanted,' Jedkah said, waving some sheets of paper. 'Copied it out by hand.'

'They really *don't* pay you enough, do they?'

'I'm not getting caught using computers like Makkersvil,' Jedkah said. 'They caught him downloading and...' Jedkah mimed a knife slitting his throat.

'How do I know the data is genuine?'

'It is. Making something up would've taken me longer, wouldn't it, eh?'

The Doctor tutted. 'No imagination?'

'No head for figures.' Jedkah grinned nastily. 'Not numerical ones anyway.'

The Doctor didn't smile back. 'So let me see the papers.'

'When I say so,' Jedkah said, hoarsely. 'Take off your shoes.'

'Shouldn't I be saying that to you?' the Doctor said, stalling him. 'You're my guest, after all. Make yourself at home.'

Jedkah produced a syringe. 'I'm taking a blood sample and some tissue for a biopsy,' he announced, waving the papers again. 'You want these, you have to pay the price. So, like I say – take off your shoes.'

'That it should come to this. Selling my sole.' The Doctor grimaced. 'You're quite sure about this? I can't persuade you to take some fluff from my –'

'Just take them off!' Jedkah hissed urgently.

'Toe the line, eh?' The Doctor sat down on the bunk and as he raised his foot to remove the shoe he kicked out at Jedkah's hand, sending the papers flying. With an angry squawk Jedkah flew after them, but the Doctor was too quick for him, covering them with his body.

With a snarl, Jedkah raised the hypodermic – just as a guard entered the room. Jedkah leapt backwards like a cat on a hotplate.

'Get out of here, Jedkah,' the guard said, ignoring the scene entirely. 'Dam's on his way.'

Jedkah's face fell about a mile. 'No! I paid you well to let me in here!'

'Not well enough for Dam to find out I've let you in,' he said, heaving Jedkah out by the scruff of his neck. 'Now move it.'

'I'll get you for this, Doctor!' Jedkah squeaked as the guard hauled the door shut.

'Shoo,' muttered the Doctor, desperately folding up the papers and shoving them down the neck of his prison suit.

When Dam entered a minute or so later, the Doctor was the very image of the bored inmate.

'Oh, hello,' he said distantly.

'You're to be interrogated with one of your saboteur friends,' Dam announced.

The Doctor closed his eyes in weary disbelief. 'How many more times...?'

'Well with one of the people who helped your companion to escape, then,' Dam said, irritably. 'A girl called Karron. So you see, it really doesn't matter that Makkersvil can't speak to us now.'

The Doctor drew his hand across his throat as Jedkah had earlier, quizzically.

'Shot while attempting to escape from Jessen. But he'll pull through. His testimony may well yet count against you.'

'I wouldn't count on that,' the Doctor said. 'You know, you sound to me, Dam, like a man who's trying to act convinced of my guilt when really he's not.' The Doctor gave a small smile. 'Or is that just wishful thinking?'

Dam avoided both the question and the Doctor's eyes. 'Narkompros is out for blood, you know.'

'Is he, now?' the Doctor muttered.

'He's getting desperate for results. Your work on the computers has only slowed things down. It's already failing.'

'What?' the Doctor looked up at him, appalled. 'That should have held things stable for a good few days!'

'Perhaps you've overestimated your abilities,' said Dam, not unkindly. 'And now that Terma and Narkompros have realised this, the importance of keeping you in one piece – and sane – has diminished.' He paused. 'I'm actually sorry for you, Doctor.'

'You believe me, don't you?' the Doctor said, rising to his feet, a grin spreading over his face. 'You think I'm telling the truth.'

'I think there's more to this whole thing than –' Dam's communicator started beeping, and with a scowl he activated it. 'Jessen?' He slapped a hand to his forehead in disbelief. 'You didn't check for concealed weaponry? Jessen, what were you thinking of? We'll...' As the Doctor watched, Dam seemed to visibly deflate. 'No. No, I'll tell Narkompros... There'll have to be an enquiry. I'm sorry... Yes, take your rest-stretch now, if you must. Keep out of the way. *Well* out.' Swearing, he switched off the communicator.

'Karron?' the Doctor asked, tentatively.

'Found dead in her cell,' Dam muttered, his face hangdog again. 'Suicide. Seems my overstretched security administrator failed to find a knife in among the girl's personal effects.' He paused, shook his head. 'Couldn't have been much more than a teenager.'

'You know, Jessen strikes me as the very model of efficiency,' the Doctor said, thoughtfully. 'And yet she has rather been dogged by disaster just lately.'

Dam looked at him suspiciously. 'What are you getting at?'

The Doctor shrugged, feeling Jedkah's papers sliding down towards his waist as he did so. 'A man shot while trying to escape... A suicide mere hours later...'

'Ever since you arrived, security of every kind has gone to hell,' Dam pointed out, punching a code bitterly into his communicator. 'Narkompros will have my hide for this.'

'Look on the bright side,' said the Doctor, stretching a leg, feeling the papers slip safely down to his knee. 'Perhaps you'll catch him in a really good mood!'

Jessen walked back to her quarters, grateful Dam had let her off the hook so easily. She felt bad she'd upset him at what was already a bad time, but was confident he'd feel better about it all in the morning. If nothing else, he'd appreciate that the girl being dead meant at least he was spared the unpleasantness of their having to interrogate her. And Karron looked the type that screamed. Dam would've hated that.

Besides. What did it really matter? Soon, the Project – and the Facility, the saboteurs and the terrorists alongside it – would be history. And a secret history; the full truth of whatever occurred here would never get back to the rest of 59. Like everyone else, she'd be looked after by the Government, fitted up with some other position somewhere far from here. A blameless employee.

The thought made her smile, and she quickened her step back to her quarters.

Narkompros cursed inwardly, wishing he'd returned to his room. Sitting there in Strategy One, the nerve centre of all forward planning for the Facility, there was no avoiding video link-up now Government had called in for an unscheduled progress update. Every time Narkompros attempted a confident smile, his guts would lurch and it would become a sneer. Not that he felt anyone in government would settle for a smile as reassurance right now.

'Your projected targets remain unmet, Narkompros,' the thin, sour-faced man stated. His glower was no less intimidating on a screen than when given in person earlier that day. 'We *must* be able to activate by the declared date to take full advantage of the alignments, and before the launches of Parallel 6 reach any further outward into space.'

'I am aware of my responsibilities, gentlemen,' Narkompros stated flatly.

'Then you shirk them deliberately?' Another face, bloated and red.

'There have been security matters…'

Red-face cut him off. 'Which you have failed to deal with, even when granted conventional military resources to deploy.'

'We have just made a major breakthrough with the discovery of

170

a terrorist base and the apprehension of a suspect,' Narkompros announced. 'I am confident of successfully meeting all targets with only minimal delays.' He swallowed. 'Everything possible is being done, I assure you.'

'We've all heard this before. I assure *you*,' the thin man said gravely, 'that there shall be the fullest possible enquiry into your conduct as Head of Facility.'

Narkompros bridled inwardly. 'Of course, if you feel such an act necessary…'

But the link had been cut. Only the familiar, geometric logo of Parallel 59 remained on the monitor. Narkompros regarded it dispassionately for a few moments, then wrenched a handful of wires from the video terminal, sending the screen sparking into blankness.

His stomach lurched again, but he tried to ignore it. He could still act. He'd contact his associates, they'd have to help him out. If a full enquiry *was* on the cards, he could implicate them. Buy some immunity. Salvage *something*.

Part of him, an old, wrung-out part of him, just couldn't accept that any of this was really happening. To have lived through such stress, for so many years… to get *so* close…

He stabbed a button on the control desk, contacting his aide.

'Head Narkompros?'

'I'm going to work on in my quarters. All calls to be fielded there.'

Just then his communicator activated. He swore and slid it open to see what it was Dam had to report now.

'I don't believe it!'

The call was like a prearranged signal for a small chorus of disbelieving voices to start up. Terma, who'd been too hot, tired and depressed even to shamble back to his quarters and sleep, squinted into the lights bathing the upper gallery to see what the fuss was about.

'Deputy Terma!' someone shouted from the gantry.

'Well? Patch whatever you've found through to the strat-screen!'

A few seconds later data started scrolling across the screen in enlarged, chunky numerals. Codes that made sense. Figures that weren't mathematical contradictions.

'She's coming back to us!' someone shouted. The chorus of voices was getting louder all the time. 'Power's building!'

Terma peered at the screen, checking and rechecking the information. It seemed to be true. Somehow, as if a blockage had been cleared, the power drain affecting the network was easing and the cause of it, 634, was starting to respond to their signals again. It would take time before all units were running again at optimum level, but the Doctor's lash-up could hold the Bastion out of the Project equation while they set about either repairing or replacing it.

A smile spread over his face. The news, he decided, put a decidedly different complexion on everything.

'All right!' he bellowed over the whistles and the cheering. 'Down here, everyone. This might be nothing more than an aberration. We've got to grab 634 by whatever we can get hold of, in case she sinks again.'

'Does this mean Narkompros won't have our heads on a stick, Deputy Terma?' an operator shouted from the throng.

'Bonuses, all round!' another chipped in.

'We're not telling Narkompros yet, nor anyone else.' Good-humoured moans ensued. 'Not until we know it's all for definite.' Terma allowed himself a smile. 'Then I'll tell him in person.'

Dam slid the communicator slowly shut.

The Doctor looked consolingly up at him. 'I take it that didn't go too well for you.'

Dam knew he was shaking visibly. 'Nor for you,' he said, his voice clipped and soulless. 'Narkompros wants to go ahead with your interrogation immediately.'

'And he told you not to spare the horses, eh?'

'Like I said before, he needs results. At any cost. He's desperate.'

'And what do you need, Dam?' the Doctor asked softly. 'Another pointless death on your conscience?'

Dam shook his head, trying to clear it, trying not to listen. He saw Ilsa in his mind, babies and children waiting in her, heard all the things he'd been telling himself these last few years to keep himself sane. *Keep it straight and simple. Just do the job. Finish your stretch.* Ilsa opened her mouth to speak. *Then you can come home and we can begin at last. Ready for the last possible moment.*

'I'm sorry, Doctor,' he said. 'Whatever the truth is about you, I can't stop Narkompros.'

The Doctor considered. 'Well, I hate waiting around,' he said, leaping to his feet. 'Let's go and get this over… with…' He stopped, clutching his chest, suddenly short of breath.

'Doctor?' Dam stared at him in alarm. 'What is it?'

'Oh dear,' the Doctor gasped, doubling up and shaking. 'You know, I really hate to contribute to the already embarrassing statistics relating to healthy prisoners in your care, but…'

He toppled over, face down, on to the bunk.

Dam saw the Doctor wasn't breathing. Frantically felt for a pulse. Tried to resuscitate him. Breathed into his mouth. Thumped his chest.

Nothing.

He sat there, dazed, beside the Doctor's corpse for a little while – just to be sure – before calling for the medics.

The Doctor was pronounced clinically dead by Chief Clinician Tonfran at 0235 hours. She was coming to the end of a very long work-stretch, and not particularly interested in giving Dam civil explanations. The prisoner had died of some kind of cardiovascular failure; he'd keep in the morgue till Jedkah responded to calls and could open him up to determine exactly what had happened.

Fine, thought Dam. He'd give Narkompros a full report later, when he had all the facts – whatever they might be. He couldn't take another conversation like their last one right now.

Dam wandered aimlessly through sickbay. He remembered Makkersvil commenting on evidence of cardiosurgery during the

Doctor's scan. Spying was hardly a vocation for a man with weak hearts

Makkersvil wouldn't be saying much more for a while, it seemed. Dam looked in on him briefly; he was sleeping, his vital signs mysteriously low. Tonfran had explained that if his health continued to decline, he could be dead by morning. She hadn't seemed bothered. Clearly, enemies of the state didn't count among her favourite patients.

Dam shook his head. Maybe his instincts were shot to hell, but he couldn't bring himself to believe that either the Doctor or Makkersvil was the real problem here.

You can come home and we can begin, Ilsa was saying.

He checked in on Yve while he was there. She looked terrible, and was still comatose, but her stats suggested she was going to pull through. In what state, and what Narkompros might do to her then, he didn't like to think.

'I really wouldn't hurry back to join us,' Dam told her quietly.

He should get some sleep. There wasn't much he could do now, with everyone pertinent to his investigation either dead or dying. All very convenient… He yawned. Jessen was back on duty in a few hours. The automatics could handle things in the meantime. Maybe he could make more sense of all this in the morning.

Dam headed off to his quarters to dream of being home again.

The Doctor's eyes snapped open to take in harsh blue lighting. He shivered not just with the cold, but at the sight of his morbid surroundings. He hadn't been in a morgue since he lost his life in San Francisco.

He wasn't happy pulling the old respiratory-bypass trick too often these days, not least because the older you got, the less certain you became that you could snap out of it again. He guessed he'd been out a few hours, and that they'd just dumped him on a trolley and wheeled him here.

Next to him lay a skinny young girl, her dark hair splayed out over the slab like ivy growing over stone. He looked at her, sadly, then peered more closely at the wound in her side, examining it.

'Suicide, Karron?' he whispered softly to her. 'No. I think you'd tell me a different story if you could.' He squeezed her cold hand. 'You don't look strong enough to make a wound like that.'

Suddenly he heard a noise from outside, and clambered swiftly back on to the hospital trolley. He heard the door open, and footsteps approach. Heavy breathing, and a low chuckle of satisfaction.

'Hello, Jedkah!' the Doctor cried, jumping up and sending his trolley careering backwards.

The squat little man screamed with terror and threw his scalpel into the air.

The Doctor caught it neatly and winced as the gurney smashed into the far wall. 'Whoops,' he said, the blade gleaming in the blue electric lights. 'That's the trouble with us men of Haltiel. The high gravity there makes us all terribly tough. Impossible to kill, and totally off our trolleys. Still, I can't stay chatting all night. I'm going back to Haltiel for reinforcements so we can blow you all to kingdom come.' He pinched his nose. 'WE-WILL-EXTERMINATE-ALL-OF-SKAAAAAAAAAALE!'

Jedkah fainted dead away, falling to the floor with a thud.

Allowing himself a quick smile of satisfaction, the Doctor located some shrouds and bundled Jedkah up in them, tying his hands and feet together. Then he started snooping about. With a thrill, he noticed his clothes and belongings, dumped on the floor in a corner. Compassion's, too. They were a bit crusty, but otherwise fine. Of course, fresh from Jedkah's studies – the morgue would have to be his little den. He would go about his forensic business here, performing autopsies, and whatever else he did in his spare time.

Deciding he'd rather not think about that, the Doctor hurriedly changed, thrusting his bits and pieces – and the vital notes from Jedkah – safely into his coat pockets. It felt gloriously decadent to have pockets again. He looked at Compassion's things. She wouldn't care about the clothes, but she'd want him to look after her earpiece, wretched thing that it was. He slipped it into his waistcoat pocket alongside his fob watch.

The Doctor stepped out into the corridor, wondering where it would lead and how far he could get.

Chapter Thirty-One
That's That, Then

'Any time now, then,' Nikol said quietly.

Filippa nodded, sitting by Fitz on the bench opposite Central, stroking his hair. He was grateful for the contact, the warmth of her beside him. Her hazel eyes met his own and probed them searchingly. Such a warm contrast to the glassy eyes of the zombies in the lift.

He shuddered. Relieved, not resisting, he'd gladly let the correctioners throw him out of the building. The crowd had already vanished, its fighting spirit broken as quickly as it had ignited. It was only the usual suspects gathered outside now. No threat to anybody. But at least Filippa, unharmed and apparently of the belief this was due to his actions, seemed a little more back on side. He squeezed her hand.

Then, just as Nikol had prophesied, the zombies came stepping cheerfully out from Central and into the sunshine, off on their silent way home again to sit in darkness until the next morning.

'That's that, then,' Serjey said, his eyes pointing in the right direction but seeming not to see a thing. 'Nobody works in Central at all. It's all a sham.'

Nikol cradled the stump of his missing arm with his fingers. 'Just like their records,' he whispered.

Anya, hovering by his side, put two good arms around him. 'It's all right. You'll find out what happened. When you go home.'

'Home,' Nikol echoed. 'Whatever that is.'

'No wonder you and Anya couldn't make that lift go anywhere all night,' Serjey said, miserable and bitter. 'Never meant to move, was it? No wonder the lights are on all the time: no one can get up there to turn them off.'

His tone of voice was getting on Fitz's nerves. 'Yeah, I think we'd worked that out for ourselves, thanks, Serjey.'

Suddenly the soft stroking of Filippa's fingers stopped. 'You and

Anya were in the lift together?'

Fitz shut his eyes, his heart sinking even as Anya haltingly spoke. 'Well, yes. It was –'

'You never said, Fitz. And Anya said you were alone there.'

Fitz was still too rattled to deal with this right now. 'You… I'm sorry. I… But, you didn't know Anya then…'

Filippa was smiling, a real 'Christ-I-don't-believe-how-stupid-I've-been' kind of smile. 'Right,' she said, getting stiffly to her feet. 'I'm not sure I really know you, either.'

'But nothing happened!' Fitz protested, looking to Anya for support. 'Did it?'

Anya cast a worried look at Nikol, clearly afraid he would start wondering what was amiss in his loyal wife spending a night in a lift with Fitz, but he seemed away in his own private reverie.

Filippa nodded knowingly at the woman's silence. 'I can't do this,' she announced, tight-lipped. 'I'm going.'

Fitz sighed. 'Don't, Fil–'

'Goodbye, Fitz.'

'What are you going to do?'

'Nothing. Think a bit, maybe.'

'I could think with you!' Fitz implored her, but she just turned and walked away. 'Please!'

'There's nothing else to be done,' Nikol murmured.

'I think we should go back home ourselves,' said Anya, awkwardly. 'See you all later.'

Nikol didn't say another word to anyone, didn't try to impress upon them the importance of the next meeting or how vital their work was. Fitz felt a puzzling absence beyond Filippa's going, left outside Central alone with Serjey.

'Thanks for dropping me in it, mate,' he said stonily.

Serjey seemed not to hear him. 'You know, I can't believe they set up this whole illusion for any bad reason.'

'Excuse me, Serjey, I'm talking to you.'

'It has to be for our benefit. *Everything* here's for our benefit.'

Fitz snorted. 'All part of the treatment. Right.'

'We'll find out when the time comes.'

'Back on Homeplanet?'

Serjey stood up, and again Fitz got the feeling he was looking around without actually seeing anything. 'Homeplanet, yeah. We'll laugh about how worked up we got back here, just you wait. About how we tried to wreck everything they wanted to do for us. Bye, Fitz.'

Serjey set off without another word, and Fitz couldn't help shouting after him.

'What if you're never going back home, Serjey? What if you're going somewhere else? How're you going to know until it's too late?'

His questions echoed round the plaza, as if Central itself was pointing out that no one was listening. And now the sun was following Serjey's lead, beginning to move hesitantly from view. Soon, it would be marking time with another blood-red sunset.

Fitz shuddered. This would be the perfect moment for the black stain he'd seen before to encroach on him again, as he was standing all alone in the square. That in turn made him think of Denna, and a fleeting thought of physical comfort.

He let it go. Then he got up and walked home. He'd have an early night. See how he felt in the morning.

No one called round that night. In the bored quiet of his apartment, Fitz found he was stupidly hungry no matter how much he ate, and that his throat remained stubbornly parched all night, defiant of the empty bottles racked up around the small kitchen.

Chapter Thirty-Two
Visiting

Compassion sat next to Tod in the guard transport. The muddy sky was lightening. It would be dawn soon.

Rojin was driving again, while the others sat tensely in the back.

'The plan's changed, but only slightly,' Tod told them all. 'We breach the Facility through the launch bay. Karron's cell door will have been left unlocked and unguarded. If it was Rojin banged up he'd be able to meet us in the bay – he checked out the route last time he was there. But this still works for us, now.'

'Yeah, right,' Rojin muttered from the cab.

'Rojin leads us to the cells. We grab Karron, we spring Compassion's mate, we get out.'

'Why should we risk dying for *her* mate?' Amman asked, not looking happy at the prospect.

Compassion turned doe-eyes on Tod.

'Because,' Tod explained, patiently, 'we can't fly her secret ship and bring the whole network tumbling down without him.' He looked at Compassion and winked. 'Can we, spacegirl?'

Compassion shook her head wearily, imagining what she might do to him if he called her spacegirl one more time.

Narkompros sat hunched over his private comms system. Transmission channel was set, all he had to do was signal his people and...

A drip of sweat fell on to the controls. He was burning up, shaking with fever. Maybe he shouldn't threaten them with discovery yet. He could tell the same lies as he'd told his masters in government; they'd be easier to convince. He could still turn the situation round. There was time.

The controls were blurring before his eyes. The soft static of the open channel sounded like the sea lapping against the Northern Shores, and he was lying there, drenched, his surroundings rippling, as if he was seeing the world from underwater and someone was dropping pebbles.

Moaning with panic, he staggered to Medik, found the right buttons to slide out the support harness. He hung his arms over the apparatus and slumped, like a winded athlete. 'Report, Medik,' he croaked. 'What's happening? I'm dying, I'm dying.'

'This medication will help you feel better,' Medik promised, and produced a handful of blue pills. Narkompros grabbed for them, clumsily, sending some clattering from the dispensing tray to the floor. Medik dispensed others to replace them. Narkompros crammed them into his mouth, gagging as he tried to swallow them down his burning, swollen throat.

It had taken him a painfully long while, but Makkersvil was actually out of his bed. Now, he found walking wasn't as hard as he thought it would be. He wondered if he'd still be thinking that when the drugs wore off.

There seemed to be no one about. Good old Narkompros and his cost-cutting. Makkersvil was able to totter along the corridor to Yve's room unmolested.

Knowing he mustn't be caught was good for him in a way. It meant he couldn't agonise over pushing open Yve's door, had to shuffle inside before anyone discovered him.

Once the door was closed, the steady bleeping of Yve's life-support monitor marked time for him. Twenty, and he had turned around. Another ten, and his hearts had climbed into his mouth. Another ten, he was by her side.

There she was. Barely recognisable as his cool, cruel Chief Supervisor Yve. He stared at her in fascination, at the flakes of crispy black skin littering the pillow, trying to reconcile the image he held of the last time he'd seen her with this charred relic.

'Neither of us have really changed so much, have we, Yve?' he breathed, as her image grew watery in his eyes. He pressed his finger against a patch of undamaged skin on her hand. 'Still can't stop playing with fire.'

The click of a door closing outside made him jump, and wince with the pain of using his stomach muscles. As quietly as he could, he hid behind a cabinet in the shadowy corner of the room.

The door opened, and a silhouette appeared, black and thick against the light from outside that spilled on to the wall. Makkersvil's eyes widened as the figure approached Yve's bedside, holding a pillow in both hands.

'Jessen,' he said.

She whirled round to face him, shock all over her face. It gave him a grim satisfaction.

'You're looking well for the man they said might not survive the night,' Jessen said, recovering herself.

'Sorry to disappoint you.'

'Came here to give her a kiss good night, did you?'

Makkersvil indicated the pillow. 'Did *you*? What the hell is going on, Jessen?'

She started walking slowly towards him, her usual self-assured self. 'Thank you for coming here, Makkersvil. You'll make it a far more elegant scenario.'

'You came here to kill Yve.'

She drew a gun. 'No. You did. I just caught you in the act and stopped you. But it was too late, of course...' She gestured with the gun that he should move towards the bed. 'Too late for either of you.'

'So you're the traitor,' Makkersvil marvelled. 'That's rich, isn't it, right under Dam's nose? You set me up, then thought you could get rid of me before I could prove it wasn't true!'

'But you *are* the traitor,' Jessen said reasonably. 'And now no one will ever think otherwise.'

'This is crazy.' It was all he could think of to say.

'Kiss her goodbye, Makkersvil. Come on, now.' Jessen smiled, tossed him the pillow and aimed the gun at his head. 'Smother her with kisses.'

'Hey.'

Both Makkersvil and Jessen swung round at the sound of the soft voice. Before Jessen could react, the newcomer had grabbed

181

the pistol from her hand and had it trained on her chest.

'Visiting hours are from three to seven-thirty,' the Doctor said. 'I hope you can both explain what you're doing here.'

Chapter Thirty-Three
Change the World

I've got the shakes. Starving, barely able to swallow, my mouth's so dry. It hurts to speak; it even hurts to gibber like a raving lunatic, which I think I must be turning into, so I'm writing stuff down again. Collecting my thoughts before they slip away. I'm hiding right now in a building I think – hope – is empty. Safer here. It's so hard to concentrate. It's been like this all day.

Last night I went to bed wishing so hard that I might be allowed to dream. Pathetic, isn't it? I'm that desperate for some kind of distraction from the bloody mess I've made in the real world. No chance, of course. Woke up early, thirsty and hungry just like the night before, but my stomach felt full of rusty nails. Decided I'd skip breakfast, go straight to the doctor's. By the look of the crowds outside his office, plenty of others had had the same idea. But the word was about that the doctors had all vanished. Some people, less lazy than myself, had been trawling all over Southside looking for them.

Not sure what to do, I thought I'd get stuck into work instead to take my mind off things. If *I* was scared, then how would the kids be feeling? I'd been neglecting them, with everything that had been going on. I knew it, and it wasn't fair. The little mites deserved more.

Well, I only hope they've got it, wherever they've gone. There was no one there when I arrived, only Rencer, the big, surly sod. He told me the whole lot of them had cleared out, that it must've happened in the night. He got the hump when I asked if he'd checked with the admin centre, said that of course he had, and that there was no explanation, the staff there had no idea what could've happened. No sign of the correctioners snooping about. Nothing. Really helpful, dear old Rencer. It was good riddance to the children, I think, as far as he was concerned.

I reminded him about Feelix, the boy with no legs – how could

he have gone anywhere? Then Rencer really lost it. Said if I didn't
stop asking him stuff he couldn't answer he'd use my face as a rag
to clean those new stains the filthy kids had left behind off the
walls. He must've seen I reacted to that, and cheered up a bit, got
more cocky. 'Probably messed themselves', he went on, 'when
whatever came to clear them away turned up.' That seemed to
make him question what he was still doing here, and with another
scowl at me he announced he was pushing off.

I didn't hang around there to see the stains myself. I followed
Rencer out into the sunny streets.

There was a new buzz in the air, a smell almost, eating the fresh
air. Sickly. The people looked just the same: healthy, tanned, every
one a picture-perfect Mechtan citizen. But something was wrong;
every panicked face reflected it, but no one seemed able to admit
to it. People were checking their reflections in every window –
like me, wondering why they didn't look as terrible as they felt.
There were huge crowds in the bars, a trickle of people leaving
every office doorway in search of food and drink. Squabbles and
disagreements started to break out. I even heard one woman
accuse a barman of tricking her into thinking there was liquid in
her glass when it didn't wet her tongue. I guess that made more
sense to her than her stupid thirst.

I made my way through the stumbling crowds to Filippa's place,
looking out for any of the kids on the way. I was gasping myself,
not just for a drink but for a Woodbine. I could murder one right
now, I'm telling you, and no jury in the land would convict me.
Weird, I'd pretty much forgotten about the ciggies. Other things
on my mind, I guess.

My co-ordination was shot; still is. My legs, apparently bored
with holding me up or steering me in a straight line, seem keen
to play this new game of aching and cramping instead.

Filippa wasn't at work. She wasn't at home, either. I banged on
her door for what seemed like an age, but there was no answer.

On my way out I saw an old woman slumped against the wall,
crying her eyes out. A frantic girl, must've been a bit younger than
Filippa, was crouched over the old dear, licking up the tears from

her wrinkled prune face as they fell.

I wondered if things were the same all over Mechta, and found myself on the tram going Northside once again. Just the fact it was running was a comfort. The people round me were doubled up in pain, hugging themselves, not saying a word. No community to turn to because everyone was the same.

And I kept glimpsing the air cancers, always seemingly just out of view. I got bored of this game, of turning my head from side to side only to find there was nothing to see after all. I willed the blackness to come out and just show itself, to do whatever it was here to do, whatever that might mean for me and everybody else. Selfish, I know, but I've never been great with pain.

I went looking for Denna. Well, I couldn't find anyone else, could I? And, typically, Denna *was* at home.

She was lying in her bed, curled up on her side and retching. She didn't really look ill as such, but you didn't need to be Richard Chamberlain to see something was badly wrong with her. She seemed to look straight past me. I don't know if she even recognised me. I never heard her say a word the whole time I was there. I fetched a cloth to try to cool her temperature down, but could see she needed proper care, not my half-arsed efforts.

The hospital unit wasn't far away, and I knew I had to hurry. I had to practically haul her neighbour out of his apartment to sit and wait with her while I went for help. It occurred to me halfway there that I'd left a guy I didn't know from Adam alone with a helpless girl half-naked in bed, and that gave me the strength to stumble on a bit faster.

I saw red cars motoring through the streets, and Centreside's departure area was thronged with shouting people waving Notification forms. The taxis might clear this nightmare panic away person by person, I thought, face by frightened face. But what would happen then?

The hospital was swamped with people, and, just as back Southside, I couldn't see any lavender tunics in the crowd denoting a doctor's presence, only grey patients milling around, increasingly frantic. I saw a medicine cabinet being heaved off the wall and its locked doors prised open, the liberators fighting among themselves over their right to whatever was inside.

We've been abandoned, I realised, with the first semblance of anything approaching clarity that day. Me and Rencer had left our positions, realising there was no point in staying, but the doctors, the correctioners, the signifiers of care and authority had already beaten us to it.

All gone. Leaving the lunatics to make a piss-poor attempt at taking over their asylum.

I turned around and ran back to Denna's, with the shadows, always the shadows, flapping just out of sight like old curtains catching in a breeze.

I got back and found Denna wasn't there any more. Just vanished, leaving wet bedsheets and a dent in the mattress. The guy from next door was still sitting where I'd left him, staring at his hands like bloody Lady Macbeth and ignoring me. I grabbed hold of him, shouted at him, swore, tried to make him tell me where Denna was, where she'd gone. He acted like he didn't know what I was talking about, and so I started shaking him. He told me he hadn't seen her go anywhere and I lost patience, hit him. It wasn't much of a knock but he folded up on to the bed.

'I can't tell you where she's gone,' he said, quietly, turning his face away from me. 'I didn't see a thing. I think I've gone blind.'

I thought he was making it up, for a second. Making excuses. But I knew it had to be true when the pale wall he was facing became suddenly dark, like a filthy rot had suddenly set in, and he didn't react. Just lay there, facing it as it opened up around him, dank and cold like a massive, ancient hole dug deep into a bank of wet earth.

I should've helped him, I suppose, pulled him away or something. But I just ran. I'm not even sure when I stopped running. I remember opening my eyes, finding myself flat on my back on the pavement, struggling for air, watching the frantic crowds push past, their heads eclipsing the sun every few seconds. I just lay there like dirt to be trodden in.

I hauled myself up in the end, of course. Didn't know where I was, but from the position of Central, dominating the skyline with its dozens of empty floors, I clearly hadn't run that far. Still Northside. Not much between me and the black stuff. Maybe it was only the north it had a hold of, I thought, like that other building I'd been in. Anyway, I knew I had to get back home. Back to somewhere safe.

There was no sign of Denna anywhere as I headed for the tram line, but then I hadn't really expected there to be.

The journey was a nightmare. I kept expecting the power to go and the tram to trundle to a halt at any minute. There seemed to be fewer people travelling on the way back.

I wonder how many will be riding the tram tomorrow.

Filippa still wasn't in, though the door to her apartment was open now. I hated her for making me worry so much. I called for Serjey, but he wasn't there, either. I felt like you do when you're a kid in a department store, when you get that horrible realisation that you've lost your mum. All the people I cared about here I'd left on bad terms, with no proper goodbyes. And now they were all gone.

I knocked Serjey's door down, in the end, actually kicked the thing until I broke it off its hinges. There was no one to stop me. No sign of Serjey inside, either. Everything in his apartment in place, as it should've been. I was tempted to stay a while, to sit down and pretend nothing was wrong. But even *my* imagination isn't that good.

See, the doors only lock from the inside; the windows were shut and there's no back way out.

I just don't understand what can be happening. I've just never been so scared. Ever, ever, ever. And writing this stuff down is meant to be helping me. It isn't. I think I'll carry on when I'm sitting somewhere a little brighter.

If I can find anywhere.

Anywhere at all.

Part Three
Getting Out

Chapter Thirty-four
Now That We're Gathered Here

'You must be Makkersvil,' the Doctor said, beaming. 'Shot while trying to escape, I understand.'

'It was a setup,' said Makkersvil.

'It's funny, they all say that,' the Doctor observed. 'But when it comes to your word over hers, I'm inclined to believe you.' He turned to Jessen, who was eyeing him coolly. 'I knew you were up to no good when you arrived at the launch bay.'

Jessen shrugged. 'The deranged fantasy of a dangerous terrorist. Who'd believe you?'

'When I showed you the fragments of that electromagnetic device, you asked me what they proved before I'd even shown you what they were. And you seemed very concerned that Yve had been hiding on that damaged ship. She might have seen you plant the device.'

'So you came here to kill her in her sleep, just in case,' Makkersvil added, sneering.

'Just as you killed Karron because you knew she wouldn't back up your allegations against Makkersvil,' said the Doctor. He smiled thinly. 'No loose ends. I imagine I would've been next if I hadn't saved you the trouble.'

At that, Jessen laughed. 'Good guess, Doctor, but you don't know why I'm doing this. You're not seeing the bigger picture.'

'I'll readily admit that. So suppose you describe it for me?'

Jessen remained silent.

The Doctor looked at Makkersvil. 'We're both escaped prisoners. Will you help me, or do your loyalties still lie here with the Facility?'

'I'm as good as dead whatever I do,' Makkersvil said. 'No one will ever believe I'm innocent.'

'Good. Let's start a gang.'

'Why should I trust you any more than I should her?' argued Makkersvil.

The Doctor shrugged. 'You can have this gun, if you like.'

A moment later, Makkersvil had the gun rammed up against Jessen's neck. 'Careful,' the Doctor warned him. 'I need some answers from her.'

Jessen's cool seemed to have been shaken. 'Listen to me, Doctor,' she said. 'I don't know who you're working for or where you're from, and I don't really care. All that matters to me is that you're against the Project, like I am. You've practically done my job for me. I'm not your enemy.'

The Doctor raised an eyebrow. 'But I'm your scapegoat?'

'I'm getting out of here. I can take you with me.'

Makkersvil rammed the gun barrel up under her chin. 'You can't kill us, so you'll let us run with you?' he snarled.

'I can deliver your friend to you, Doctor,' Jessen gasped, her teeth gritted.

'Compassion?' The Doctor leaned forward. 'You know where she is?'

'If she's still with the people who helped her escape, then she's on her way here right now. The activists... I'm their source here.'

'I thought that was me.' Makkersvil stared at her, shaking his head. 'You think I'd want to go *anywhere* with you?'

'You have a better offer?' Jessen mumbled.

'We'll move later,' the Doctor said. 'We're safe here for now. I helped a medic outside get some sleep – he looked like he could use it.'

'What about security?' Makkersvil asked.

'Dam's next shift isn't till morning,' Jessen said. 'And I've blanked the cameras here, anyway.'

The Doctor nodded approvingly. 'It wouldn't do to catch yourself in the act on film, would it?' He clapped his hands together. 'So, there's plenty of time then for one of you to tell me what exactly is the purpose of those Bastions, and how I can get to Mechta. I think a friend of mine may've ended up there and I'm worried about him.'

Makkersvil and Jessen looked at each other in surprise.

'Shouldn't I be?'

Jessen smiled faintly. 'You remember the mindwalker?'

The Doctor nodded, puzzled. 'The machine that took me on that virtual stroll through Parallel 59.'

'Technology has moved on a little since then.' She shuddered. 'Imagine yourself arriving in an off-world colony for convalescents. Practically all you know is your name, and that you were sent away to recover here by a benevolent power...'

Compassion wriggled forward to the driver's cab. 'Are you planning to drive through the main gates?' she asked Rojin.

'Even the thickest of guards would probably be wise to a stolen transport making an unscheduled reappearance,' Rojin said.

'Our source has left us an entry point in the perimeter fence,' Tod said.

'Do you mean a hole?' Kurd asked.

'In which case, will we all fit through it?' Amman said, smirking at Slatin.

'It'll be a short open run, then we'll be in the cover of the missile silos,' Tod went on. 'From there we can make our way to the launch bay. Easy.'

'Easy,' Slatin said in her soft little voice. 'Flexible word.'

'Isn't it?' agreed Compassion, as the Facility loomed up on their horizon.

The warmth in the Doctor's eyes seemed to have dropped several degrees, but Makkersvil kept the explanations coming with some enthusiasm. He put his hyperactivity down to the pain-blockers. 'Each of the Bastions holds three hundred of Skale's undesirables.'

'Such a clinical term, isn't it?' Jessen said, still looking nervously down at the pistol he was pointing at her neck. 'The diseased, the handicapped, political criminals...'

Makkersvil ignored her. 'Little by little, using 59's legitimate space interests as a cover, they've been placed in capsules, stored in the Bastions, then sent out into space.'

'Six hundred thousand people?' the Doctor asked, aghast.

'They're only the ones aboard the Bastions,' Jessen said. 'There are already tens of thousands more people hanging in space in their life capsules.'

'The Bastions have been constructed at strategic points round the planet, further out into space than any other Parallel has yet reached. From there, the capsules are launched out into key positions in deep space, all linked together in a vast psychic network, creating a sensory barrier. If the network is breached at any point, the capsule at that point will explode.'

The Doctor screwed up his eyes. 'With the person inside?'

'And with devastating effect.'

The Doctor frowned. 'You mean, when Compassion and I came down –'

'We were terrified, basically,' Makkersvil admitted. 'But since you'd dropped out of the network, the charge wasn't triggered on splashdown.'

'So what's the real purpose of this network, then? Some kind of planet-wide minefield?'

Makkersvil nodded. 'Protecting Skale and its new spacelanes from possible attack.'

'From Haltiel?'

'From anyone. And tipping us off if any other Parallels try to get above themselves, moving any further out into space. The mines can see them coming.'

'Ludicrous, callous paranoia,' the Doctor said, coldly.

Jessen agreed. 'Only Parallel 59 will have the safe path *out* through the barrier, thus ensuring every other power on the planet stays grounded, kept in place by the threat of our human bombs falling on their key cities... while space becomes ours and ours alone.' Her voice became satirically pompous. 'The breakthrough in our glorious struggle for supremacy as we establish a new frontier without interference.'

'"The key to securing safe, interstellar travel",' the Doctor murmured. 'Dam used that description when I asked him what Mechta was.'

'Apparently it's only active minds that can power this... "intuitive" minefield,' Jessen said, angrily. 'Once they reach the

Bastion they're placed in storage and prepared for service. Each person is in a dream state, all six hundred thousand linked together and steered by the controllers of each Bastion in a kind of group operating system. And each controller is in turn linked to the governing systems of the computer-simulated world these people find themselves in.'

As Makkersvil watched, the Doctor pulled out pages of scribbles from his pocket and surveyed them gloomily.'The co-ordinates for Mechta... exactly the same as for the Bastion network.' He sighed, screwing the page into a ball.'It's simply a shared sensory illusion.'

'Oh, come on, Mechta's much more than that,' Makkersvil protested.'I took part in the demos, I feel like I've *been* there. It might as well be a real place. The things that happen to the people there, good or bad, are indistinguishable from the real thing because wherever possible the sensation comes from the individual's past experience. The controllers only govern their behaviour if it threatens to become too damaging.'

'More subtly I hope than the way your helping hand chose my direction in the mindwalker,' the Doctor said to Jessen.

'They won't know what's happening to them,' she assured him grimly.'They can't.'

'And what happens when a harnessed mind is exhausted?' the Doctor demanded.'A man's friends wake up and forget he was ever there?'

'It's quite neat, actually,' Makkersvil enthused.'Everyone burns out at a different rate, and there's always someone else in storage on a Bastion waiting to take their place. So the person about to croak gets an eight-day warning that he's shipping out. He has a great send-off, a big celebration, and off he goes. All very humane. His mates all think he's well again and going back home.'

The Doctor glared at him.'And instead he's ejected from the network and left to drift through space for ever, I suppose.'

'Or until he hits something, anyway.'

The Doctor shut his eyes.'This entire twisted scheme is nothing more than the most basic cruelty.'

'Oh come on, it's not really cruel,' Makkersvil said.'Running current through their heads to get results would be cruel.'

'The research proved that the brain lasts longer when it's stimulated in this way,' Jessen said. 'That's the only reason Mechta was built. That and the research angle. They're looking into stimulating the minds of future astronauts in suspended animation on deep-space voyages. Mechta's excellent groudwork.'

'But why use human minds at all?' The Doctor looked seriously distressed. 'It's...' He slapped his forehead. 'Of course. Why wouldn't you? Your technology is founded on flesh-tech.'

Jessen snorted. 'Not using human brains. But animals weren't considered good enough for the Project.'

'Less precision,' Makkersvil chipped in. 'Human brain adapts faster. Hey, that's progress.'

'And so much cheaper, too – why spend welfare money caring for your "undesirables"? Put them to good use in the defence of their country. Why replace hardware every time a capsule explodes? Just use another dissident!'

The Doctor's eyes showed that he shared Jessen's anger, but he mimed with his hands that she should keep her voice down.

Makkersvil sat painfully on the bed by Yve's side, still covering Jessen with the gun. God, the women in his life. 'What are you getting so worked up for, anyway, Jessen?'

'It's wrong. It's all of it wrong.' She seemed genuinely distraught, tugging morosely at her short blonde hair, and for a second he wanted to reach out and comfort her. 'Even the penal camps offer a better existence than that.'

'But why take things into your own hands?' the Doctor asked.

'Someone had to –'

The Doctor waved her excuse aside almost immediately. 'Why not go to the press?'

'Maybe you *are* from Haltiel,' Jessen scoffed. 'You think anyone would believe me?'

The Doctor shrugged. 'Another Parallel could –'

'– start a war over it, or try to co-opt the Project for its own use.'

'So to stop them you are prepared to destroy what's left of those poor people up there.'

'And anyone else who might get in your way,' Makkersvil said.

'Listen to yourselves,' Jessen snapped, rounding on them. 'Self-righteous, self-satisfied hypocrites. This place has left six hundred thousand people to die for some –'

'They *will* die, too, if we can't help them,' the Doctor retorted, pacing the room and thrusting his hands in his pockets.

'Help them?' Jessen almost laughed with disbelief. 'There *is* no helping them! They're already as good as dead, all of them. Can't you see that?'

'No. No, they're not,' the Doctor said, putting his hands over his ears, not wanting to hear it. 'Though I can see why you'd find it convenient to think so.'

'You're just as callous as the people that put them up there,' Makkersvil sneered.

'Well, what about you?' Jessen yelled at the Doctor. There was a heavy pause. 'What about the people you killed up there, doing whatever you were –'

'I know!' The Doctor was shouting himself now, trembling. 'It was an accident. When my TARDIS landed there, I swear I had no idea what the consequences would be!'

He looked like he was about to cry.

'Keep it down, you two,' Makkersvil said, unnecessarily as it turned out. They'd both gone very quiet.

'You're trying to take your own guilt out on me, that's all,' Jessen said more quietly, wiping her eyes. 'My only hope was to join up with the activists hiding out in the marshlands with the mineships.'

'Mineships?' Makkersvil looked puzzled. 'How would they –'

'That doesn't matter now.' Jessen sighed. 'I was going to give them the co-ordinates for the weakest point. The chance of success wasn't great, but it was the only chance, as far as I could see. Until you came along.'

The Doctor looked into her eyes as if to make her see that every word he said was vital. 'The ships you were trying to sabotage with the electromagnetic-field generator, to stop anyone standing a chance of getting up there for themselves; we can take one of those, I'm sure I can pilot it. We can get up to one of the Bastions, get sterile suits from my ship –'

Jessen was laughing. 'You're crazy!'

Makkersvil had to agree. 'You'd have to dock with one of the Primeiras first, and the alignments won't be right –'

'We'll go straight there. I can do it, I know I can.' The Doctor was standing there, arms outstretched, his whole body screaming *Give me a chance*.

Makkersvil gestured at the rolls of wadding round his stomach. 'Doctor, even if I didn't think you were totally mad, I don't think I can get far like this.'

The Doctor pouted. 'Oh. I was forgetting that.' He brightened. 'Let me have a look, perhaps I can –'

'Those rockets aren't going anywhere,' Jessen said quietly.

The Doctor turned warily back to her. 'What have you done?'

'My activists are coming here because they think we're still working to the old plan, the one I'd worked on before you arrived. We'd capture one of their people. I was to give the co-ordinates of the network's weakest stress point to the prisoner –'

'Her name was Karron,' the Doctor reminded her stonily.

'– and arrange for her cell to be left unguarded. The other activists would then arrive to take her and the co-ordinates away to safety, ready to launch their mineships.'

'So why did you have to kill her, then?' Makkersvil asked.

'You saw the state of her,' Jessen said. 'She'd have cracked in two minutes under interrogation.'

'But the rest of the cell is still coming on schedule?' the Doctor demanded. 'Don't you think they might be a little upset, and with good reason?'

Jessen looked away.

A terrible thought seemed to strike the Doctor. His lips curled downwards. 'It's a trap, isn't it?'

Jessen said nothing. The Doctor stalked over and grabbed Makkersvil's gun arm, pointing it closer to her. Makkersvil cried out as his shattered stomach muscles pulled, but the Doctor seemed oblivious to anything but the gun and Jessen. 'Tell me what you're planning,' he demanded. 'I'll give you to the count of three.'

'And if I do, you'll do what? Kill me?'

'One'

She spat out the word: 'Hypocrite.'

'Two...'

He's going to do it, thought Makkersvil, feeling the Doctor's fingers digging still more tightly into his arm, feeling the trigger being squeezed for him. He's actually going to do it.

Chapter Thirty-Five
A Significant Betrayal

The missile silo towered over Tod's ragged band, a huge grey mountain. They huddled against it for cover.

'So far so good,' Tod breathed. 'We're going to do this.'

'It could be a trap, of course,' Compassion said. 'They'd want us to get well in before tightening the net on us.'

'No,' Tod said. 'I checked out our source very thoroughly.' He smirked. 'More thoroughly than her employers did, obviously.'

'She comes from a whole family of dissidents,' Rojin said. 'Half of them are up there, brain-dead on Mechta.'

'She?' Compassion enquired. Then she frowned. 'It's not that dreadful Jessen woman, is it?'

Tod smacked Rojin round the head. 'You absolute tosser.'

'Who cares if I know or not?' Compassion pointed out.

Tod sighed. 'She falsified her birth papers, escaped connection and so persecution. She's got a long history of this kind of thing. She's on the level. Legit.'

'Legit-*imate*,' Compassion said huffily.

The small band sprinted for the next piece of cover.

'Tell me!'

There was a wild look in the Doctor's eyes. Still, Jessen said nothing. A few moments later, the Doctor released Makkersvil's arm with disgust, though with Jessen or with himself it was hard to tell.

For a minute or so, all Makkersvil could hear was the sound of the Doctor's and Jessen's hoarse breathing. An impasse had been reached. It needed to be broken.

'I don't mind you calling *me* names,' Makkersvil said, pointing the gun once again at Jessen's head. 'I've got some lovely ones to shout back at you. A bullet might clear your ears out.'

The Doctor waved him aside. 'No, Makkersvil. No, no... That's not the way.' He clicked his fingers. 'It's something to do with the repair ships, isn't it?' he said. 'That's where Compassion was last seen, *ergo* there's a good chance that was where she met the activists and hence their way out of the Facility building. And hence also their most likely entry point.'

Makkersvil saw the flicker of a reaction on Jessen's face, and the Doctor clearly caught it too. He folded his arms. 'So what is it, then? An ambush? Guards posted in the cover of the repair ships, with you making sure every rocket gets a good pasting and will never fly again?' He marched over to her. 'Those people could be killed. Compassion too.' He stamped his foot like a bad-tempered child. 'It's not going to happen!'

Jessen didn't look at him.

'When was this planned for?' the Doctor asked her, pleasantly. Makkersvil had never seen one man get through as many emotions in so few minutes, as if he were trying on moods to see which suited him best. 'Tell me, please.' He drew closer to her, held her hand, wouldn't let her pull it away. 'You've painted such a terrible picture. Shown me thousands of souls pinned to the most hateful canvas. It hurts you just knowing that it's hanging there above you. But to simply rip it down and turn your back on it… You can't do that.' He tried to look into her eyes, she wouldn't let him. 'I want to end the Project.' His tone was fervent now. 'I don't want another soul to suffer because of it. But I have a friend up there, and he's helpless. If I could get up there, maybe I could save him, save others, everyone I can. I have to, you see. And you *have* to let me.' He paused. 'So when are the activists coming?'

Still she wouldn't look at him.

So with a great shout of annoyance, the Doctor started tickling Jessen. Making her double up with protests and pained laughter. Makkersvil thought he must be delirious, dreaming all this himself.

'Tell me!' the Doctor insisted, his fingers remorseless. 'Tell me, tell me, tell me!'

She did. When the Doctor stopped, Jessen was lying sobbing on the floor, with relief, first of all. Then she was just crying.

The Doctor stood back up. 'Do you suppose she's all right?' he asked Makkersvil.

The figures, Terma concluded with a self-satisfied smile, confirmed it. The Project was definitely recovering. In another thirty-six hours it would be practically at optimum level again. Whatever the Doctor had planted on board 634 could be destroyed by a team sent up from the Primeiras, and the damage fully repaired.

Suddenly, everything had again become possible.

He checked his watch. Yes, now he could tell Narkompros the news.

Makkersvil had been pumped full of still more drugs, but was already finding it hard to keep up with the Doctor and Jessen as they walked swiftly through the corridors.

He'd left Yve's room without another glance back at her. Everything had changed; his old life was effectively over, and from this moment he would only ever know a life on the run. Or on the limp, for the time being. He just hoped he'd live long enough to speed up the pace.

He wasn't sure if Jessen had truly come round to the Doctor's way of thinking, but she'd agreed to scatter the guards on duty as far from the launch bay as was feasible. She'd let the Doctor try things his way. It was weird: she seemed a little less uptight since their bizarre confrontation on the floor, apparently embarrassed now to look at Makkersvil, no longer acting angrily defiant. The Doctor was clearly good with his hands.

They reached the launch bay without incident. In the gloom, the ships were lined up neatly, a giant's ornaments in storage. The Doctor brought the main lights clanging into life, then suddenly turned to Jessen, frowning.

'Fixing these ships was a priority, right?'

'Right.'

He pointed at the only ship with a flimsy barrier of hazard tape round it. 'So why not that one? Is it permanently out of commission?'

Makkersvil could see scorch marks all over its hull, and shivered. I'm not thinking of Yve, he told himself. Not any more. From now.

'You know the cutbacks here,' Jessen pointed out.

Without another word, the Doctor ducked under the tape and ran inside the ship.

'Doctor, we've only got a few minutes until they're here!' Makkersvil called.

The Doctor's head poked out of the door. 'Jessen, did you ever contact your activist friends from this ship?'

She shook her head. 'I hid things there, sometimes. It was our pick-up point, about the safest bet. Couldn't risk transmitting, it was too dangerous.'

'Mmm,' said the Doctor absently. 'Do you remember what Yve said in the launch bay? About the communications panel being warm?'

'A slight understatement I'd say. She was delirious.'

The Doctor shook his head. 'I think she meant it was warm from use.'

'Why would anyone want to use the comms system of a damaged supply ship?'

'Come in here, you two,' the Doctor said. 'Quickly.'

Makkersvil was last in of course, holding his gut and definitely not thinking of the woman who'd been here before him. Once in the cockpit, he joined Jessen in a puzzled stare.

In the melted, blackened instrumentation panel, a brand-new shiny silver comms system had been installed.

'To answer your question,' the Doctor continued, 'someone could conceivably use this comms unit to route through a signal that would bypass standard channels used on the Facility.' His voice dropped to a pantomime whisper. 'For transmitting and receiving *secret* messages!'

'Clever,' Jessen commented.

'The panel's warm now,' the Doctor commented. 'Maybe it's in use!' Excitedly, he turned up the volume, only to hear nothing but garbled static. Undeterred, he then produced a dainty silver tube with a red bulb on the end from his pocket and started taking the front panel off.

Jessen rubbed the back of her neck uneasily. 'Who would have the opportunity – or the authority – to set something like this up undetected?'

Makkersvil looked back at her, wide-eyed. Maybe the drugs were stopping his jaw from hitting the floor in shocked realisation. 'Who do you think?'

Narkompros was still slumped in Medik, wretched with fever, when the door slid open and Terma came inside. He felt naked envy at the sight of his old colleague, fit, well. Happy. It wasn't fair. Narkompros wanted to be happy.

Terma looked at Narkompros, bloated, hot and pasty-faced. In thirty years, Terma had never seen him look so truly dreadful.

'The medication will help you feel better,' Medik said, bleeping as a blue tablet dropped down the chute. Mindlessly, Narkompros took it and shoved it into his mouth.

Terma sniggered.

'What are you *doing*, Doctor?' Makkersvil asked, glancing outside every few seconds.

'Descrambling this signal,' the Doctor said. 'I wouldn't normally dream of eavesdropping, but…'

The Doctor finished his fiddling and two familiar voices suddenly filled the cockpit.

Makkersvil looked at Jessen. 'Whoops.'

'It can't be…' Jessen said, shock leaving her voice little more than a whisper.

'Things aren't going well for you, are they, Narkompros?' said Terma, his voice heavy with mock sympathy.

Narkompros snarled at him. '*Head* Nar–'

'I know what you've been planning these last few years, and the toll it's taken on you,' Terma continued, his voice hardening. 'The stresses of belonging to a global consortium of frustrated old men, climbing so far and achieving so much, only to be denied the real power they crave over the world… and so dreaming instead of wielding it over the stars.'

Narkompros bellowed something incoherent. Terma ignored him. 'It's placed a terrible strain on your heart, all the dealings and *détente* with those other Parallels… waiting for the day when you might seize the Project for yourselves to dictate your terms to the world.' He clapped sardonically in appreciation. 'A super-elite ruling over all Skale and plucking the stars from the skies one by one. Until the Project started to fail, started spoiling your dreams of empire…'

'Transmission must be patched through from Narkompros's quarters,' Jessen whispered.

They heard Narkompros answer Terma, but his words were so slurred as to be indecipherable.

'Well, you'll be pleased to hear the Project is back up and running,' Terma was saying. 'In thirty-six hours we'll be more or less back at full strength.'

The Doctor and Jessen looked at each other. 'How?' the Doctor asked, desperately puzzled. 'How can that be?'

'They must've put it right, regained control over 634,' Jessen said, hugging herself.

'I saw the figures…' the Doctor shook his head. 'How could they have reversed the entropic effect?'

'Poor, clever, foolish old Narkompros,' Terma said. 'Led us to victory despite everything, but led himself to an early grave.' He sauntered up to Narkompros, saw the stubborn fury in the old goat's eyes even now.

'How… How did…?'

'I found you out quite by chance,' Terma said. 'An accidental parsing of the signals bleeding through from the relief ship's comms unit. I became a regular listener, you know, never missed a broadcast. And that's when I started hatching plans of my own.'

'Your own?' Narkompros mumbled.

'Once I knew what you were up to, I had to plan for my own future. I never honestly believed your plans would work, or that you'd keep it all going with no one else finding out, but by God!' Terma slapped Narkompros almost affectionately on both cheeks. 'You're tenacious, I'll give you that.' He smiled. 'But then, so am I. I'm afraid I've taken other liberties, such as tampering with dear Medik here. I've been manipulating the dosage of her medicinal chemicals for so many years now.'

Narkompros's face twisted in horror. 'You... poisoned me?'

'Every sweet little tablet, laced with traces of a toxic agent Jedkah would never even think to look for. Every pill pushing you a little closer to the end.' Terma sighed theatrically, savouring the moment. 'I've waited inviolate while you've taken all the risks. Now it seems they've paid off at last. I can simply pick up where you left off. Your colleagues will accept me as their leader. The Project is, after all, now in my hands.' He chuckled. 'It's a terrible threat to have hanging over your head, isn't it? I really think you're better off out of things...'

Narkompros gripped Medik's supports and tried to pull himself up, that steely will back in his eyes. Terma backed away, laughing at the sight of his old leader struggling even to stand.

'You know, when I thought the Project was finished I decided I'd kill you anyway, before Facility One was shut down and I lost my chance. The blue ones contain a faster-acting poison, you see. And now I find my timing really couldn't have been better!'

For a few seconds, Narkompros balanced unaided, staring at Terma, his face crimson with the exertion. Then he crashed to the floor.

'Condition terminal,' purred Medik.

'Terma,' Makkersvil muttered. 'All this time, him and Narkompros... the *pair* of them!'

Jessen laughed bitterly. 'Can't you believe it?'

'I have to believe it, don't I?' Makkersvil retorted. 'Just find it hard to accept, that's all.'

A burst of feedback whooped into their ears as if the comms unit shared their incredulity. Gasping with pain, the Doctor flicked a switch on the comms panel.

'What happened there?' Jessen asked, alarmed.

The Doctor started punching buttons uncertainly. 'The systems didn't like my improvisations. The signal's folded back on itself.'

'Will Terma have heard that?'

Suddenly Jessen's communicator started beeping. She looked at it. 'Blanket security call. Directed here. This place will be teeming with every guard we have.'

Makkersvil groaned. 'Take that as a yes, then, shall we? Where are the sirens?'

Jessen shrugged. 'Why give us time to run until the guards are in position? He doesn't know I'm here to tip you off.'

'Quickly. Outside.' The Doctor shepherded them out of the blackened shuttle and then set off for the far wall, hands in pockets, head down.

'Doctor,' Jessen said, but he carried on walking. 'The Project, Doctor. I...' She pulled him round to face her. 'What can we do? They can't just pick up where they left off, it can't just go on and on. It can't all have been for nothing.'

'If only we had proof we could go to your Government, tell them what Terma's done, what he's planning...'

Jessen shook her head. 'Even *with* proof, they'd kill us as soon as look at us. Put it down to a Haltien invasion by stealth –'

Just then, with a noisy clatter, the door in the hangar wall swung open. Makkersvil stared in alarm as a bizarre assortment of people started bundling through, then stopped to stare at the three of them in alarmed surprise. The first man into the hangar, a skinny guy with white spiky hair and earrings, pulled out a gun, but the woman behind him – he realised it was the Doctor's friend – stopped him using it.

The Doctor disengaged himself from Jessen and bounced over to the new arrivals. 'Ah, there you all are. Hello, Compassion,' he said, beaming broadly. 'Who's in charge of this little outing?'

'I am,' said the white-haired man.

The Doctor shook his hand. 'Please may we borrow your mineship?'

Then the lights turned blue as the main alarm finally sounded.

When the first guards signalled they'd reached the launch bay, Terma had activated the general alarm from Narkompros's quarters, cursing the dreadful noise it made. His ears had barely recovered from the signal feedback which had practically blown the speaker. He'd been careless: he hadn't even noticed that Narkompros had left the unit on. While he was relieved to find there was no carrier, that meant the noise had most probably originated from some fool poking about in the shuttle's comms system for some reason. They needed to be stopped, captured and killed.

He took out his communicator and tried Dam again. Where was the idiot? That man had botched his responsibilities once too often, and it was time something was done about it.

I can do anything, he realised. I have only to say a word, or to press a button, and I can do anything I choose.

The sound of the alarm, his clarion call to arms, began to take on a more pleasing cadence.

Dam lay sweating on his bunk in the cool blue light, listening to the communicator bleeping under the droning of the alarm. He knew he couldn't ignore it a second time, but found he was scared of what he might hear when he picked it up.

Whatever he'd been expecting, it hadn't been that Narkompros was dead, that Terma had taken control, or that the Project, far from being on the point of collapse, was now back on track for meeting all planned targets. Nothing must be allowed to jeopardise that, Acting Head Terma had dictated. Nothing and no one.

Dam dressed in a daze, and, as instructed, hurried to the launch bay.

Before the Doctor could say another word, the launch bay

flooded with guards. Compassion felt for the gun that Tod had given her.

'Two of you men, over here,' Jessen snapped at the guards, her voice ringing with authority. She'd grabbed the blond man's gun and was suddenly covering Tod and the others, who lowered their weapons. The Doctor and the man shuffled over to Compassion's side.

'I've got the situation under control here,' Jessen said. 'The rest of you, move out. There's another lot in here, heading for the cells.'

For a moment, it looked as if the guards were going to obey. Two of them wavered uncertainly, while the others started to back away.

'Go on, then, move! Get after them!' Jessen ordered, her words echoing again and again, as if attempting to instruct each man in turn.

Then Compassion saw Dam walk into the bay.

The Doctor cursed under his breath.

Dam looked from person to person, his expression unreadable. 'Jessen?'

'You know, I imagine Caesar probably asked "*Et tu, Brute?*" in just the same way,' the Doctor muttered.

But then, Kurd's nerve finally broke. Compassion dropped to the ground for cover as he screamed and brought his gun up to bear on the nearest guard and fired, blowing the man backwards. He fired again and another guard fell clutching his arm, before yet another blew Kurd's head off in retaliation.

'Run!' the Doctor yelled.

Dam stood in the devastated launch bay, trying to take it all in. The Doctor alive, Makkersvil well again and clearly part of the terrorist sect after all. Jessen. *Jessen*... And Narkompros was dead, and Terma was in control and the crisis that had gripped them all was past history...

He felt the entire world had changed while he'd been sleeping; all certainties dissolved in just a few tired hours. Now the dead walked, the friend was an enemy, icons were falling.

Guards jostled past him, knocking him to his knees. Gunfire rattled round the room, every noise amplified and repeated endlessly by the acoustics in the launch bay. Light and shade became confused in his head; he couldn't make out anything clearly, only snatches. The Doctor helping Makkersvil out through the door. The Doctor's associate, Compassion, scrambling up from the floor, firing into the crowd of guards alongside a lean, dark-haired man, using the body of the idiot who'd fired first as a shield. A snot-nosed kid, terror all over his face, throwing a grenade *you should duck you should dive for cover.* A large man, greasy hair flapping as he jerked and jumped with three holes in his chest, falling against an even larger woman who must be *another* terrorist *it's going to go off, you should dive, just do your job and keep it straight.* The woman was screaming as she tumbled over and started crawling for the door *why do you always leave things to the last minute –*

The grenade went off, a deafening burst of light, and guards were sent flying, shrieking through the air. Then it was as if his ears had stopped working, the scene ran on but in silence. There was nothing but flame and smoke for a moment; then the smoke cleared, and he saw Jessen, and her eyes met his. She was upset, she was shouting at him, but something wet had started pouring down into his eyes and now he couldn't see, perhaps he was sleeping again. Perhaps everything would be all right if he could just wake up.

Chapter Thirty-Six
Ambition in Motion

Compassion watched the Doctor sprint ahead, leading the way through the compound.

'Wait!' he shouted, skidding to a halt.

'What?' Compassion asked him.

'I have no idea where I'm going,' he admitted. 'Who wants to go first?'

Tod pushed him aside, silently, and led the way. Slatin followed him, the operator with the stomach wound scooped up in her arms. She was puffing and panting but clearly determined.

Rojin was trying to confront Jessen, on the move, as to Karron's whereabouts.

'Leave me alone,' she snapped, her pale eyes narrowed with pain. 'Dam was... Dam was –'

'I'm so sorry, Jessen,' the Doctor said; Compassion reckoned he was probably the only person on the planet who could say something so facile and imbue it with such feeling that it didn't sound inadequate. 'But we really have to get moving now.' He ran on, beckoning them urgently to follow.

'What about Karron?' Rojin insisted. 'She's still in there!'

'She's dead,' Jessen shouted, knocking his hands away. 'She tried to escape. I saw it happen.' Leaving him, she ran on ahead.

Rojin stared after her like he'd been told a joke and didn't understand the punchline. Compassion shoved him forward, repeatedly, until he finally broke into a stumbling run, just as heavy footsteps started pounding across the concrete towards them.

By the time the ambulance buggy arrived in the launch bay, the action was over. There was only smoke again and the cries of the dying.

Dam wasn't dead, but his balding head looked like a split fruit.

The medics froze the wound and racked him up to go.

They went on to find three more guards alive, and one of the terrorists, squirming in his own blood and whimpering for help. He was promising anyone who'd listen that he'd tell them anything they wanted to know, if only they wouldn't let him die.

Compassion dodged sharply as Tod hurled another grenade behind him, nearly catching Rojin full in the chest with it. It bounced against the missile silo, then detonated.

The shock wave of the explosion threw everyone forward.

'Stop throwing those things!' the Doctor said, catching hold of Tod's arms. 'Don't you think enough people have died already?'

'I never asked Kurd to start firing off like that!' Tod protested, clearly terrified. 'Typical of that stupid bastard. But I'm in charge,' he blustered. 'And I make the calls.'

'If that explosion had set off one of the missiles in that silo we'd *all* be dead now, all of us!' the Doctor stormed.

'This way,' Compassion said, ignoring them both and coolly taking the lead. 'The gap in the fence is round here.'

Two more guards came pelting towards them along the perimeter fence. Compassion shot one in the chest, and the guard behind stumbled over the body. Rojin shot him before he could get back up. Slatin stared at the carnage, white-faced.

'We're leaving. Now!' the Doctor insisted, bundling Compassion down to the hole in the fence. She felt the netting pulling at her hair as she scrambled through into the rough long grass on the other side, Jessen close behind her.

'How far to the transport?' the Doctor asked as the others scrambled through.

'Half a kilometre,' Tod said. 'Maybe less.'

The Doctor's face fell. 'We'd better move fast.'

'With him?' Compassion gestured at the man leaning heavily against Slatin.

'How are you doing, Makkersvil?' the Doctor asked.

'We should leave him, you know,' Compassion said flatly. 'I know you won't, but we really should.'

The Doctor smiled faintly at her, then turned back to Makkersvil. 'And I don't want to hear any noble self-sacrificial cries of "go on without me" from you, OK?'

Makkersvil looked appalled. 'Don't worry, you won't!' With a grunt of effort, Slatin scooped him back into her arms. 'Thank you,' Makkersvil said, and she smiled.

'Let's just move it, shall we?' Tod muttered, hefting another grenade.

'Try to throw it as far behind the fence as you can,' the Doctor said. 'Blow a bigger hole in it and they'll get to us even faster. Don't you think?'

Tod was still swearing at him when the grenade went off, lighting up the adumbral sky behind them.

Terma sat in Narkompros's old chair in Strategy One, watching patiently as an engineer fixed the wiring in the video screen. His prerecorded message, outlining the tragic death of Head Narkompros but urging the Facility staff to do all they could for the Project's success in tribute to his memory, was playing over the loudspeaker system. He would linger here respectfully until it had played out, then make his presence felt as Head Terma, touring his Facility.

The engineer stepped away from the screen as Parallel 59's proud emblem cut abruptly into existence. 'Should be all right now, Head Terma,' he reported.

'Not before time. Get out.'

The engineer left hurriedly and Terma lounged back in his chair and addressed the silent screen. 'Everything is now proceeding perfectly,' he announced grandly. 'That my ascendance to executive power –' No, too wordy – 'That my new appointment coincides with the Project's unexpected reversal in fortune is no mere chance. Narkompros was a sick man neglecting his duties. Now I am Head of Facility One, I shall sweep away needless officialdom. I shall remove inept and inefficient workers...' He laughed, '...possibly settling a few old scores at the same time. I shall of course then replace them with a hand-picked staff whose ideals mirror my own, ready for the full activation of the Project whenever I decide the political situation is most expedient. And then…'

Sighing contentedly he spun round in his chair, turning his back on the display. The only problem now outstanding was the destruction of the intruders in the launch bay. He'd taken charge of capturing the terrorist spies himself, appointing Havdar as his adjutant since Dam was wounded, unconscious, and Jessen was not responding to any calls.

It didn't matter. Both Dam and Jessen would be replaced in his new order, because they'd failed him. And, soon now, his last remaining opposition would be crushed.

'They're not coming after us,' Jessen said, a few minutes later.

Everyone came to a grateful, breathless halt as they realised she was right.

'They've given up?' Makkersvil asked in disbelief.

'More likely they've got a better plan than just chasing us cross-country,' Compassion observed.

The Doctor turned to Jessen. 'Well? What do you think?'

'Isn't it possible they've already found the transport, that they're waiting for us?' Makkersvil worried.

'More likely they're transporting more guards by road,' Jessen said. 'They'll form a circle round us and close in. Cut off the safe paths so no transport can get through.'

The Doctor blinked. 'Safe paths?'

'This area was seeded with mines a couple of centuries back,' Compassion explained.

Tod butted in. 'The precise locations were lost in the war with 67. Trial and error found there were safe paths marked – but leave them for open marshland and you'll end up as dog meat.'

The Doctor grinned, leading them off again. 'Miaow,' he said.

Jedkah had been lying bound and gagged on the morgue floor for what had to be hours. Now, at last, he could feel his bonds slipping under his constant writhing.

His arms came free, and he pulled the bag from his head with a squeal of triumph. Gulping in fresh air, he pushed away the other body bags that had been laid upon him, then furiously struggled to his feet.

He stared around, wildly. On a trolley by the dark-haired girl on the slab, he saw Narkompros, stiff and dead.

Speculating as to what might have happened during his captivity, and uncertain how best to react, Jedkah opted to run in headlong panic from the morgue.

At last Compassion saw the transport come into sight. It coaxed the exhausted fugitives into one last sprint for its protection.

'Everyone aboard, chop-chop,' the Doctor said.

Tod shot him a proprietorial look. 'Rojin, up here with me, you can drive. The rest of you in the back. Move!'

Rojin went to obey without a word. He was a different man from the wise-cracking fool Compassion had escaped with yesterday.

'I'm not sure I'm happy about a recently bereaved man steering us through a minefield,' said Compassion. 'I'll drive.'

Tod looked at Rojin. 'Agreed?'

Rojin just walked round and got in the back. Compassion decided she preferred him this way. She revved the engine.

'You're really serious, then?' Makkersvil asked, wincing as Slatin helped him to lie down. 'We're going to cut through a wasteland littered with high explosives?'

The Doctor gave him a lunatic smile. 'If we're to stand a chance of reaching the mineships at these people's main base, I don't see how we can avoid it.'

'We'll take the road as far as we can,' Tod insisted, and the Doctor nodded in agreement.

Havdar's voice sounded over the receiver in Strategy One. 'Sighting terrorist transport now, sir,'

'Then instruct your men to destroy it,' said Terma. 'Whatever it takes. Ensure there are no survivors.'

* * *

'Roadblock ahead,' Compassion warned.

'I was right,' Jessen observed without triumph.

'Take her off-road!' the Doctor said, adjusting the sonic screwdriver's calibration. He hadn't tried anything like this for quite a while, but hopefully the knack hadn't escaped him. 'Now!'

Bullets and laser bolts thudded against the side of the transport as Compassion swung the wheel and the vehicle skidded on to the marshlands.

'They're coming after us!' Tod shouted.

The Doctor flung open the transport's double doors. 'Let's see if we can't dissuade them.'

Jessen gripped on to her handhold all the tighter. 'You maniac, you're giving them a clear shot at us!'

The wind tore at the Doctor as he leaned out of the back of the vehicle and aimed his sonic screwdriver in a broad sweep in front of him. A colossal explosion tossed tonnes of the landscape to their right up in the air, and the jolt nearly threw the Doctor out of the transport. Rebalancing, he swung himself back inside.

'They're not about to give up!' Slatin shouted, crouching protectively over Makkersvil. 'If they stay in our wake they know they'll be safe – *we're* the ones taking the risks!'

The Doctor saw a huge, rugged pursuit vehicle accelerate on to the marshland, following their trail. He could see the flashes of guns, but they weren't yet in range. 'Compassion! Zigzags!' the Doctor ordered. A moment later he was almost flung out of the truck again by the sudden turn. 'Efficient as always,' he muttered.

'Pass that thing to me!' Tod yelled from the cab.

'No,' the Doctor shouted back. 'I've got more range out here!' To demonstrate his point, his outstretched arm described a wide arc from right to left over the roof of the transport.

Tod nodded. 'All right. But even if our luck holds we'll end up leading them straight to main base.'

'Take a detour. Tell Compassion where to head for.'

'We usually make most of this journey underground!'

'More exhilarating this way, though, isn't it?'

As the Doctor activated the sonic screwdriver again, another mine exploded practically next to them. Compassion swerved to ride the shock wave, and the Doctor, his ears ringing, lost his foothold on the back of the transport.

For a sickening instant he thought he would fall to the scrubby grassland flashing past below him, but with his free hand he grabbed hold of one of the wildly swinging back doors. Riding with it, he gasped as the hinges reached their extent and threatened to come loose.

A laser bolt flashed past his head, making him flinch. The pursuit vehicle was gaining on them, not following Compassion's careering path but instead thundering straight ahead. It seemed they wouldn't give up until they blew themselves to pieces. Or until Compassion blew the transport to pieces first.

Jessen had moved to the back doors, presumably to check he was still hanging on. He gave her a thumbs up. 'I'm going to try the roof!' he shouted. 'Shield yourselves, close the doors after me!'

She looked at him as if he was mad, but nodded her understanding.

Trusting the door to remain steady for a moment, the Doctor clambered up it until he could hoist himself on to the ridged roof of the transport. Another bolt seared past his head, and he felt the impact of another into the back of the vehicle. Falling forward, he pressed himself flat against the roof.

Squinting into the wind, he inched forward, wielding the screwdriver like a vampire hunter with a crucifix. Yet another terrific explosion bloomed ahead to their left. Compassion drove towards it, and huge clods of debris rained down on the Doctor's back. The jolting as they rattled over the churned-up ground made it hard to keep his grip. He could feel himself slipping backwards, and, as he turned to check on the pursuit vehicle, the closest laser blast yet burnt past his face, sending sparks racing from the roof.

Then the pursuit vehicle ran out of luck. A mine exploded directly beneath it, with enough force to lift its front end entirely off the ground in a torrent of flame. The vehicle hung in the air like some rearing animal caught mid-charge as the thunder of the explosion rumbled out across the marshland.

The Doctor laid his head against the roof, the wind whipping water from his eyes, streaking his face. He could hear cheering from inside as the transport slowed down to a halt. Sliding down the side of the vehicle to the ground, he walked round the side of the transport on wobbly legs, and tapped at Compassion's window. 'I think we can take it a little easier, now.'

Tod looked at her appreciatively. 'That was nice driving, spacegirl.'

'Oh, shut up,' said Compassion.

Chapter Thirty-Seven
Fall Back, Regroup

Terma took the news of the pursuit craft's destruction and the losing of the terrorist vessel badly – until he remembered Tonfran reporting that one of the terrorists, badly wounded, was among the casualties from the launch bay. He could be made to talk. He'd explain exactly where to find his comrades before he was executed.

His train of thought prompted him to think of Narkompros lying in state, and Terma found himself smiling again at his own cleverness and patience. Perhaps he should attend the autopsy, just to make sure Jedkah didn't enjoy himself with his scalpels *too* much.

As if the thought of the little man had somehow conjured him from the ether, Jedkah came screaming into Strategy One. Terma recoiled at the sight of him flapping about, red-faced and panting, black bags billowing out from round his ankles and wrists.

'Narkompros is dead!' Jedkah squealed.

Terma looked hard at him. 'I know. I am now Acting Head of the Facility.'

Jedkah stared back for a few moments longer, uncomprehending, before starting to flap again. 'Then you've got to do something,' he gasped. 'It's the Doctor. He's not dead! He can't be killed! He's from Haltiel, isn't he, eh?'

'What are you talking about?'

'Tonfran, she told me the Doctor was dead, that he died in his cell when Dam was there with him. I knew he was from Haltiel, all along, I knew it!' Jedkah sank to his knees, terrified. 'And now he's going back for reinforcements, isn't he?'

Terma didn't need this irritation. 'Reinforcements? You're babbling, man.'

'The Doctor rose from the dead! *Sat right up from it!*' Jedkah waved his attached body bags, on the verge of tears. 'I fought him, of course, but he was too strong for me. It's Haltiel's high gravity: makes them tough to –'

Terma stood up and smacked Jedkah round the face with the back of his hand. Jedkah yelped, fell back, then stayed very quiet.

'Tell me what happened in a way I can understand,' Terma hissed. 'Then we'll decide exactly what needs to be done about it.'

The Doctor looked round the mission room in the underground bunker and laughed with delight.

'This is really quite something, Tod!'

'Course it is,' Tod answered gruffly, but Makkersvil could tell he was pleased that the Doctor seemed so impressed. 'We're a serious outfit, aren't we?'

After coming such a long way, expectations of this place had been high. Both Jessen and the Doctor had been fretting all through the nightmare journey that even if they weren't all blown to bits, their hopes could be dashed regardless if Tod had just been shooting his mouth off about this place. When Compassion had driven as instructed into a hide overlooking a waste dump, no one had got too excited. But then no one surveying the desolate landscape above could've dreamed this technological storehouse lay hidden below.

Tod had built his own mission control, and kitted it out with the latest gear that made Main back at the Facility look almost antiquated. It was all silver spheres, walls of computer banks and big vats – the vats, apparently, contained a self-generating power supply that ran the place. There was a strat-screen dominating the floor area, larger and better than Main's own, and three work stations; even so, Makkersvil suspected the control room was automated as far as possible. Even the air conditioning worked. And all this, as Compassion had pointed out so dryly, simply to steer a couple of remote-controlled rockets. Tod took his hobby seriously.

As a child, Makkersvil had dreamed of working in a place just like this, of protecting Parallel 59 from the shadow men of Haltiel and the evil schemes of the rest of the world. Now he was helping those who would destroy it. He remembered the vow he'd made back in his cell, and smiled. This counted as doing things differently, he decided.

He'd said as much to sweet, solemn Slatin when they were finding out a little about each other during the long haul in the transport. She'd just shrugged. 'Don't worry about feeling so messed up. It's just where you find yourself right now.'

'And then, the next minute, you find yourself dead,' he'd said. 'Like your friends back in the bay.'

Slatin had shrugged, a little crestfallen. 'Oh. Well. They were all arseholes, anyway.'

Makkersvil had tried again, determined to wallow for a few moments. 'I just… I'm not sure I *want* to find myself here right now.'

'That can happen in any life you might lead.'

She had a point, he reflected, looking back on the last twenty-four hours.

She'd given him her solemn little smile. 'Look… We're not doing this because we hate 59. We just hate what they've done. What they want to do.'

'I was helping them to do it myself, yesterday,' he'd said, then looked at Jessen with a pang of emotion. 'And that's not all I was doing.'

He watched Jessen now as she took in all the technology, nodding thoughtfully to herself. How many years had she been killing time, waiting to act? How many months had the two of them been…?

Jessen saw he was looking at her, and smiled at him, a distant, sympathetic smile. He realised she felt guilty about what she'd done to him; but then, he realised, too, that she'd do it all over again if it kept her alive, kept her free and able to do what she did. *This* was the real her he was seeing, weirdly at home in this mad, improbable, dangerous place. The career-girl-security-guard persona had already been discarded, just as she'd discarded him when he was no longer of value.

He knew they'd never be lovers again. And from the corner of his eye he caught Slatin watching him and enjoyed a second of astonishment to think that his own life could go anywhere at all, anywhere he dreamed, from this moment onwards.

'And so where are your redoubtable mineships?' the Doctor was asking Tod, cutting to the chase as if he hadn't had enough of pursuit yet.

'Through here,' Tod said, acting casual. 'I'll show you.'

Jedkah looked even more dishevelled than usual as he stared grumpily at Terma across the grand table. 'You don't believe me,' he said. 'I knew nobody would. I went to the morgue to get proof, *real* proof, that the Doctor wasn't human. That Haltiel is preparing to attack.'

Terma sighed. Jedkah was an unsavoury little man, but a first-class forensic scientist. Ambitious, but easily manipulated, he could prove useful in Terma's intended coup. If only the man wasn't so obsessed with his alien aggressors.

'What would you have me do, Jedkah?'

'When the Project is fully functional, we must plan to attack Haltiel before they can attack us.'

Terma leaned back, amused. 'Must we, indeed?'

Jedkah moved forward importantly, practically babbling. 'It's vital we recapture the Doctor so that I may take him apart cell by cell. We *have* to know our enemy, and I need to be given more funding in order to –'

'*I* decide what is vital, Jedkah,' Terma boomed, sending the scientist scurrying back a few paces. 'The Doctor's recapture is not a priority. His destruction, however – and that of his friends and their ludicrous ideals – most certainly is.' He paused, considering. 'There are cameras monitoring the launch bay. Dam put in an order for their repair after the fire. I'm going to arrange to view the security tapes. And then –' he smiled – 'I think we'll pay a little visit to the hospital.'

After Compassion had listened to Tod lecture about his grandiose, self-assembled mineships, she was not all that surprised when she saw they were actually small and unimpressive.

Each was around six metres in length – twice as long as the life capsule she and the Doctor had taken from the Bastion, and the lower section was a little wider. They stood vertically on a circular dais.

'We're right beneath the waste dump here,' Tod explained. 'The ports you can see up in the ceiling open directly on to it.'

The Doctor frowned. 'Concealed from observation, I take it.'

'We've placed lightweight debris over them, easy to shift. When we initiate the launching procedure, the dais rises up to the roof of the bunker, the ports open and the mineships launch through them, steered by radio signal from mission control.'

It all sounded very far-fetched to Compassion. So the Doctor, of course, was lapping it up, giving Tod plenty of 'mm's and 'ah's and 'Oh, I'm sure that's feasible's.

'So we're going up to get the TARDIS in those things, are we?' she asked.

'Well… in one of them, actually. Tod won't risk both and I can't say I blame him. It's not as if we can bring them back when we've finished, is it?'

'And Jessen's trusting you to go and destroy the Project for her?' Compassion sniffed. 'I doubt that.'

'That's one more reason for squeezing us both into one,' the Doctor said. 'In case we fail.'

'I can't believe you're going to seriously try to wrench six hundred thousand people from a life of peace and happiness and give them straight back to the people who put them there. I mean, I understand why you want to get Fitz out, but what did any of those other people ever do to you?'

'Their world's not real, it's all meaningless,' the Doctor said. 'They're being used, used horribly.'

'It's a better world than their real one if you ask me.'

'I didn't,' the Doctor snapped, signalling the end of the discussion. 'Now give Makkersvil a hand programming in the approach vectors,' he said, waving a crumpled piece of paper taken from his pocket.

'And what will you be doing?'

'Tod is going to help me remove the explosives from that nose cone and then strip out some of the circuitry to create some living space for you and me.' He smiled apologetically. 'It'll be a bit of a tight squeeze again, I'm afraid.'

'Obviously.' She paused, suddenly troubled. 'Doctor, I had a dream while we were travelling, last time...'

'Yes, you talked a lot about that in your sleep when we were in the cell.'

Compassion glared at him. 'You never said.'

'I didn't like to. Dreams can be very private things.'

She showed she disagreed by telling him about it again, in some depth – the platform overlooking the void, the feeling of belonging, it was all still so vivid. The Doctor nodded, attentively. By rights she should've found herself on Mechta, so what had happened?

The Doctor scratched his head. 'There were some strong signals being given out by the injured controller of that space station. Your earpiece must've been trying to tune you out of the Mechtan simulation so you could better receive them, and presented you with a different interface. I wonder...' He abruptly jumped off that train of thought. 'Oh yes, that reminds me...'

He reached into his waistcoat pocket and presented her with her earpiece. She smiled and placed it against her lobe, gasping with delight as it seemed to grip the soft flesh before sliding easily into place. The buzz of the planet, the fear, the tensions, the secrets all tingled through her. It was a rush for a while, but soon it faded. The TARDIS she supposed, even out in space, was 'helpfully' making the signals little more than background chatter for her.

Compassion turned to go, but the Doctor caught her arm. 'Hey... I've been meaning to say. I'm sorry if I upset you earlier. Back at the Facility, I mean.'

'Forget it,' Compassion said, pulling away and choosing to focus on the signals. *Secrecy. Paranoia. Give nothing away.* 'I really don't want to talk about it. OK?'

* * *

Dam lay absolutely still. The room kept tilting, and he felt that if he moved at all he might roll out of the bed and shatter on the floor like glass. The top of his head felt like someone had gouged his brain out with a spoon and chucked firecrackers inside, and his ears were screaming white noise at him.

He could hear something else screaming, too. It sounded like a man, a man in terrible pain, from the room next door. Dam knew very well what men in pain could sound like. He could hear Terma's voice, and other noises. A machine was being used.

The man, Dam was certain, would be telling Terma everything he knew. The screams had reached a kind of peak, and he knew that from that point the man would keep babbling for as long as possible, not wanting to give his persecutor the chance to give him the pain again.

Dam would've frowned if he'd dared move a muscle. A hospital was no place for an interrogation, and Terma was a lead scientist, not a security administrator.

But maybe Terma was everything now.

They'd done as much as they could, the Doctor decided, with a kind of tired satisfaction. The mineship had been stripped down to its absolute bare minimum components. The fact that it was based in part on a life capsule meant that – as long as Makkersvil transmitted the appropriate access codes at the crucial point – they could actually dock with 634, and enter the Bastion as if they were fresh fodder for Mechta. There'd be the automated systems to bypass when they arrived, of course, but he'd worry about that when the time came. They should have just about enough oxygen to last the journey. All in all, he was reasonably confident they'd at least arrive in one piece.

Makkersvil had been a godsend, picking up on a few errors Tod's tech team had overlooked and generally working like a demon even with his injuries. They were lucky that Tod had medical supplies stored here. Slatin had changed the dressing on Makkersvil's wound. He smiled. It hadn't taken her long to become proprietorial of their new recruit.

He'd had a long chat with Jessen. She didn't believe that he could fit every single person up on the Bastions in his ship if he chose to; how could she? And even now, she didn't trust him. She was terrified he was simply going to leave as soon as he reached the TARDIS.

He hadn't realised that so much of what she did was motivated by her family's political history, by the way they'd been used in the Project. Taken from her parents at birth for her own protection, Jessen had finally managed to track them down... or up, anyway. She'd spent all these years knowing they were still alive, just out of reach, changing slowly under the ceaseless attention of insidious machines.

He'd promised her that, whatever it took, he would bring it all to an end. He would let the dream die.

Now they were sitting on the floor, having a last supper of protein wafers and beer before making the final checks. Only Slatin was missing. She and Rojin had been clearing debris from the enormous hatch above which would open to allow them to launch. Now Rojin had come back while Slatin remained outside, placing the explosives removed from the mineship round the perimeter of the base, for extra protection in case anyone came looking. It had been her own idea. As Tod so often said, Slatin was the thinker.

Periodically, the Doctor noticed, Tod would try to start a conversation with Compassion. She would terminate it with a couple of well-chosen words, chewing her food sullenly in silence, her finger idly playing with her earpiece. Touching the world from a distance.

Jessen and Makkersvil ate in silence, but Rojin's plate lay untouched. He swigged from his beer can, staring into space.

Loss, thought the Doctor. How come there's an endless number of things we can lose in our lives, but it's always pain that we find to take their place? And yet, here he was, intending to inflict that pain on hundreds of thousands of people. Taking them from a world where they were safe and free, and giving them back to a cold and cruel society that had already turned its backs on them.

225

'What have they ever done to you?' Compassion had said.

Then, the Doctor wondered how many thousand more people were staring into space even now, just like Rojin, wishing that the person they loved could somehow be returned to them.

He swigged back his beer and checked his pocket watch. Soon be with you, Fitz. It was nearly time they were off.

Off to destroy the world, for a change.

Chapter Thirty-Eight
Leaving This Place Behind

Dam had heard the screams stop with a kind of detached satisfaction that he'd been right. They hadn't started up again. He didn't imagine they would now.

Then he'd received his special visitor.

'I've viewed the security recordings from the launch bay,' Terma told him, towering menacingly above him. 'And there you all are: Security Administrator Jessen – your closest colleague. The Doctor – who you claim died before your very eyes. Operator Makkersvil – whose death Jessen clearly faked, probably on your orders. And all fraternising with known terrorists who were *on site*, prowling the Facility for our secrets. You'd have gone to join them yourself if you hadn't been hit.'

Dam stared dead ahead, saying nothing, the words barely sinking in.

'Even now I am moving to crush your friends, Dam,' Terma whispered. 'I've been told most clearly where to find them. So perhaps you should mourn them now, while you can. Before you and Yve take a little journey.'

Dam waited for the inevitable explanation.

'I can't very well keep *you* on my payroll, now, can I? And it's a shame to waste Yve's mind, even if her body's been destroyed. Besides, you'll be in fine company: I'm rounding up anyone I think might cause trouble for my new regime just as soon as I can... Not that you'll remember them, of course. Yes, a fine solution to my staffing problems, don't you think?' He chuckled at the thought of it, leaned down so his nose was practically touching Dam's own. 'You're all going to Mechta.'

Terma turned and left without another word. Dam was glad when he was alone again. Now, if only the ringing in his ears would go, too, maybe he could listen properly to the voice that was trying to convince him desperately that he'd wake up soon.

* * *

The mineship was being given the final checks for its one and only voyage.

The Doctor was squeezed in next to Compassion, his feet by her head and vice versa. The harsh lighting of the makeshift hangar made a silhouette of Jessen as she closed the pressurised hatch over them, then the interior became black as pitch.

'You two all right in there?' Jessen's voice crackled over the speaker Tod had installed in the tiny vessel.

'Very cosy,' the Doctor replied into his tiny microphone. Jessen's voice guided him through a hastily improvised assortment of pre-launch checks.

'All systems go,' the Doctor confirmed at length.

'Right. I'm going through into the mission room.' Jessen paused. 'Good luck.'

They listened to her footsteps grow fainter as she left the mike. Then there was nothing but the quiet and the darkness.

'Have you ever played sardines?' the Doctor asked. Compassion tutted and didn't bother to answer.

Makkersvil scrutinised the data scrolling down the strat-screen. Launching this rickety thing off into space was far more exciting than the sort of stuff he had to do back at Main.

Tod hovered over his shoulder, watching him as he worked, pointing out things needlessly and drawing his attention to problems he'd already noted. Makkersvil let him carry on. It was his setup, after all, and the kid clearly wanted to be seen to be contributing. And perhaps it was helping him take his mind off the way Compassion hadn't even bothered to say goodbye to him.

Suddenly, Slatin jumped down from her work station at the far side of the room and jogged over to Tod, calling his name.

'What is it?'

'Forward scanner's picked up pursuit vehicles, coming our way.'

Tod swore. 'When are they due to arrive?'

'About five minutes.'

'How long left till launch?'

'Eight minutes,' Makkersvil answered, not letting himself feel the fear, his eyes scanning the flight data streaming down the strat-screen now as he searched for any possible error.

Jessen entered from the launch room in time to hear what was going on. 'What armaments have we got?' she asked, instantly.

'There's some heavy-duty stuff by the main entrance,' Rojin said, in a dull voice.

'Let's go get it,' Jessen said, leaving with Rojin.

'Thinks she's it, doesn't she?' Tod said, clearly feeling a little undermined.

'I'm not sure *what* she thinks she is,' Makkersvil muttered. '*She* probably isn't, either.'

'The first pursuit vehicle's here,' Slatin called urgently. 'I've got visual!'

Tod ran over to see, while Makkersvil kept staring at the strat-screen. At seven minutes, a real-time, forced-perspective image of the mineship from an upward-pointing camera helpfully appeared, inset in the lower left corner, so he'd be able to see the roof hatch as it opened automatically at three minutes. If not, the countdown would have to be aborted.

'When was the last time you tested the roof hatches, Tod?' Makkersvil called over, nervously.

'Never,' Tod said.

Leading from the front, Havdar decided, made a pleasant change from the norm. Good for morale, too; and this terrorist scum had severely tested that.

The pursuit vehicle rolled steadily along. 'Checking the thermal readings, sir,' a technician said. 'Must be right on top of them.'

Havdar checked the readings himself and smiled. 'They might as well have put on a fireworks display. Higs, bear right, thirty-six degrees.'

Higs, beside him, obeyed with a curt 'Sir!'

There was a concealed crater site not far from the road; clearly this area had been well checked for mines. Now a squad of thirty should be sufficient to smoke this vermin out and string them up.

There was an air of excited expectation about the men as they waited, tense and eager to do their job

Havdar smiled indulgently at Higs. 'This time, the bastards are going nowhere,' he announced.

Just as the pursuit vehicle exploded.

The rumble of the blast reverberated through the mineship, rattling Compassion against the thinly-insulated walls. She was convinced for a moment the ship was going to topple over on to its side.

'What do you think that was?' she hissed into the close blackness.

'Trouble,' answered the Doctor.

The whole base shook, and the strat-screen flickered alarmingly.

Makkersvil lost concentration for a moment as the inner door opened, but it was only Jessen and Rojin returning with heavy-duty laser rifles slung over their shoulders. Rojin threw one over to Tod, who tried to catch it with one hand and nearly collapsed under its weight.

'Got them!' yelled Slatin. 'They drove right over the explosive charge!'

'That should even things up a little,' said Jessen.

'No. We're in trouble.' Tod pointed to the screen in front of him. 'Look.'

'What is it?' Makkersvil called, trying to keep up with the information on the screen. Five minutes to go.

'Wreckage from the pursuit vehicle,' Jessen said. 'It's fallen, blocking the roof ports.'

'The other one's stopping now,' Slatin said urgently. 'At least thirty guards, coming in on foot.'

'We've got to hold them off,' Jessen said.

'We'll have to abort!' Makkersvil shouted. 'If those doors won't slide –'

'No!' Jessen snapped. 'You know the countdown defaults back to thirty minutes if interrupted. They could've totalled this base by then.'

'I'll hold that thought,' called Makkersvil. 'Thanks.'

'Rojin, you take –'

'I decide what we do here, Jessen!' Tod said, raising his voice. 'Not you. And I say we go outside and try to clear the ports.'

'There's half a truck on top of them,' Rojin argued. 'We'd never shift it.'

'And you'd get shot to pieces while you tried!' Jessen snapped. 'You're not combat-trained, Tod, you don't know what you're –'

'Roof ports off-line!' Makkersvil practically shrieked. 'The automatics just –'

'No,' Slatin said, calmly. 'That's me. I've switched to manual. If those ports won't open we need to know soonest, don't we?'

'If they won't open, there's nothing we can do about it anyway,' Rojin said, his voice rising. The crisis seemed to be bringing him back to life.

'Are you coming or not?' Tod demanded.

'They're moving!' Slatin cried. 'They're starting to open!'

'Don't open them too far,' Jessen warned her. 'You'll expose the ship to their fire!'

Makkersvil heard someone rush past and the inner door slam.

'Tod!' shouted Rojin, and ran after him.

Dumping the two spare laser rifles at Makkersvil's feet, Jessen grimly set off after Rojin. 'Do what you can. We'll hold them.'

The door slammed shut behind her. Makkersvil wondered whether the next person to come through it might be someone who could shoot him dead where he sat.

'Oh, no!' Slatin growled.

Just over four minutes to go. Makkersvil glanced nervously at the source of her frustration. The roof ports had barely moved.

'Jammed,' he breathed.

'Do you think they'll come back in here for the last bit of the countdown?' the Doctor asked Compassion, tapping his feet together in excitement, narrowly missing her nose. 'That's the most exciting thing about this sort of space travel, I find.'

'Be quiet and listen,' Compassion ordered, as the thick, heavy sound of metal rending sounded through the speaker. 'What's making that noise?'

'Oh dear,' said the Doctor. 'Nothing very healthy, by the sound of it.'

'What are you doing?' Rojin shouted after Tod. 'Think you're a one-man army, or something?'

'Whatever happens now,' Tod said, turning to face him, 'things will never be the same, will they? I mean, with Amman dead, and…' He never finished the sentence, started grinning fiercely at Rojin instead. 'I made this place happen. Got to protect my investment, haven't I?'

Rojin strode up to him. 'You are so full of –'

'I'm not asking you to follow me!' Tod said. 'Take your orders from her like a good boy, if you want.'

Rojin lost all patience. 'What is this, just a bloody great sulk?'

'How about fighting the enemy?' Jessen suggested, priming her rifle as she ran past the two of them. Tod watched her go, speechless.

Rojin found himself faintly smiling. 'Well, I suppose she has got a point,' he said.

'And she's got the big plans, too. I'll give her that.' Tod smiled back at him, but there was something not quite right in his eyes. 'It'll be all right, you know, Rojin. We're going to do this.' Then the moment passed, and Tod cranked up his voice to match the size of the dumb-bastard grin plastered all over his face. 'So let's get going.'

Three minutes fifty. Makkersvil's raw stomach muscles kept wanting to tense with the stress, it was agony. 'Try closing the ports again, Slatin.'

She did, and they responded. 'I'll try opening them now…' She swore. 'No, the wreckage is too heavy, it won't shift!'

In the narrow wedge of sky revealed by the jammed port shield, Makkersvil thought he caught a glimpse of blazing sunlight. Then the sparks leaping from the hull of the mineship told him that the guards must've seen what was happening down below and opened fire.

Jessen saw the Facility guards assembling on a wide ridge on the other side of the dump. The loss of the first pursuit vehicle had made them cautious; there was plenty of cover on the ridge and they had the advantage of the higher ground. At the moment they were just firing occasional blasts into the long grass, waiting to see what resistance they met.

As soon as they see our numbers are small, Jessen realised, they'll move in and crush us. And in the meantime, from their position over the dump, the guards could shoot straight down at the mineship. The opening and closing of the roof-port shields was already attracting their fire.

Jessen considered her group's options. The long grass disguised their position but offered no protection. The guards were too far away for a grenade to stand any chance of hitting home, so it seemed there was little choice but to engage them in laser fire. Maybe if she and the others darted here and there behind the grasses it would fool the guards into thinking they had more than three people to deal with.

Cancel that. Two, it seemed. 'Where's Tod?' she hissed at Rojin. He shrugged.

Another blast of laser fire smashed into the roof shield. Jessen winced. 'We've got to draw their fire!' she whispered.

Rojin showed he agreed with her by letting loose a salvo of shots at the guards.

'It's no good,' Slatin said. 'It's not going to shift.'

Makkersvil slammed his hand down on the console in frustration. 'Two and a half minutes. For God's sake, keep trying!'

Compassion tried to stay calm. Unable to move, lying in pitch blackness, it was like being trapped in a metal coffin buried deep in the ground.

'Something's gone wrong. They'll have to abort,' Compassion

said. 'We should get out now.'

'No. There's still a couple of minutes,' the Doctor said.

'But we don't know what's happening! They could all be dead!'

'We'd hear something over the speaker,' the Doctor pointed out.

Compassion tried to shift her position. 'I don't like feeling so helpless.' She felt the air getting warmer as, somewhere below them, the rocket engines started firing up.

The grasses were ablaze around Jessen and Rojin from the fierce heat of the laser blasts.

Half-blinded by smoke, his eyes streaming, Rojin began to fall back.

'Hold your position,' Jessen shouted. It wasn't an order: she was imploring him to stay. 'We *have* to stop them attacking the ship, for just another few minutes!'

'Where *is* Tod? What's he playing at?' Rojin said, frantically wiping his eyes. 'They must know there's only two of us.' Rojin jumped back as enemy fire charred the ground in front of him. 'They'll be on us in minutes.'

'I'm going to have to abort,' Makkersvil said.

'No,' Slatin insisted, still wrestling helplessly with the manual controls. 'You can't.'

'I must! If that rocket lifts with the port shields closed this whole place will go up, and all of us with it!'

Chapter Thirty-Nine
Over

Rojin dived aside as the laser bolts scorched the air between him and Jessen. He dropped his gun, kept rolling and rolling as gunfire raked the ground about him. Then he heard Jessen shout a warning, and a new noise in the mix. It took him a few seconds to identify it as an engine, a second more to instinctively roll out of its way.

He caught a glimpse of Tod in the guards' transport, white knuckles gripping the wheels, eyes closed but laughing like a maniac.

'Cocky little bastard,' breathed Rojin, feeling his throat grow tight.

Bursting through the wall of smoke and fire, the transport piled over the ridge and hit the slope leading down to the dumping ground, gathering momentum.

'Brace yourself,' the Doctor ordered Compassion. 'We'll be lifting off any second now.'

The noise and vibration in the tiny craft was reaching a crescendo, but Compassion could still hear the sound of metal grinding against metal over the speaker. 'I don't think the shield's open!' she shouted.

'One minute.'

'What the...' Slatin was staring at the external view on the forward scanner.

'Well?' Makkersvil demanded, flicking off the senestic locks as the strat-screen instructed.

'Someone's in the guard transport...' Slatin shook her head in disbelief. 'I think it's Tod. I think he's trying to ram the wreckage from the port shields!'

* * *

Tod yelled at the top of his lungs all the way down the bumpy side of the crater. He stepped on the accelerator and pushed himself back in his seat, bracing himself. The transport was hit by laser fire, it lurched and he smelt burning, but it was too late to stop him now. His rocket was going to fly and that was that.

The yell choked off into wild, hysterical laughter. He aimed for the tail end of the giant slab of metal blocking the ports. The windscreen shattered, the inside of the transport caught fire, but travelling at this speed nothing could stop him smashing – into –

A split second before the impact, Tod decided this was the best fun he'd had in his life.

Jessen kept firing as Rojin yelled out Tod's name. With so much around them already ablaze, she barely noticed the explosion blossom up from the waste ground below as the transport blew to pieces.

Again, the mission-control room shook with the impact.

'Tod…' Slatin stared at the screen, white with shock, and fell silent.

'Forty seconds!' Makkersvil yelled at her. 'Well, did it work?'

'I… He's moved it, but…' She wiped her eyes, squinted at the smoke trailing across the bleary image. 'I don't know if it's enough!'

'For God's sake, try it!'

'That's it,' the Doctor's voice still carried through the clinging darkness despite the vibration, the noise, the heat. 'You hear it? That's –'

A clang. More grinding metal. 'No.' Compassion started banging on the side of the ship, reaching out for the hatch. 'No, there's something still wrong! We've got to get out!'

'No, Compassion, don't!'

'Closing and opening one more time *might* do it,' Slatin said calmly, operating the control.

Makkersvil's finger hovered over the abort button as the countdown reached twenty seconds. He watched the hatch cover sliding shut, then sliding back open, reaching halfway then slowly, painfully slowly, pushing against the obstruction.

At ten seconds it was almost three-quarters clear.

'Like being in a cocktail shaker,' the Doctor yelled as the vibrations rocked him and Compassion helplessly about the narrow confines of the mineship. He kept his shoes pressed against Compassion's arms, trying to hold her still, ignoring her angry shouting.

Then his stomach ploughed down into his knees as the mineship began to take off.

Jessen almost missed the rocket's take-off entirely when it cleared the enveloping smoke and burst into the sky. Within seconds it had vanished from view.

She laughed in disbelief. 'You did see that, didn't you?'

Rojin was still looking up at the sky. 'I saw it.' Jessen's laughter made him smile despite himself. 'A good, big plan, Tod,' he added quietly.

More laser fire scythed through the smoke, getting closer. Then there was the sound of an enormous blast. Another of Slatin's concealed explosives, Jessen guessed, nodding approvingly. But the troops were still coming, and still firing.

'Let's move,' she said.

But Rojin was already running.

Slatin closed the roof port again and grabbed Makkersvil so tightly he nearly passed out from the pain in his stomach. She was apologising and laughing and crying all at once when Rojin burst in.

'Did you see any of that?' he asked.

'We *lived* through it,' Makkersvil assured him. 'Believe me.'

'Wish Tod had,' Rojin said simply.

Slatin's eyes welled up and she turned away.

'Where's Jessen?' Makkersvil asked.

'Burying us alive with a tonne of grenades,' Rojin said. 'Those troops might just think we've achieved our objective and so have killed ourselves like good little fanatics. And if not, well, if we can't get out, they can't get in, can they?'

'That's our plan?' Makkersvil asked, incredulously. 'You're letting her do that?'

Rojin misunderstood his meaning and shrugged. 'Well, if she *wants* to be the leader…' he said as a massive explosion knocked them to the floor and blew half the lights out, 'let *her* get her hands dirty.'

Dam had given up trying to hear voices in his head. Instead he had determined to listen in on more conventional conversations. They hadn't thought to take his communicator from him. Amateurs. He knew the wavelengths of most key personnel on the Facility, and was trying to focus his mind while he gathered his strength by working out who was where, what they were up to, and more importantly, when they were planning to… prepare him.

He thought of Ilsa. The humiliation she'd endure as their privileges were stripped away, and social standing reduced. No babies for Ilsa, now. After waiting so long.

'I'm so sorry,' he whispered to the wife he would never really know.

The communicator was like a radio, tuning in to random dramas. Jedkah was currently in the morgue, muttering to himself, his melancholy at no one taking him seriously only mildly relieved by the prospect of opening up Narkompros's cadaver. Most of the guards were out after Jessen and the Doctor; Terma had been receiving updates on their progress. Things hadn't gone well: the activists had wiped out half Havdar's forces and managed to launch a rocket before burying themselves alive. Terma was refusing to be downcast, however. He reckoned the Doctor was trying to get to Bastion 634, and had apparently changed the recognised acceptance signal already. Nothing could breach that Bastion now.

But if anyone could prove Terma wrong, Dam reckoned, it was the Doctor.

In Main Control, Head Terma stood savouring the moment.

The progress of the little ship on the strat-screen as it approached Bastion 634 had amused him. Soon, with access denied, the ship would simply hang in the tiny gravity field of the Bastion, helpless.

'Forgive me, Head Terma,' an operator said, deferentially. It was Ansu, a small, serious woman who had previously worked under Yve on projections. 'I felt you should see these figures.'

Respectful girl, Terma ruminated. She might well make a competent supervisor; he would have to consider. 'Talk me through them,' he said benignly.

'They show network power recovery is exceeding targeted levels by twelve per cent.'

'Excellent.'

Ansu looked uncomfortable. 'Head Terma, Bastion 634 is not taking the power flow. The Doctor's equations are still holding it in a low-power stasis.'

Terma's beatific smile curdled on his lips. 'It's not accepting the boost in power?'

'It's too damaged, hanging on to the group mind by a thread. If the network continues to power up at the increased rate while 634 remains crippled inside it, the imbalance –'

Terma started to scroll through the information more rapidly. 'All right, all right, I understand. There'll be burn-out, the *opposite* problem from before.'

Ansu nodded nervously. 'But the end result will be exactly the same.'

'It will *not*, girl,' Terma thundered, pushing the display unit back into her arms and stalking off to the strat-screen. 'Sever 634's links with the network.'

'We've tried, but it's going to take –'

'Without further delay!'

'Immediately, Head Terma,' Ansu said, racing back to her

position on the upper gallery to get back on with it.

Fuming, Terma tried to console himself by considering again the plight of the tiny ship shut out from 634. He forced a smile.

If anyone *was* aboard, they'd die a drawn-out, claustrophobic death by suffocation.

Compassion had blacked out during take-off. She'd woken to find herself weightless, bumping gently against the confines of the capsule. She didn't know how long she'd been unconscious, but now she found, easily in the absolute darkness, that every time she closed her eyes she was back in the dream she'd had before. The platform that looked out over anywhere was drawing her to it once again.

'Why is that?' she asked the Doctor. 'How can it be?'

'The decay of the flesh–tech interface must be resulting in a considerable amount of energy bleeding out into space,' the Doctor theorised. 'I can feel something's wrong myself, but your earpiece is accentuating the feeling, defining it for you.'

A high-pitched whistling tone, almost beyond human hearing, started up.

'Signals…' she whispered. 'So basic, like building blocks… building me pictures.'

'Compassion,' the Doctor said warningly. 'We're close to Bastion 634 now. The codes allowing us entry to the Bastion will have stirred the datacore of the damaged controller. You could be interfacing with it directly. Please, be very careful.'

Something was coming for her out of the mist. Wide and dark, like an open mouth. A mouth screaming a warning even as it licked its lips.

'Something's wrong, Doctor,' she said, suddenly rigid, her breath coming in rasps. 'It doesn't want us. It *hates* us.'

'Compassion –'

'It's not going to let us in!' she whispered.

Makkersvil had reached the same conclusion back at the

entombed base. They'd had nothing to do except stare at the tiny icon of the mineship as it sped towards its target. Now that the two had almost merged into one a warning alert had appeared on the strategy screen.

'The Bastion's not responding to our signal. The access codes must have been changed,' Makkersvil said. 'They're screwed.'

'What can we do?' Jessen asked, already on her feet.

'Know any good prayers?' Makkersvil enquired.

'They're going to die, then,' Rojin surmised, a bitterness in his soft tone. 'Just like everyone else.'

Chapter Forty
Change Yourself

I'm back.

This must be the longest night of my life. Time has always passed so quickly here, a real blur… It's weird – I've checked over what I've written so far and I can barely remember writing it. Seems like hours ago.

Getting harder to concentrate, to keep everything in focus. Maybe I should just give in, lie down and try to forget all of it, but I'm scared that if I do that, it might get a hold on me. Like it did with Denna. So I can't let myself stop thinking.

From Serjey's, I started making my way back to my apartment, as fast as I could. Maybe Filippa was waiting for me there, I thought; it seemed plausible, sensible even, just the sort of thing she'd do. Maybe she'd have found Serjey on the way, and he could explain away his Houdini act.

There *was* someone waiting for me when I got home. Anya, curled up in my bed, hiding under the covers like a child from a thunderstorm.

'Nikol's gone,' she announced, her face sliding out from beneath the white blanket.

'Gone?' I'd never heard her sound timid before.

'Gone. For good. Early departure.' She shrugged. 'A new Notification came for him this morning. Red car took him at lunchtime.'

'Have you seen Filippa?'

'I'm alone, now, Fitz.'

'But have you seen Filippa?'

'I can't believe he just went like that, so quietly, when the time came. Just left me standing there.'

I didn't have time for this. 'Anya, listen…'

'Yes, I saw your precious Filippa,' she said, suddenly angry. 'And she's gone. She took the next red car after Nikol and she said she never wanted to see you again.'

I was floored. 'What?'

'Don't make me say it again.'

Anya looked away as I started on a dozen protesting sentences, discarding each after a single word.

'I'll stay with you, Fitz,' Anya said, slowly. 'I can come and stay with you here. Nothing in the way, remember?'

I couldn't believe what I was hearing. 'Have you missed what's happening out there? I was up Northside and it's a nightmare, it –'

'It'll pass. Whatever's gone wrong, it *will* pass in the end.'

I wanted to believe she was right, but I couldn't. I just looked at her, empty of everything. She must've taken that as a sign to go on talking.

'It has to pass, doesn't it? *Nothing* lasts for ever. And I'll do whatever you want, Fitz.' She was trying to hold my gaze with her own in the way she knew I used to love. 'Whatever you say. Anything. Just don't leave me alone.'

I looked at her, this hard, desperate creature clinging to the wreckage of the woman I'd once thought I'd cared about. It was hateful, wrong, as wrong as anything happening outside.

Her voice caught. 'Please, Fitz.'

'You didn't see Filippa at all, did you?' I breathed. She didn't answer. 'Tell me.'

'Nikol's date was pulled forward and so was –'

'*Tell me.*'

She threw the pillow at me, lips pulled back in a sneer. 'She's gone, Fitz, accept it. She might as well be dead for all the hope you have of reaching her now –'

'No.' I grabbed hold of her arms, pulled her out of the bed. She whimpered and kicked me with her bare feet. I saw the scars on her hands as she tried to scratch my face, and I was just saying 'tell me, tell me,' shifting her struggling, skinny body round the room like she was my protesting partner in some sick dance. In the end she crumpled in my arms, bawling her eyes out, shaking her head and owning up. She'd not seen Filippa. Didn't know where she was. I let her fall to the floor and she crawled away back to my bed. She made so much noise.

I found myself going back to her, putting my arms around her, shushing her down. The important thing was Filippa might still be around, there was still a chance. I was thinking so hard of what I might do next that I barely noticed Anya eventually reaching a shocked calm in my arms.

'It's the end of the world,' she whispered. 'And no one even knows why.'

I left her a few hours ago, sleeping in my bed. Just like I left Alura. But no note this time. Only this one, to myself. Her face and body were hidden under the blanket, but her hair streaked out across the pillow like the legs of a spider.

I know I shan't ever see her again.

So I'm camping out under the Mechtan stars tonight – well, under a streetlamp, more accurately – watching over the Centreside departure area in case Filippa goes by.

It's quite quiet out here tonight. And I don't think there'll be as many people about tomorrow as there were today. I don't think they'll have the strength.

So much for thinking things through on paper. Things don't look any better written down. I suppose it's passed some time, anyway. Should be dawn soon. Thank God the streetlights are still working, keeping back the darkness.

So much for running being the lazy option. The amount of Mechta I've covered today…

Tomorrow I'm going to find Filippa.

I'll be less scared then.

I only wish I could shake the feeling that whatever I do now, it doesn't really matter.

DESPERATION
A ROPE ENDS IT

Chapter Forty-One
Knocking At the Door

'Find the key, Compassion,' the Doctor urged, feeling the air growing thinner. 'The signal that will let us in. You can do it, I know you can.' There were no allowances for delays on this flight. If she hadn't got them in by the time the air ran out, she'd be unconscious in two minutes, dead in under ten.

'It can't recognise... things... any more.' Compassion was mumbling, her voice quiet and breathy. 'Everything's changed.'

'It's still communicating, Compassion, you can understand it. Please, you must hurry!'

'Hurts... It hurts...'

'I know, I know, but hold on to it. Don't lose it.' His head was tingling. He gripped her by the leg and shook her. 'You *must* hold on, Compassion!'

Compassion had been swallowed, her sky was the roof of a mouth. There were half-glimpsed things all around her, images half chewed and rotting in folds of shadowy skin. She knelt on the thick, wet tongue, trying to fit pieces of sound and shape together into a pattern that made sense to whatever force held her, but it wasn't listening. It was sick, distracted. Angry.

She knew she must appease it. She stopped fighting, let herself fall down its throat.

The Doctor lost his grip on Compassion's leg as she went into convulsions, feet and arms clanging against the cramped interior. He tried cooing to her as if she were a teething baby; then stopped, realising he was using up the scant air too quickly. Something sparked as Compassion must've pulled out a wire, and the Doctor choked as smoke filled the dark little chamber.

Then the capsule lurched forward.

* * *

'No…' Terma watched in horror as the two icons on the screen became one. 'That's impossible! How is this happening?'

No one could answer him, and he turned angrily to Ansu. 'Bastion 634 *must* be excised from the network! Status report!'

'We're boosting the radio link, Head Terma,' Ansu reported coolly from where she was surrounded by pale and sweaty operators. 'Bastion controller starting to respond. If it stays on-line long enough we'll have full access to shutdown codes shortly.'

'They've done it!' Jessen shouted as Slatin led a whooping cheer from the others. 'They're into the Bastion!'

Makkersvil wiped his brow theatrically. 'What did the entombed *do* in the days before television?'

Jessen's smile had slipped a little. 'I wonder what the Doctor will do now.'

The lever that unlocked the pressurised door was by the Doctor's head. Weakly, he reached out and pulled it. There was barely enough air for him to hold his breath, but he considered it the respectful thing to do while waiting in suspense for the door to open.

Finally, reluctantly, it did so. Worming his way out, rather squashing poor Compassion in the process, he found the capsule had come to berth in a ribbed, circular docking tube. His body was aching for a stretch, but it was too cramped in here – and too dark and shadowy to feel comfortable about even trying.

Above him the Doctor discerned some kind of harness, evidently a lifting and carrying device, fixed by magnetic wheels to the low roof and heavy with those curious Skalen wires, hanging down to the floor. He remembered there was a similar affair hanging down from the ceiling in the chamber they'd arrived in. Clearly, when functional, the machinery was designed to process new recruits on their one-way journey to Mechta. He tried now to shift the harness, but it wouldn't budge.

Checking Compassion was OK, he awkwardly manhandled her out of the capsule. She was out cold; the strain of communicating with the controller must've been too great. Still, at least if the Bastion was still operational despite everything then Fitz, provided his capsule was still berthed here, should be all right. But dragging Compassion with him would take too long. He needed to know Fitz was OK right now.

'Be back soon,' he whispered, and crawled off through the service tunnel alone.

A minute or so after he'd gone, the wires trailing from the body harness twitched into life, reaching down to caress Compassion's prone body.

The docking tube led to a hatch, which in turn led to a dark, narrow channel just wide enough to accommodate a life capsule. Crawling along, bunched up on his hands and knees, the Doctor realised that if the processing system was fully automated – and if it was functioning correctly – then at some point the wire harnesses they'd seen on the ceiling should start operating. They'd take him for a capsule and lift him out, manoeuvring him into whatever position was vacant. If it *wasn't* functioning, he'd just have to keep crawling until he got somewhere.

Compassion awoke to find the intuitive wires caressing her face, hovering centimetres from her eyes.

'Yes,' she whispered, and the presence inside her seemed to approve. 'Yes, it's me.'

The wires slipped round her throat.

Impatient with the apparently never-ending tunnel, the Doctor had loosened a section of its ceiling with the sonic screwdriver and, to his relief, was able to kick it open. He'd emerged into one of the many chambers of capsules, but the peaceful sonorous hum he'd noticed on their earlier arrival had gone, replaced with silence. Several of the capsules had gone with it, launched pointlessly out into space.

The thought that Fitz *could* be out there in the darkness chilled him to the bone. Fitz and all these poor people.

Selecting a capsule, the Doctor opened it. An old woman lay inside, her emaciated arms raised up as if she'd been trying to bang on the lid for help. She was dead. He tried another. A boy of ten or so was face down in the amber gel. The Doctor gently turned him over, and found he was dead too.

The lights suddenly flared in the chamber, dazzling his eyes. A power surge of some kind. Some systems were still functional, there still could be time. If he could locate the TARDIS then he'd find Fitz in the chamber adjacent to it. Fitz *had* to be here still.

The Doctor took the inner door and sprinted for the control room.

Compassion was back standing on the platform she had dreamed of – the maw she'd fallen down had led nowhere. Gaping before her now was just grey nothing.

There was a different darkness from before visible against the void. Damage.

Compassion reached out to it at the same second that she realised it could kill her.

Chapter Forty-Two
The Reunion

The noise of taxis in the departure area finally filtered through to Fitz's exhausted brain, and he woke. The sun was well up in the sky, but it had still been dark when he'd allowed his eyes to close. That's me, he thought. Never mind fiddling while Rome burns, I'd be having a nice kip in the atrium.

His whole body ached, but at least the sun was still warm on his skin. He'd had some instinctive fear the sun would never rise again. Now, the departure area was bustling with people, though not as busily as it had been yesterday. A queue of red taxis – how many of the things could there be on Mechta? – lined the terminus, waiting patiently for squabbles to be resolved and for the right people to get inside. It seemed the red cars wouldn't roll without the designated passenger inside them. Very efficient; but on whose instructions, Fitz had given up caring.

He got up painfully, pushing his scribbles of paper into his pocket, then moved over to the departure area. He tried to lick his dry lips but there seemed to be no moisture in his mouth. He was sick, no doubt about it, just like Mechta itself. The white concrete of the buildings all around was stained with rotten shadows, making the pyramids in the distance seem like mountains dusted with dark snow. Even Central was showing signs of the decay now, grey patches scabbing its pristine surface. As Fitz watched, this last bastion of Mechtan authority seemed to flicker as its many windows reflected the morning sun, as if each flash of dazzling light was mortar fire that might sometime soon bring the whole building crashing down.

Everywhere he looked, anxious faces were checking their Notification papers and peering at the taxis, no longer privileged travellers but evacuees, not knowing where they were going, only praying they could get away at all. Bystanders regarded the taxis with a cold wanting, like starving animals eyeing food. Fitz sensed the violence in the air, wondered if it was borne with the shadows and the stains. How could everything here have broken down so quickly?

'Fitz…'

He whirled round at the familiar voice, lips cracking as he grinned in disbelief. Filippa was here. She smiled at him sleepily for a moment, swaying on her feet, then he just managed to grab her before she fell. Typical – he'd been so wrapped up in his own worrying *she'd* had to find *him*. And she wasn't looking too clever, her face pale, shivering with cold despite the sun.

'I was looking for you.' Her speech was slurred.

He smoothed damp hair away from her face. 'I was looking for you, too.'

'Forgot where you lived,' she said, forcing a laugh.

'Stupid,' he teased. But as she looked at him, terrified, he knew it was pointless trying to conceal his worry.

'What's wrong with me?' Filippa whispered.

Fitz prised a piece of brown paper from her fist, and checked the details with a measure of relief. 'You'll be OK. Fine. You're getting a red car out of here.'

Filippa nodded weakly. 'Early summons. This afternoon.'

'Not long now.'

'What about you?'

'I'm sure they won't mind me coming along for the ride.'

Fitz pressed his face against her neck. When Filippa had told him about her Notification, it had seemed like the end of the world. Now the world *was* ending; taking a red car had become their only hope.

He was quite heartened on some level that he could still appreciate the irony in that.

They waited like vagrants, slumped in a doorway looking out over the departure area. A large crowd was milling about, spilling out into the road, mobbing each red car upon its arrival. A noisy, lengthy group inquisition ensued as to whose taxi was whose, before one more person made their escape, squeezing into the back of the taxi and pushing away anyone else who tried to get in, to the frustrated jeers and shouts of other onlookers.

Escape would take for ever at this rate, Fitz fretted, as the same scene was re-enacted over and over. Why didn't more of them try to pile in? Surely as long as one of the occupants had Notification, others could travel with them? Perhaps there were weight restrictions. He wouldn't fancy Rencer's chances of stowing away, but Filippa weighed next to nothing and he was hardly a heavyweight himself.

At one point the monotony was broken by a man driving a blue car across the pavement and into the departure area, trying to block the road so no one could get out, insisting he be taken next. No one spared the protester much time. A group of people descended on him, shifting the entire car to one side, dumping it on the grass. When the man promptly tried to block the road again he was hauled roughly from the vehicle and sent on his way.

Filippa was still shivering beside him. 'They might try to stop *us* going,' she said.

Fitz squeezed her reassuringly, and wished someone would do the same for him. 'Don't worry. I've played places rougher than this before. We'll be fine.'

A woman tried to push to the front as another red car arrived, but fell amid the heaving crowd, trampled out of view. Someone was trying to bring some order to the proceedings, his shrill exhortations for calm going unheeded.

Filippa just looked at him. Her skin was blotchy, her eyes shot with red. 'Will we?'

Chapter Forty-Three
The Revelation

The Doctor skidded to a halt, recoiling from the terrible smell of decaying meat that was wafting out from the control room. The lighting had failed again. Only LEDs flashing on the control panels offered tiny candles to the darkness.

Bracing himself, he walked inside.

There was a stinking mass in the middle of the room – the damaged controller. Peering closer, forcing himself to examine it, he made out gangrenous flesh thick with wires and hair, veins stitched into cables and bristling sensors spiking from the bulk like protruding nails. The encrusted black matter he'd noticed on the hands and head of the dying man when he'd been here last time had spread like hot tar slowly enveloping the body.

Something sagged open in the morass, and the Doctor took a step back.

Too late.

He realised it was a mouth. The voice was halting, disguised by static, and seemed pitched at many timbres.

'I am or you are?'

Too late. The network is falling to our control.

'Who is this?' the Doctor asked, puzzled. 'Terma, is that you speaking through this –'

Skale not reach out into space... Caged in. People will be dead.

The lights surged on again, and the Doctor looked away from the monstrosity twitching in its seeping chair. He punched a few controls – the basic setup was the same as the console he'd operated back at the Facility – feeling a prickling feeling rise up the back of his neck as he took in the readouts on the screen.

The network was recovering, and quickly; Mechta was rebuilding itself. This crippled lump behind him, housing the on-line systems of Bastion 634, was the only thing holding back its full regeneration. If he could tap into the other Bastions from here, shut off their remote access from Parallel 59, then he could extricate each Bastion in turn from the network and save its people. Save Fitz.

Simple. But by the look of things, Terma was trying to cut 634 away from the network like so much dead skin. There wasn't much time.

He started to work, then heard a slither behind him. He turned instinctively to see that the mouth of the dying cyborg creature had reopened.

Doctor... Pash... Com Pash...

There was something in the tone of the unearthly voice he recognised.

Doctor, can't... inside... Passion I'm...

'Compassion?' the Doctor demanded. Of course, it had to be her, the earpiece still allowing her communion with the datacore deep inside the controller. 'Compassion, you must stabilise –'

The power failed again, and the screens behind him flickered and went dead. The Doctor thumped the top of a monitor with his fist, and, while he nursed his sore hand, he blinked as the whine of the generators started up again and a picture formed out of the static.

Forward scan...

The image represented the view outside the Bastion. A snapshot of space. And something else. Long, curved, a shadow eclipsing stars.

Shielded by the same cloaking that kept the Bastions hidden from Skale, something immense was waiting to be let in.

It wants us.

'Compassion, what is it?' The Doctor was practically tearing his hair out. 'What's out there?'

It's from Haltiel.

The Doctor froze, and his mouth gaped open like the controller's own. 'Haltiel? A spaceship from Haltiel?' He paused. 'A battleship?'

People will be contained. Caged.

'They've seen what's coming,' the Doctor whispered. 'And they've found the perfect way to ensure no one on Skale will ever leave the planet, ready made.' He jumped up, slapped his forehead. 'Of course! The resurgence in the power...' Frantically he manipulated the controls. 'Jedkah was right all along. I have to warn Terma, warn the whole *planet*!' he shouted to the ruined controller. 'Haltiel is taking control of Mechta!'

Chapter Forty-Four
Brick Walls

'It's time,' said Fitz.

Helping Filippa to her feet, he led her slowly and cautiously towards the packed thoroughfare.

'That's my Notification she's got!' a woman shouted. 'Her with the red hair! I'm next, not her!'

Immediately the crowd turned on Fitz and Filippa. He clutched her to him. 'Yeah? What's your name, then?' he shouted, taking the damp piece of paper from Filippa's sweaty hand. The woman didn't answer and Fitz nodded knowingly at the hostile faces gathered round him. They softened a little and parted to let the couple through.

He smiled at Filippa but her eyes were still closed. Together they staggered forward a few more steps, and people grudgingly made way for them, accepting that the sooner people found their red cars, the quicker more cars would arrive.

Fitz tried four taxis, fending off angry shouts and accusations as he and Filippa stumbled in search of the car that would take them away from here.

'Here, Fitz,' Filippa said, breathless, as a rear door opened for her and she collapsed inside.

'Filippa Cian,' a tinny voice announced apparently recognising its occupant.

Fitz felt his heart leap so high it almost overbalanced him, and he struggled in beside her. 'Right, then, driver,' he said, 'don't spare the horses.'

The car didn't move.

'Filippa Cian only,' came the driver's voice through a grille in the frosted partition.

Fitz looked at Filippa, who had screwed up her eyes at the announcement.

'One person only in a red car.'

'No!' Fitz shouted, slamming his fist against the partition. 'I need to look after her –'

'One person only in a red car.'

Fitz felt the last of his strength slipping away, and turned to Filippa. 'I was afraid of this... Stupid. I couldn't bear to think I might not leave with you. Didn't want to... Well. You know.'

Filippa nodded. 'You didn't want to give up.' She looked at him, helplessly, then they held each other.

'Don't think I'm leaving you behind,' Filippa said.

'Don't think you've got much choice, love.'

The taxi was being rocked by the people outside anxious to move them on.

'No. Come on.' Filippa feebly pushed him, protesting, towards the door. 'The car will wait – if it's in my name, it's got to.'

She tottered out drunkenly, and Fitz helped pull her out of reach of the mob. Luckily, no one wanted to lose their positions at the front of the queue by following them across the road, settling for shouting abuse for wasting others' time.

'Sticks and stones,' Fitz shouted back, politely extending two fingers. Gently, he seated Filippa on the grass near the blue car the protester had abandoned. 'They're right, though. Look at you. You *need* to take that taxi.'

'And you don't?'

'My Notification will come –'

'Come from where?' Her voice was bitter. 'Mechta's finished. If I leave you behind I'm leaving you for dead.'

'Bastion 634 signalling back to us, Head Terma,' Ansu reported. Then she peered in disbelief at the display. 'It's a priority message... from the Doctor.'

Terma looked as if he was developing a facial tic, his eye twitching madly, but Ansu felt she should at least deliver the message. 'He claims the forces of Haltiel are poised to strike against us the moment we remove 634 from the network,' she said, deadpan. 'That they've been causing our power fluctuations and that the Bastion is the only thing preventing them taking full control.'

Terma stared at her as if she had heaped curses on his mother. 'He claims *what*?' Then he started to laugh, harder and harder. 'Oh, Doctor. Oh, *very* good...'

The Doctor stood poised over the computer controls, racked by indecision. If he simply destroyed the Mechtan program, the forces of Haltiel would be unable to gain control, but the people trapped within its parameters would all die. And if he didn't succeed, Mechta *would* be taken over, and all Skale would be at Haltiel's mercy. Hundreds and thousands of uncaring stars ready to fall from the sky.

He felt a flare of anger that these stupid, petty people should force him to make such decisions; then he remembered that no one was forcing him to do anything, remembered saying once, long ago, that he didn't work for anyone, he was just having fun.

Which way should he jump?

The voice that was partly Compassion and partly unknowable, dark things, gurgled as if being strangled. *Doctor, they have me, Doctor.*

'No!' The Doctor turned and stared helplessly at the glistening thing in the chair. 'Compassion!'

'Bastion 634 can be brought off-line permanently,' Ansu said, glowing with pride as Terma smiled at her with an almost passionate intensity.

'No more games, Doctor,' he said. 'Disconnect!'

Chapter Forty-Five
The Strike

The console of the ruined Bastion pinged plaintively, then the low hum of power that had been already barely audible in the control room decreased to a fragile murmur.

The thing that had been the controller screamed with Compassion's voice.

'Oh, you've done it now,' the Doctor whispered, as the temperature began to drop.

Terma walked out of Main, the cheering of his staff ringing in his ears. The Project was saved.

Ansu wriggled free of the overenthusiastic embrace of a young operator and staggered back to her station. The strain on the Main crew over the last few days had been replaced at last by a heady euphoria.

Ansu decided their first priority should be to run a full correction check on the Mechtan program, to ensure the ebbing and flowing of power had left no lasting damage on the systems.

As the cheering carried on around her, she found that there was no response to her commands. She tried again, and was forced to reach the same conclusion.

They were locked out of the system.

Program parameters collapsing.

'No!' The decision taken for him, the Doctor leaned heavily on the console, shaking his head. 'Fitz...' the Doctor muttered. 'Compassion, if you're there...'

Doctor, it's cold... I'm lost.

'You must stabilise a portion of the datacore for me, Compassion.'

Haltiel has me.

'Sift through the systems for any survivors here, Compassion. I can save their bodies but only you can save their minds. They're lost, excised from Mechta. We're their only hope. They have to be our first priority.'

He imagined for a second what Mechta could become with Haltien technology infiltrating the systems, what could befall the people caught within its confines.

Only for a second.

Haltiel broadcasting now, Compassion said through the black, crusty mouth. *Teach Skale a lesson.*

Fitz had an idea.

He turned to Filippa and gripped her with an energy that surprised them both. 'The car. Maybe I can't ride with you, but if I got that thing to *tow* me along…'

He tailed off; he could see from the smile on Filippa's face she knew what he was driving at. Or steering towards, anyway. The red car could do the driving for them both.

The smiles stopped as the grass beneath them turned suddenly black. Jumping to his feet as if he were sitting on hot coals, Fitz helped Filippa up so they were at a more convenient height for staring at each other, speechless.

Dam had been lying quietly on the bunk, planning a daring escape he knew deep down he would never be able to carry out. He felt worse for Yve, funnily. As if there was something he could possibly do for her.

What is the right thing to do? he wondered.

All this time he'd been obsessed with that question, not questioning anything else. He'd distracted himself with self-advancement, every move calculated to raise him through the strata of society as quickly and unobtrusively as possible, as if that was enough. Always putting off the big decisions. *Turn a blind eye. Do your best for the state that spawned you.* That was what you were *supposed* to do as a good citizen. That was success. And that was what had brought him here. To help make his own death sentence possible.

'They'll put you in a box and bury you on Mechta,' he whispered as if Yve could hear him. 'Would you want that? Your old face back, your dream body. A new start, new friends and no responsibilities... No idea at all that...'

He closed his eyes. He'd let his life drift for fear of making choices; now he'd drift through the stars, join a world where choice was taken away.

You weren't romantic, Ilsa was saying. *You were just weak.*

'Maybe we'll meet again, Yve,' he whispered. 'And we'll both be better people.'

After the grass, the pavement was next to turn black. The entire departure area seemed ringed with burnt rubber.

Without another word Fitz squeezed Filippa's arms and ran forward to inspect the back of her waiting red car. The crowd had lost some of its helpless anger to fear at the sight of the dry, black tide, but Fitz knew that didn't make the people any less dangerous.

There was no towbar on the taxi, of course, but there was the emblem of a globe raised up from the back of the vehicle which might be strong enough to tug the little blue car along. Fitz pulled off his tunic and twizzled it round into a plaited rope, cursing his clumsy fingers as the knot kept slipping loosely off the metal extension. Filippa stumbled over and helped him, a feverish look in her eyes as she yanked at the grey material.

He jogged over to the blue car, started it up and steered it over to park behind the red car. He heard people shouting at him, telling him to clear the way, ignored them. How long before they shifted him by force? He got out of the car and went to help Filippa, who was already trying to attach the other end of his tunic to the wing mirror on the right-hand side, the only thing that might hold. A couple of bruisers started moving towards them, and Fitz braced himself to stand up to them.

Then the shadows came back. In force, this time.

Formless shapes and stains, like the ones he'd seen Northside, were suddenly blowing like clouds of oily soot over the people lining the side of the departure area. People screamed and ran as more defined shapes began to coagulate from the air, huge black stick men towering above the crowds.

Fitz yelled at Filippa to get in the red car, and finished knotting the fabric around the mirror himself. He was unable to stop himself risking a glance at the chaos on the concrete beside him. It was like looking through a fish-eye lens: the perspective was all wrong. Dark fingers like soily roots stabbed down at the panicking people who just melted into the filthy air one by one.

As he jumped into the blue car, Fitz got a crazy sense that the dark figures were like the correctioners in some way.

Then the car lurched forward as the red car roared away, throwing him to one side. The mirror seemed to be holding as the taut fabric towed him wonkily away down the street. It was working. Jesus Christ, it was actually *working*.

In the wobbling wing mirror Fitz saw the darkness swamp the departure area, the stick figures poised over it like the shadows of great wicker men. Then the two cars awkwardly took a bend in the road and sped along brighter streets that were still crowded with the sick and the infirm. He glimpsed disbelieving, angry faces as the people watched the colourful convoy go by.

That's nothing, Fitz thought, gripping the wheel so tightly he thought it might break. Just wait till you find out what's waiting round the corner.

Looks like Mechta's under new management.

Terma seated himself at Narkompros's desk with a relaxed smile and switched on the personal communicator. It was time to announce his succession to Narkompros's exalted position to this shadow Elite. To claim his inheritance.

When the voice came both screaming and whispering at the same time over all transmitters in the Facility, Terma thought it was some kind of fantastic prank, just high spirits.

This is the Haltiel Presence. Surrender or be destroyed. Be contained, or be killed. Haltiel controls your defence network and will now demonstrate our destructive capability. Skalen powers will never be tolerated in Haltien space. Any missile fired against our presence will be construed as an act of war and we shall respond accordingly.

Terma contacted Main. 'What is this?' he demanded, uneasy. 'What's going on?'

The naked panic in the voice of the operator who responded shook him just a little. Terma learned that most of the systems in Main were down, or jammed.

'None of the Bastions are responding to signals,' the operator stammered. 'Mechta's fully functional again, but it's not responding to our computers. Something else has control.'

'Something else? What "something else"? Haltiel, for God's sake? Is that what you're asking me to believe?'

'Government confirm…' The operator's voice trailed off. 'Seems the voice isn't just broadcasting over every transmitter we have here. It's being heard everywhere. The same voice and the same message. All over the world.'

'It's a trick,' Terma insisted. 'You hear me? A trick. None of this is happening!'

Billions of men and women all over the planet reacted in exactly the same way. But no matter how many times the voice and its message was dismissed by people in the street and by parliaments the world over as an elaborate hoax, the fear grew.

Haltiel was just a speck in the sky, an evening star. It had inspired scientists and poets alike, spawned a thousand theories and countless fictions of invasion and exploration. When the first pioneering probes had detected life there, Haltiel gave Skale an impetus for reaching out to the stars, a distant, anonymous, impersonal presence. A focus for vague unease as to what was waiting for them as the inevitable journey out into space began.

Now Haltiel had been given a voice.

As night fell, a fearful people stared up into the dark and saw that distant point of light, glimmering uncaring in the sky as it always had. Nothing seemed to have changed, but still the harsh, terrible voice rang out over the cities and the seas. People found their fear turning to irritation. This wasn't Haltiel talking. It was just a joke. A sick, twisted, clever joke.

A lot of people thought the same when the news first filtered through that Parallel 6's Great City had been bombed to destruction, with two million dead.

Chapter Forty-Six
Emergency Exit

Makkersvil stared wildly round at the others as the hideous voice that had reverberated once again round mission control in the half-light fell silent at last. 'What the hell is happening?' he said. 'This is crazy. Crazy. I don't believe it. '

Rojin was white-faced. 'No.' He kept muttering the word, again and again.

'The Bastion network is shielded. We can't see beyond it. None of us know what could be gathering out there in space,' Slatin said quietly.

'And only we know what's *being* gathered. Hundreds and thousands of our people.' Jessen slumped down in a chair. 'What does it matter now? Any of it?'

Filippa and Fitz's luck held, as did Fitz's tunic. Clothes maketh the escape, if nothing else, he thought wryly as the red car pulled him awkwardly along through the stained streets. He watched the crowds grow thinner, the sky grow darker, even though it was only mid-afternoon.

Then they were out of the city, the road stretching out dead straight, like a surgical scar on the golden landscape.

Feeling faint, nauseous, Fitz watched Filippa's head through the red car's rear window as it lolled from side to side. The noise of the car's engine was soporific now. Looking past the taxi, he could see nothing but a flat horizon far in the distance. In the wing mirror, Mechta had already faded from view.

Jedkah had been elbow-deep in Narkompros's guts, and deciding he still hated them even now he knew them more intimately, when he first heard the Haltien broadcast. Unlike Terma, he believed in it immediately. That inhuman voice couldn't be faked. Every syllable sounded like thousands of jet-black beetles scattering into darkness.

He knew he should be terrified, alone in the cold blue light of the morgue, but all he could feel was a kind of dislocation from reality, a satisfaction coupled with a frustration that no one had ever believed him.

The paranoid man, he told himself, is paranoid only until he's proved right. Then he becomes a prophet.

Jedkah had decided that the voice probably heralded the end of the world.

Fitz willed himself not to lose concentration, to focus on Filippa's head, on the tresses of her red hair. He was rocked gently from side to side now the road had run out. In a blue cradle, soothed to sleep.

Then he was gliding, barely any sensation of movement at all. The sky was peculiarly dense with stars, as if the whole of the night had been draped over one single point above them.

A shadow passed over him as if they'd driven under a bridge. Distracted for a second, Fitz now found he couldn't see Filippa any more, or even the car in front.

He was about to shout out when the sky and the car and the ground all turned to grey glass around him.

Compassion could feel them. Identities broken down into signals and cells, transmitting through the dead meat of the datacore.

Two were close by, outside all protocols. The others were stranded in shadow.

She could harvest them, reroute them through the main systems. Give them back to the living meat of the organics as her user wished.

The blackness was spitting everywhere like fat from a roast. The alien power, strangulated in the systems shutdown, was still consuming her systems even as it ebbed away.

Fitz was balled up, stuck like gum under a table in some smoky waiting room, unsure whether or not he should call for help for fear of what might come. The nurses would be monsters now.

A door opened, and a woman he knew with auburn hair entered, peering about as if impatient to disappear again. She found him quickly even through the smoke. She'd come for him. It was his turn.

The Doctor will see you now.

The echoing announcement had left Dam chilled, shivering in a cold sweat on his sickbed. Ironic really. After all his deliberating, the voice had removed his way out, and Yve's, too.

And given him back choice.

He'd wondered how Terma would be responding, and used his communicator to listen in.

Compassion's voice had spoken the ultimatum over and over along with the Haltien Presence. Transmitting across all bandwidths, the Doctor imagined. Letting this world know the Presence was here, and that it meant business.

Now it came again. Distorted, multi-timbral. *So many dead.*

'So give me the good news,' the Doctor snapped, still wrestling with the controls. If truth be told, he had no idea whether she was actually speaking to him or just communing with the dying controller. 'How many could you save? How many survivors from this Bastion?'

Six.

'Six? Out of three hundred?' He stared at the controls forlornly, then carefully hunted down their locations on a schematic and activated the opening mechanisms in the lids of their caskets. 'Be lucky,' he whispered.

Doctor, so many people killed below. The voice choked off from the stinking morass. *Only a warning.*

The bleary blackness of the Haltien ship filled the screen. 'She's still part of it, still tapped in,' the Doctor breathed in realisation. He gripped the ripe, black flesh of the creature in the chair and addressed it urgently. 'Compassion, you need to go deeper. The Haltien Presence is still touching the systems here. I don't know whether it's a natural entity or some kind of electronic program itself, but you can follow it back to that vessel outside. We need information, Compassion, do you understand? Numbers. Weak points. Weaponry specifications.'

There was nothing but silence from the shuddering bulk. The lights dimmed still lower.

Then the Bastion lurched violently to one side. The Doctor lost his balance and the mess of the controller threatened to splatter out of its fragile housing.

Bright-green letters chattered over the blackness of a monitor screen as the information the Doctor had requested began to materialise. He turned to the controller, ready to give it a big kiss; then decided instead that he'd perhaps settle for patting Compassion on the back. Assuming he ever saw her again, and that he had enough time to do anything with the information.

The temperature was rising again. He guessed that the Bastion, no longer sustained by the harmonics of the network, was slipping out of its orbit and into the atmosphere of Skale.

It knows I'm here.

'Compassion!' the Doctor cried. 'Get out of there. Disconnect. Now!'

It's coming.

A spray of stinking ichor burst from the controller.

'*Now*, Compassion!' the Doctor shouted.

Chapter Forty-Seven
The Retribution

Slatin was sitting at her work station, logging on to a news server. The weight of her silence was such that, one by one, the others went to look over her shoulder.

'Great City 6 has been destroyed,' breathed Makkersvil, reading the summary.

'Rubbish,' said Rojin uneasily. 'How can a whole city just go like that? It would take... Well, it would take...'

Makkersvil finished his sentence for him. 'It would take three or four visitors from Mechta. That's all.' He carried on reading. '"No fix on enemy location renders retaliation futile."'

'Damn it, they *are* shielded by the network,' Jessen said, smashing her fist against the work station. 'No one will be able to get a fix.'

Makkersvil stared at her. 'We've spent thirty years committing suicide.'

The Doctor tapped out a message as fast as he could, wishing he could bring himself to stop having to correct his spelling. A covering note; and the download address for the electronic information that needed to be passed on to all Parallels on the planet via 59.

Provided there was enough power to send it. Provided anywhere at all was able to receive it. Provided anyone was even prepared to listen to a sabotaging stranger in the sky.

A weak red light glowed in its glass housing. 'Message sent,' muttered the Doctor to himself, triumphantly.

They know you did something.

The voice was less Compassion and more the gurgling controller, now. Was that good or bad?

Know where you sent it.

The Doctor wiped sweat from his forehead as the temperature in the listing Bastion increased still further.

* * *

The message purporting to be from Haltiel was broadcasting once again over all frequencies, despite Ansu's best efforts to shut it off. She was the only one still sitting at her post. Fear and panic was spreading throughout the staff in Main – not a single Bastion would respond to their control, and yet five capsules had dropped on Parallel 6. It seemed the impossible voice was right.

The people here now needed firm leadership, someone to unite them. But Terma was still hiding in Narkompros's room, insisting that all this was a trick. She thought about broadcasting the instruction to evacuate. But even if she dared, who would listen to her?

Finally, Ansu got a response from her endless test signals to the Bastions: another message from 634, linked only tenuously now it was excised from the network, running on the last vestiges of its power, ready to burn up in the atmosphere any time now. The Doctor again.

Perhaps his cheek would goad Terma into action as before.

'Head Terma, I have another message from the Doctor,' she shouted into her communicator, above the alien voice. 'He claims to have information on the Haltiel Presence, and there's a download address.'

Terma's voice sounded dull and heavy. 'It's a trick, I told you.'

Ansu glanced furtively round Main. People were actually leaving their posts, just walking away. She had to keep trying. 'Our log-ons are jammed, non-operational since Mechta ceased responding. You might be able to access it from your own terminal – download address is 11.269.11791…'

'It's a trick!' Terma raged back at her. 'The Doctor is a saboteur, an enemy of the state. Why would he help us? It's a trick!'

Ansu wanted to argue it was at least worth trying. But then she saw so many people left in the stifling heat, shouting, wrangling, even destroying equipment in their panic and frustration. No one was listening to anyone, any more.

It was the end for this place. The thought terrified her.

'Please, Head Terma,' Ansu said shakily. 'Please do something.'

* * *

'If I tell you it's a trick, it's a trick!' Terma screamed into the communicator, at both Ansu and the voice from Haltiel. 'Don't you understand that?' He threw the communicator against the door, and stared at it, red-faced, shoulders heaving. He clutched his head, shook it, felt his breath wheezing out through gritted teeth.

Just then, there was a soft *ping* from Medik. There in the prescription tray was a single, large blue pill.

Terma stared at it in horrified amazement.

Dam turned the tuning dial on his communicator and Terma's tantrum was silenced. Perhaps he couldn't do anything for Yve, or for himself. But there was *something* he could do now. A course of action he could choose.

He didn't know whether the range on his communicator was enough, but he had to try.

He sent the calling signal to Jessen and peered at his bedclothes, checking he could read his own writing. In scrawled blue figures, he'd noted the download address Ansu had broadcast.

The wires didn't want to let go of Compassion's neck. Her consciousness struggled out of the heavy sack of her trance and fell flat on its face. Her eyes blinked open.

Then the wires tightened round her throat. They wanted vengeance now, for the secrets she had stolen. She pulled at them, but other wires were constricting her chest, squeezing the life from her.

Jessen's communicator bleeped mournfully as if in treacherous respect for the millions dead in Parallel 6. She peered at the coded frequency, and her stomach turned.

Activating it, she cursed as she realised the signal was distorted too much by her being underground. 'Slatin, we must have some kind of external comms setup here?'

Slatin blinked at her, as if coming out of a trance. 'Uh… Nothing too powerful.'

'Could you patch through a message from the Facility if I give you the wavelength?'

'Sure.'

Jessen passed her the communicator. 'Boost this for me. Here's the frequency…'

'TARDIS… Come on, old girl… Where are you…?'

The Doctor had a feeling he was pushing his luck with this last request, and wasn't totally surprised when a mass of sparks blew up in his face. But just before he'd hidden his eyes from the flash, the location of the 'contaminant' had been revealed.

Recoiling, he fell into the controller's sluglike body, crying out in disgust as the flesh burst over him and the wiring dug into his body. On his knees, as if praying before the console, the Doctor keyed in a command to open all bulkheads.

The gnat-thin whine of the operating systems seemed to stop altogether. There was no telling how long life-support might last now.

Twisting himself free from the unfortunate creature's remains, the Doctor fled the control room.

Compassion felt the wires slacken as the power cut off, and tore herself free from their embrace.

'Gone,' she whispered, rubbing her neck. The lights shut down leaving her in darkness again. Disorientated, desperate, she started to crawl along the access tunnel, its metal floor heating up, burning into her hands and knees.

Racing along the inner corridor, his hand cupped round a lit match to guide his way, the Doctor threw open every outer doorway, looking for capsules with their lids open. He had no idea if the bulkheads would've had time to open or not before the power died completely. The TARDIS might still be out of reach. Their struggles could yet all have been for nothing.

He thought of Jessen, of how she'd begged him to put an end to the Project. She'd been so frustrated with him for wanting to do things his way. Well. At least he'd see to it that six lives were spared from this abomination.

The only way you could look at it was that anyone saved was better than no one at all.

Ansu was the only one watching the strat-screen when the tiny icon of a capsule broke away from its position and began to descend. A single person, falling out of the sky. The flicker was back on the screen. Sometimes the icon would vanish altogether, only to reappear a little further down, always a little further down.

Guided by the Facility's own radio signal, someone was coming back home to them.

Ansu hit the general alarm, suddenly decisive now she knew it didn't really matter any more. 'Evacuate. Capsule incoming. All personnel must evacuate immediately. *Immediately!*' She thought briefly of repeating the instruction, then decided she'd be better saving her breath for running like hell.

'...keep on saying this because I don't know if you can hear: Download information on the enemy's forces from 11.269.11791. Repeat, 11.269...'

Dam's voice came through loud and clear. Jessen found herself laughing. He was alive.

'You want to talk back to him?' Slatin asked.

Jessen shook her head, felt herself blush, though she didn't know quite why. 'No. No, what can I say?'

'Sorry?' Makkersvil suggested.

'Might be the last chance you get,' Rojin observed.

'This stuff's all from the Doctor,' Dam went on. There seemed to be a real din going on in the background, raised voices. 'Why we ever thought we could keep a hold on that man... I don't know how he figures in all this, or what the hell you're trying to do, Jessen, but no one here will listen. Maybe you can do something. I don't know.' A pause. 'I'm not trying to be a hero here, incidentally, if you are listening. I'd be running like hell, like everyone else is, if I was strong enough to stand. Jessen... Jessen, if you *can* hear me, if you get the download and if it makes any kind of sense...

'Well. Do what you can, eh?'

His voice cut off.

The silence in mission control grew suddenly louder.

Dam staggered to the tiny window in the hospital room and looked out over the Facility's floodlit grounds far below. People were screaming, running full-pelt in terror, desperate to escape. Milling about like ants. Dam remembered watching the tiny, distant soldiers as they crawled over the dark northern shores, and marvelling at Higs's cheery, unshakable belief in the strength and glory of Parallel 59. He heard a growing, gathering roar, and for a comforting moment he imagined it was the sound of the sea.

Dam didn't close his eyes. He held the communicator tight in his hand as the insects poured thicker and faster from the concrete blocks, even as the giant's boot fell to stamp them into the ground.

The Facility was engulfed in an explosion that could've been a sun.

Chapter Forty-Eight
Last Moments

The Doctor had found five of his survivors. Emaciated, weak, bewildered, at first they seemed unable even to walk. He had looked deep into their eyes, willing them to work with him. They had all held hands and an everlasting match, and followed him.

The Bastion was tilting ever more steeply, and the temperature was almost unbearable. He knew that life-support would soon terminate altogether.

Looking like macabre acolytes in the light of the tiny flames, the survivors gathered round the Doctor as he pulled back the lid on the sixth living remnant of Mechta. She was a red-haired girl, painfully thin with a withered arm, looking dumbly up at him with large brown eyes.

There was a rattling from the corner of the room. The Doctor stood protectively in front of his survivors, bracing himself – then relaxed as he saw it was Compassion pulling herself out from the access pipe, just as he had done. This must be where he'd broken free of the automated channels.

He ran to her and held her; and to his surprise and delight, she actually gripped him back. She was weak, exhausted, barely able to walk faster than the poor haggard souls sheltering behind him.

'Come on,' he whispered. 'Nearly home.'

All Skale fell into confused panic as the message from space continued to sound over all receivers, and as the spy cams finally proved beyond any doubt that a terrible weapon had been used against Parallel 6 – and that anyone else could be next.

Parallel 90 was the first to fire missiles into the apparent emptiness of space, formally starting the war.

Finally, the Doctor led his decrepit band into the chamber that he and Compassion had fled just a few days ago. The one empty space in the rank of capsules marked not only their departure but the location of Fitz nearby.

The Doctor dashed over, then paused, peering into the gloom at the bulkhead door.

It had raised just a fraction before the power had gone, barely enough to let a man through, let alone eight people in a hurry.

'Compassion, can you see what you can...?'

She nodded wearily and pushed the others aside, sliding her hands under the edge of the bulkhead door and pushing up with all her might. The noise of her exertions mingled with the subdued whimpering and sobbing of the survivors. They looked at themselves, at each other, at this place they'd lived in but never seen, staring about like lunatics. The Doctor wondered if they'd be strong enough to recover even as he reached into the tepid gel to bring Fitz coughing and choking to the surface.

'Where is she?' Fitz was croaking, seemingly delirious. 'Did I save her? Where is she?'

The Doctor held him close and laughed out loud, whooping for joy.

'Oi. That was right in my ear,' Fitz complained, weakly.

'I can't shift it, Doctor,' Compassion said.

'All right, everyone,' the Doctor commanded, lifting Fitz from the casket. 'I know you've all spent an inordinate amount of time lying down lately but I'm afraid I'm going to have to ask –'

The Bastion tilted still further, throwing them all to the floor. 'Come on, under that door!' the Doctor shouted, wrestling with Fitz's limp, gangly body, which had fallen on top of him. 'Move!' It was getting hard to breathe, the air so hot now it prickled his lungs.

'These people are useless,' Compassion shouted. 'Half of them are unconscious, the other half raving.'

'Get through the gap,' the Doctor ordered, examining Fitz. The fall had finished the poor boy off, he was out cold. 'We'll have to help them through ourselves. You pull, I'll push.'

'There's no time,' Compassion protested, hauling herself up the incline to the narrow gap.

The Doctor was already sliding Fitz along towards the bulkhead himself. 'Do it!'

Jessen was hard-faced again as Slatin prepared to display the downloaded data for them on the strat-screen.

Dam's message had filled Jessen with a new hope. Just the warmth in that familiar voice she'd thought she'd never hear again allowed her to believe that they could somehow *do* something more down here about whatever the hell was going on outside.

'Well, why not?' she enquired of a sceptical Makkersvil once she'd said so. 'We have a functional mineship left, don't we?'

'If Tod were here he could hack into the military servers and post the information to other Parallels,' said Rojin. 'Might make them do something.'

'Makkersvil can do it,' Jessen said. 'Can't you?'

'I can try,' Makkersvil offered. 'In my own understated manner.' He sat down painfully and started work.

'Great. We can hold a bring-a-missile party,' Rojin reflected. 'Hand ourselves over to Government at the same time. If Tod *was* here –'

'Well he's not,' Jessen said. 'Everything's changed, hasn't it? Everything.'

'That's what Tod said himself,' Rojin concurred.

'Let's see what the Doctor has to tell us,' Slatin said, as the information started to fill her monitor.

Compassion opened the TARDIS door, nearly toppling over on the threshold, her mind buzzing and dizzying as the ship welcomed her back – and as something else, bleary and dark, coiled through her receiver. She yanked the earpiece from her ear as if it was red-hot, wincing as it pulled at her flesh, and threw it into the console room. The decrepit survivors of the Bastion followed it inside.

Only the Doctor and Fitz were still to come. Typical, Compassion thought. If the Doctor were a parent carrying too many children on a school run, he'd make sure his own offspring were the ones without a safety belt.

The Doctor was almost free of the bulkhead door when life-support finally shut off altogether, and with it, gravity. Compassion watched as Fitz floated up slowly from the floor, and almost lost her footing as the TARDIS tipped to one side. Reaching out an arm from the TARDIS interior she was just able to catch hold of his straggly fringe, and to haul him inside by it. He fell on her heavily the moment he was through, and she struggled to roll him away. Looking up, she saw the Doctor swimming silently through the air towards her. Gripping the insides of the police-box doors, he pulled himself in and fell on her just as Fitz had. She groaned, winded.

The Doctor disentangled himself from his companions, and rushed to flick the switches that would close the doors and set the TARDIS spinning of on a new course. 'Right,' he said, clapping his hands together, smiling politely at his emaciated guests. 'If I can just steer the TARDIS to the other Bastions, somehow free them from –'

'No,' Compassion said softly.

'No?' He looked at her, quietly appalled, like a jilted lover.

'It's too late. I heard the signals. The Haltiel Presence has them.'

The Doctor folded his arms. 'Well, the Haltiel Presence can jolly well give them back.'

Compassion rubbed the bruised lobe of her ear, and looked away. 'That's just what they're doing,' she said.

Far below, as the bombs started falling, the cities of Skale began to blow away like pollen.

Epilogue

The war lasted three days.

We survived, thought Jessen, looking out over the wastes of the marshes. Thanks to the Doctor. Thanks to Dam.

With Dam's stolen information, they'd launched Tod's remaining ramshackle mineship, waiting in a horrible silence as it spluttered its way up to the stars to find the Haltien Presence. The missiles of every other Parallel followed its pioneering trajectory, thanks to Makkersvil making his electronic presence known; and just as the network had hidden the aggressors from view, so it had shielded their own retaliation. A planet united, just in time to be wiped out. *Almost* wiped out.

Haltiel had finally withdrawn only when every life in the sky had been taken, either thrown down like stones at a glass planet or else engulfed in Skale's own fire. Perhaps the Presence saw no point in remaining, now that the feeble hand reaching so presumptuously out into space had been broken and burnt. Perhaps, one day, the enemy would return in greater numbers, to poke about in the planet's wreckage. Well, they would find something on Skale in the future, Jessen was certain; something that would continue to fight back.

The air was still clear out here around Tod's old base, sufficiently far away from populated or military targets to escape bombardment once the Facility had been destroyed. Perhaps from here they could rebuild – not just Parallel 59, but all Skale. Already, while deep, deep wounds were being licked, statesmen were talking, however timidly, to their opposites in other Parallels. Seeing who was left alive. Swallowing pride and asking for help.

It was a start.

Jessen wondered what had become of the soldiers laying siege to them before the war, whether Slatin and Rojin would find anyone alive out there in the wasteland. Locating survivors was their little group's first objective. There was so much to do – so much to do differently. And they had to build their numbers. Anyone alive would be better than nothing.

A cold wind was whipping up, loud in Jessen's ears, so she didn't hear the noise of the large blue box as it somehow appeared on the bleak hill behind her.

None - of - it - was - real.

I thought it would take me for ever to get my head round those words at first, but I persuaded myself to wise up. No such thing as for ever; no one knows better than me, right now, just what a *mother* Old Father Time can be. How subjective the whole thing is.

I lived months on Mechta without ever leaving my pit. How much of my life have I spent wishing that was possible?

I was asleep for just five days.

None of it was real.

Sitting in my broad blue-striped pyjamas in bed, watching the fire in my room as I like to do, I felt a bit like Ebenezer Scrooge waking up on Christmas morning to find he's alive after all, and he's got the chance to change. I don't have to make the same mistakes I made in Mechta: I can break the pattern. Surely to God I can. Hey, Scrooge did.

Scrooge's dream was for him alone, though. Not one shared with thousands and thousands of people. I haven't felt like throwing gold at kids, telling them to run off and buy me the last turkey in the shop. My little kids aren't running anywhere. I've lain here crying my eyes out over them, over the friends I made that I'll never see again; that I never properly saw at all. Filippa. Serjey, Anya, Denna. Night after night after… Well, it's only been two nights so far.

I'm getting a bit stronger, though.

The Doctor sat on my bed and talked me through everything, keeping his patience and picking me back up no matter how often I flew off the handle. He really seemed to listen, too. I think he's been hit pretty hard by all this, like me, but who knows? He never really lets on.

Me and him, it's funny. There we both were, making the Big

279

Decisions, thinking we were actually making a difference. But in the end, all the choices were taken for us. I wasn't saving Filippa and me, I was just free-riding her casket out into space. But with me trailing behind, the whole car/capsule metaphor went all to hell, just as Mechta did. The program didn't allow for me being there, too.

What do you know? Fitz Kreiner finally beat the system.

Wonder how Nikol tried to do that round his way, and how long ago. What he did to get himself and Anya caught.

There's six other people from Mechta in a room down the hall, doing well, the Doctor says. Convalescence. Home from home, I'm sure. The room's meant to 'promote natural healing' or some such rubbish, all green hills, blue skies and butterflies. The Doctor's spoken to them, explained everything. They all want to go back, he told me. To face up to a new future.

I know he wants me to do the same. He tried to tuck me away in there, too, but I'm staying here, in bed. In reality. I've had enough of fakes. And of faking it.

There I go again, thinking I might change.

I remember writing before… When I was a kid, if I'd been given any one wish, more than anything else in the world I'd have wished always to remember my dreams, exactly as they were. To never know again that disappointment of waking up and feeling them slip away, of forgetting the things I'd seen or the way they'd made me feel.

Right now… well, I don't know what was in that gunk I've been sunk in, but I can recall most every step I took on Mechta. Every look, every scare, every kiss, all there for me to relive whenever I want. And it's a joy; the kid was right to want it so much. But because I know it was a dream, I can move on. I *have* to move on. With the Doctor, with whoever else might ever share our lives.

So, more and more, I find myself wanting to let myself quietly into that room of green hills and take a good look at the people inside. To see if I know any of the faces. To see if they really are ready to take on a brave new world, or if they're feeling like I am.

The Doctor thinks it's a good idea. In my own time, he says.

In my own time.

I don't think he was trying to be funny.

Still, here I am writing down how I feel again, and once again it's not helping much.

'Cause I suppose I don't *have* to keep stuff to myself any more.

The Doctor hesitated. He knew he shouldn't really follow Fitz as he left his room at last and shuffled off along the corridor. But the boy was working his feet properly for the first time in over a week. He might fall over. As the Doctor, he had a duty of care.

Quietly, he watched as Fitz walked over to the big, oak door in the stone wall and stood before it.

Then leaned against the wall beside it.

Started to walk away again. Stopped, turned, and then opened the door.

The Doctor drew closer. Fitz was walking with an exaggerated nonchalance, clearly uncomfortable, looking casually around him. The survivors, weak as they were, had spread out a fair way over the painting-book landscape.

Fitz was staring at one of them now, the one the Doctor had wondered about. A woman, spindly thin, with a bad arm, and with wispy hair that had stayed burning – even after all that time shut away in the dark – the colour of fire.

Fitz kept staring at her. The woman looked up and must've noticed him, too. She jumped to her feet. The two of them stood there dumbly as if reflecting on the enormity of the odds against their ever meeting again, that same recognition holding them apart somehow. As if they were weighed down by the numbers, too heavy to move on.

Then, Fitz started walking slowly forward in his stripy pyjamas. The woman didn't back away. She stayed standing there, watching him approach.

The Doctor turned then, and left. He didn't need to watch any more. Soon he would bring the TARDIS back to Skale, see what could be done there. Soon.

He whistled as he walked, Fitz's plaintive little melody still in his head. Thinking of loved ones, coming home.

The Eighth Doctor's adventures continue in THE SHADOWS OF AVALON by Paul Cornell, ISBN 0 563 55588 2, available February 2000.

PRESENTING

DOCTOR WHO

ALL-NEW AUDIO DRAMAS

Big Finish Productions are proud to present all-new *Doctor Who* adventures on audio!

Featuring original music and sound-effects, these full-cast plays are available on double cassette in high street stores, and on limited-edition double CD from all good specialist stores, or via mail order.

Available from January 2000
THE LAND OF THE DEAD

A four-part story by Stephen Cole.
Starring **Peter Davison** as the Doctor and **Sarah Sutton** as Nyssa.

In the cold wastes of Alaska, the Doctor and Nyssa encounter a sinister millionaire who is haunted by a secret past.

However, when a terrifying, unknown species from the dawn of time starts to awaken, the Doctor fears the past itself may prove fatal.

If you wish to order the CD version, please photocopy this form or provide all the details on paper. Delivery within 28 days of release. Send to: PO Box 1127, Maidenhead, Berkshire. SL6 3LN.
Big Finish Hotline 01628 828283.

Still available: THE SIRENS OF TIME starring Peter Davison, Colin Baker & Sylvester McCoy
PHANTASMAGORIA starring Peter Davison & Mark Strickson
WHISPERS OF TERROR starring Colin Baker & Nicola Bryant

Please send me	[ ] copies of *The Land of the Dead* @ £13.99 (£15.50 non-UK orders)
	[ ] copies of *Whispers of Terror* @ £13.99 (£15.50 non-UK orders)
	[ ] copies of *Phantasmagoria* @ £13.99 (£15.50 non-UK orders)
	[ ] copies of *The Sirens of Time* @ £13.99 (£15.50 non-UK orders) – prices inclusive of postage and
packing. Payment can be accepted by credit card or by personal cheques, payable to Big Finish Productions Ltd.

Name..

Address...

Postcode..

VISA/Mastercard number..

Expiry date..Signature...

For more details visit our website at http://www.doctorwho.co.uk